THE SANATORIUM

BY SUZANNE WILSON

Special Thanks

I would like to take this time to thank a few people who were instrumental on helping me put this book together.

Linda Donlin, for her brain storming putting together the heavenly part of this book. This addition gave the story another dimension, plus all of her time spent editing. Special thanks, Linda.

Our son-in-law, Chad Banning for all of the printing and artwork, turning my words and thoughts into an actual book. His helper Jessi, our daughter who proof read and organized the pages. Without you two my dreams of turning these pages into a book would have never materialized.

Our daughter, Elyce for always helping me out with all of the computer glitches (and there were a lot) that I would have never figured out on my own.

Then it comes down to my handsome, compassionate, loyal, and patient husband Steve (by the way Steve wrote that part), his nagging and not so patient ways kept me pushing forward to finish the book twice!! He also came up with this ending of the book, so I finished it twice but all worth it.

Love Suzanne!

Special Thanks

I would like to take this time to thank a few people who were instrumental on helping me put this book together.

Linda Donlin, for her brain storming putting together the heavenly part of this book. This addition gave the story another dimension, plus all of her time spent editing. Special thanks, Linda.

Our son-in-law, Chad Banning for all of the printing and artwork, turning my words and thoughts into an actual book. His helper Jessi, our daughter who proof read and organized the pages. Without you two my dreams of turning these pages into a book would have never materialized.

Our daughter, Elyce for always helping me out with all of the computer glitches (and there were a lot) that I would have never figured out on my own.

Then it comes down to my handsome, compassionate, loyal, and patient husband Steve (by the way Steve wrote that part), his nagging and not so patient ways kept me pushing forward to finish the book twice!! He also came up with this ending of the book, so I finished it twice but all worth it.

Love Suzanne!

The Sanatorium

Chapter 1

"The Lord shall smite thee with a
Consumption, and with fever, and
With an inflammation…and they
Shall pursue thee until though perish"

Deuteronomy 28:22

My name is Francine Carver, but everyone calls me Francie. It's 1947, and Bing Crosby's White Christmas is playing over the PA system at the Sanatorium. Today is the day I go to heaven. A dying person knows these things. I'm only 18. Pa is next to my bed, whispering goodbye, with his head in his hands. He looks so sad and defeated. Ma is praying the rosary, tears silently running down her cheeks. Her faith has always sustained her, but this may be more than she can take. So much has happened.

Even though my eyes are closed, I see them. I feel as if I'm floating above my body, looking down at them. I observe myself in the bed looking thin, drawn and pale. I want to tell Ma and Pa that everything will be all right. I start to reach for them, trying to take Pa's hand, but suddenly I feel a strong magnetic force pulling me away from my grieving parents.

I should be scared, but I'm not. A warm sensation fills my chest and spreads through my entire body. Even though it's the middle of the night in the dead of a Minnesota winter, I'm surrounded by light and beautiful colors of the rainbow, pulsing in time to the sweetest music I've ever heard. The magnetic pull continues, and I float above the sanatorium, above the lake, passing through the brilliant rainbow, and into the golden clouds.

I'm windy through a vibrant meadow, realizing I haven't been able to walk for months. The lush green foliage and gorgeous wildflowers surpass anything I've ever seen. I that's when I recognize I'm still wearing my poodle pajamas! I'm walking barefoot in the grass, and it feels wonderful, like a thick, expensive carpet. The smell of the flowers and the pure atmosphere are unbelievably sweet as I take long, deep breaths. I fill my lungs with the fragrant air, and for the first time in a long while, I don't have a coughing fit. I don't know where I am, but if this is heaven, I'm loving it. Then I hear…

"Francie! Wake up!" I freeze at the sound of my name. I look round, but nothing is familiar. Hold on! Someone is scurrying toward me. Thank goodness. Now maybe I will find out what's happening to me and what I'm doing here.

"Hello, Francie, says a very colorful person.

She looks to be middle age. I can't help staring at her. She is a plump woman with rosy cheeks, wearing a muumuu with multi-colored beads dangling around her waist. There is a bright scarlet Christmas Lily in her hair. And then I see the darndest thing—she's barefoot.

"You know my name!" I say with curiosity.

"Of course I do"

"How?"

"I've known it since the day you were born."

"I'm sorry, but I don't know you."

"Hold on, oh my, oh dear," putting her hand to her chest, fanning herself.

"I need to catch my breath." She inhales deeply. "I was supposed to be here the minute you arrived, but I got a late start and had to run. Okay, whew, now where were we? Oh, yes. You said you don't know me. Well, you should. I've been watching out for you, your whole life."

She takes hold of her muumuu, and twirls around on her tiptoes, showing off. "I'm your guardian angel—Ambriel.

"My guardian angel?

"The one and only. I was chosen just for you."

"You don't look like an angel."

"How do you know? Have you seen one before?"

"Well, no, just in books."

"Okay then, don't let the cover fool you. The books hardly ever get us right. We come in all colors. There are still a few who like to sport the white robe and wings. Me? I prefer incognito."

"I had no idea."

"You do look confused."

"I am! This is all so strange."

I look around trying to get my bearings. Instead, I get a glimpse of a golden gate with a beautifully carved C above it.

I have to ask. "Is that gate for me?"

"That's the gate you will pass through when the time is right."

"I'm not going to pass through now?"

"Not yet, you just got here. You're not ready to pass through just yet.

"This must be some sort of weird dream "Wake up! Wake up!" I say, while slapping my cheeks.

Ambriel twirls her beads, and says smugly, "Satisfied?"

"No! Not at all."

"I'll give you a minute to let it sink in."

Okay, it's not every day you meet your guardian angel, so, obviously, I have a plethora of questions.

"If you really are my guardian angel, then tell me when and where I was born?"

Ambriel acts bored, while admiring her scarlet fingernails. "Is that the best you can do? Oh, all right. I'll play along. You were born in 1928 in Fawn Oakes, Minnesota."

"Who's my best friend?"

"Millie"

"What was my sixth grade teacher's name?"

"Sister Jane Frances."

"How many kids in my family?"

"Ten counting you."

"Do you really know everything about me?"

Ambriel clasps her hands behind her back, and circles around me, sizing me up.

"Every word you uttered, every step you took, and every prank you ever played."

"Oh, oh,"

"Indeed."

"We angels are here to help you decide what's right and what's wrong—we're your conscience. Some people choose not to listen to their guardian angels, and end up going the other direction."

Well, let me tell you, I had a bad sense of direction growing up, which was something that usually got me into plenty of trouble—like the time in sixth grade when my best friend Millie and I put rubber bands around the spray nozzles on the sinks in the kitchen at school. When the cooks came in the morning and turned the faucets on, the water shot out and sprayed all over them. It was hilarious! Millie and I were hiding in a cloak closet in another room, laughing our heads off—that's how they caught us. The school sent us home, and Ma made me go to my room and pray the rosary. She said praying the rosary wasn't punishment but rather a way of asking God to help me become a better person. Pa came to my defense, and told Ma I was just spirited for my age. Ma said, just the same, I needed guidance.

Ambriel says she remembers that day, and explains, it was one of those times I chose not to listen to her. "Well, if I'm not going to pass through the gate, where do I go from here?"

"This is where I give you the divine disclosure. On Christmas Eve, just short of your 19th birthday, you passed from earth into the company of angels, where you are in a very special part of heaven."

"I'm in heaven? Don't get me wrong, being here is wonderful, and this part of heaven certainly is very beautiful and all—I mean the music sure is swell, and the colors are a nice touch, but since I can't pass through that gate yet, where do I go from here?"

"Oh my, did I leave that part out? Senior moment. My instructions are to take you on a journey. We will be going back to places and see things that will help you understand your purpose, so you can move on to a more glorious life."

"What things?"

Oh, like the ripple a stone makes when you drop it into the water."

"Huh?"

"It's a metaphor. I like using them, so try to keep up. The stone is you, and the ripples are your words and actions, reaching out and touching others. It's vital for you to understand how the way you live your life, whether good or bad, affects other people.

"My words and actions usually just get me into trouble. I can't imagine they ever touch anyone."

"You underestimate yourself. Come along with me, and we

will go to a little part of heaven I like to refer to as Memory Lane."

Ambriel skips along the path. I have to run to catch up.

"You sure are one fascinating angel, Ambriel."

"Just keeping it interesting."

Chapter 2

Growing old is mandatory,
Growing up is optional

Chili Davis

Ambriel and I are walking along a narrow path where I see a familiar figure coming towards us. She is wearing black and white, and as she gets closer, I realize it's Sister Jane Frances! She looks the same as she did when I was in the fourth grade. She's deep in conversation with an individual that looks exactly like the angels in my Bible Stories books. He has wavy blonde hair, green eyes and wearing a flowing green and gold robe. He has huge gold wings that flutter slightly behind him as he walks.

"Hi Francie," Sister Jane Frances says. "Good to see you."

Her companion waves to me, and they keep walking. It sounded like they were talking about something medical and they were both excited about their topic. It was way over my head though.

"Who in the world is that with Sister Jane Frances?" I ask Ambriel.

"Oh, first of all, we're not in the world", she says gently "but you'll get used to that as we go along."

I swallowed hard. This dying thing just got very real.

"That, my dear, is Saint Raphael," she says. He's one of the archangels and is the patron saint of physicians, also known as the angel of healing. He is always watching what is happening in the medical field and loves to talk about it with everyone."

We turn the corner where I suddenly catch a strong whiff of antiseptics.

"Ah, here we are," says Ambriel. "Let's take a look at one of the turning points in your life and the impact it had on you and all of those around you."

She bends over and magically parts the grass and the ground beneath our feet. Somehow, I'm looking down from way up high, but it feels like I'm just barely floating above a building. When I look down, I see myself sitting alone in a room in my hometown.

It's June of '45, and the room is Doc Carlson's office. I'm flipping through Life Magazine. My ankle is throbbing, and I keep leaning over to rub it. Music is playing. It's Danny Kaye singing I whistle and I hum, but I hum to whom, to whom do I hum, to whom? That sure is a swell song.

Now I know my body isn't a perfect specimen, by any stretch of the imagination, I mean boys never flip their wigs over me or anything like that. However, I haven't been feeling well since my graduation from High School. I thought it was the stress of graduation and starting my new job at Sears and Roebuck. I've been losing a lot of weight lately—a minor detail that isn't helping my bra sizes any. In addition, I have a nagging cough that is wearing me out. The way I see it, none of this is attracting the opposite sex, so I decide to see the doctor. I figure I'm old enough to see a doctor on my own without having to put any more stress on Ma. She has enough to worry about with my brother, Tom, fighting in the war. Even though the Germans surrendered to Eisenhower in May, there is still fighting with the Japanese in Okinawa, and Tom is in the thick of it. I see the worry on Ma's face when there is talk of the war.

My parents' names are Mary and Joseph, and we live on a farm in Minnesota. As fate would have it, I was born to Mary and Joseph on December 25, 1928. Christmas Day! I'm not kidding. However, Ma says, in no way does that make me Divine, and I had better learn to mind my P's and Q's.

The office door opens, and Doc Carlson sits down behind his desk. He frowns over the papers in his hands.

I have known Doc my whole life. He delivered me, as well as the other nine kids in my family. He's lost his hair, and his bulging belly tempts the fate of the buttons on his shirt—but his kind face never changes.

He smiles at me, while sticking his spectacles into his pocket. "Francie," he says.

"I called your parents, and asked them to come to my office. The chest x-rays show some patchy infiltrates in your lungs. As soon as your folks get here, I'll go over the results with all of you."

Patchy infiltrates?—doesn't sound good. So much for not worrying Ma. I look down at the magazine in my lap, trying to appear mature, while the mind-numbing ticking of the clock gives me a headache.

Finally, the nurse ushers my parents into the office, where they sit in the two empty chairs next to me.

"Joe, Mary," Doc begins, "Thank you for getting here so quickly. As I said to you over the telephone, Francie came to see me because she hasn't been feeling well."

Pa looks at me and back to Doc. "Sounds serious, Doc."

Ma sits stoic. She's like that.

Doc continues. "Francie tells me she hasn't been feeling well lately. Her weight's down, and she says she doesn't have much of an appetite. Besides the cough, she also has a lot of pain and swelling in her left foot and ankle. We took some x-rays, and…well," Doc hesitates. "The results are disturbing. I won't beat around the bush here, Joe. It's possible, Francie has tuberculosis."

Prickles of alarm dance on my arms. Did I hear him right? Bad news is like that. You don't believe it at first.

"Tuberculosis? Francie has tuberculosis?" Pa's voice trembles.

"The chest x-rays show some haziness in both upper lobes of her lungs, and the films of her foot show a destructive lesion. I've reviewed the x-rays with the radiologist, Dr. Lamb, and it's his opinion that it's tuberculosis." He looks at me and says, "The symptoms and films point to tuberculosis, Francie"

I'm usually not at a loss for words, but my throat goes dry as chalk, and I can't speak.

Doc continues. "TB has grown to epidemic proportions in our country, Joe, but heck, you already know that. Millions of people around the world are carriers, and it just keeps spreading. If she's been in contact with anyone who has it, she could have breathed it in when they cough. Or it's a good possibility that it could have come from one of your cows."

My cows? How's that possible?"

"Well you see, when a cow gets infected with the bacterium, which comes from the soil, humans can get it by eating the meat or drinking the milk from that cow. That kind of TB is called bovine, and it affects the bones, which is the case here with Francie's foot and ankle."

"My God, Doc—if that's the case then what about the rest of the family?"

"Yeah, Joe, I know…" Doc frowns. "I'd like you to bring the other children in and we'll take x-rays just to make sure. That includes you and Mary too." Doc pauses before he says, "This disease is a real monster. It doesn't spare anyone."

My mind is racing by this time. Tuberculosis! Wow! People die from that! I feel the blood rushing to my face, and I can barely speak. "Wh-what happens now?" I choke on my words.
Ma turns and looks at me with pain in her eyes. It's the first time she moves since she sat down.

Doc clears his throat, and takes the spectacles from his

pocket. He fidgets with them, focusing on me. "We really don't know what we're dealing with here, Francie. Researchers have discovered the bacterium that causes TB, but so far, they don't know how to kill it. In other words, there's no drug to cure it."

My eyes are glued on him as he struggles with his next bit of information.

"To be safe, you'll need to go to a sanatorium."

His words hang in the air like a death sentence. Sanatorium—No! People go there and never come back! Doc must have made some kind of mistake. It's just a little cough. I don't even feel that sick, for heaven's sake! The words only race through my mind. I sit dumbfounded, while the news keeps getting worse.

"Until then, it would be a good idea when you're around other people, that you cover your mouth when you cough. You might want to carry a hankie with you." Then he looks back at Pa, and delivers the final blow. "I've made some calls, Joe, there is room for her to go to the Glen Lake Sanatorium at Oak Terrace, just west of Minneapolis.

"Glen Lake!" I find my voice. "That's…that's 200 miles from here!"

Now It's Ma's turn. "Are you absolutely certain, Doc? Couldn't it be some kind of mistake?"

Doc squirms. It isn't as if he will be giving me medicine for a cold, telling me to get some rest. Nope! He has more bad news.

He looks up at the ceiling and says, "I'm sorry, Mary, but I've gone over the test results more than once, and there's no doubt. We could do a series of sputum cultures in the days to come to see if it changes, but really, the best form of action would be for her to leave today."

Today? I squeeze my eyes tight to fight back tears, unable to contain the seepage.

Pa clutches my hand and says to Ma, "Mary, we have no choice, we have to do what's right for Francie and the rest of the family. We need to get whatever help we can. If that means going to a sanatorium, then we need to prepare."

Ma's voice is soft. "Francie, God is testing us. Do you understand why we need to do this?"

I try to understand, and I want to be brave, my insides feel like I'm being squeezed through our Maytag ringer. "How long will I have to be there?"

We all look to Doc for the answer to that one.

"Well, it's hard to say. The first six weeks will be for observation and diagnosis, but my guess is you could be there up to six months."

Six months...every ounce of breath rushes from my lungs, like a popped balloon.

"They'll know more once they observe you for a few days at the sanatorium," says Doc. "Then a determination can be made as to how long the cure will take. It's never the same for anyone, Francie."

I think he is trying to be reassuring, but six months is way too long. A sanatorium is not in my plans. Millie and I are saving our money so we can leave Fawn Oakes and go to college. I just got my job at Sears as a cashier, and Millie is working the lunch counter at Woolworth's Dime Store. How can we do that if I have to go to a sanatorium for six months? The door to my future just slammed shut!

—⚭—

Heaven: Ambriel and I walk on a little further where the air feels different. It smells like pine trees, and tamaracks and wheat fields. I realize I am back at my home on the farm.

—⚭—

Pa isn't sure our ole '38 Chevy will make it the 400 miles roundtrip, so he decides he and I will travel to Glen Lake by bus. While Pa makes arrangements, I go to my room to pack. My two younger sisters, Lily and Sarah, come with me—we share a room on the second floor of our farmhouse. Lily is 13 and Sarah is 15. I am now the oldest at home since Tom left. A sliver of sunlight hovers over my suitcase with dust motes floating in its beam. My miserable thinking imagines they are tiny particles of tuberculosis just waiting to be sucked into my lungs. I'm lost in my thoughts when the sound of Lily's voice snaps me out of it. I resume throwing underwear into my suitcase. I toss aside a green pair that has a hole in the crotch.

"Francie, what's wrong? Pa says you're not feeling good," Lily says.

She looks so sweet with the sunlight glittering in her hair, and those sparkling blue eyes, just like Pa's. Sarah and I have dark hair and green eyes like Ma's, which Ma says comes from our French descent.

I sit down on the edge of the bed next to Lily, and take hold of her hand. It feels tiny, like the dolls we have in frilly dresses sitting on shelves over our beds. "Actually, I feel swell, I say. I just have a little cough, but the doctors say I have a disease called tuberculosis, and if I cough around you, I could make you sick too. So, I can't be near you kids right now."

Sarah sits on the bed, and the mattress sags, forcing the lid of my suitcase to slam shut.

"Where do you have to go?" Lily asks.

"It's a place called Glen Lake Sanatorium."

"How far away is that?"

"Well, it's pretty far. Pa says it should take us about five hours on the bus. I think we'll get there around 8 o'clock tonight." I keep my composure. My voice doesn't give away how I feel about losing the world the three of us share in this room.

Just then, my two youngest brothers, Michael and Johnny, come running into the house, slamming the screen door behind them. The warm summer temperatures keep them playing outside most of the day, and the holes in the knees of their pants are proof of how hard they work at it. Since school let out, they like to play in the barn, or on the tire-swing hanging from the oak near the house, or crawl around on their hands and knees with their toy trucks, making roads in the dirt. Michael is ten and Johnny is seven—the youngest of the Carver clan.

Pa had asked Ma, a while back, if maybe it was time she held another baby in her arms. But Ma asked him if he had gone and lost his fool mind.

The boys race each other up the stairs to our room. When Johnny sees my suitcase he says, "Francie, Pa told us to come and say goodbye. Are you running away from home?"

I start to laugh, but Sarah, who has been very quiet all this time, gets angry. "No stupid! She's not running away!"

Johnny ignores her, and looks at me, with innocent eyes. His voice is so small. "Why are you packing your suitcase?"

Sarah jumps to her feet and blurts, "Because she's sick, that's why! And she has to go live in a big ole scary sanatorium!"

Sarah and I lock eyes, and an anxious feeling rushes through me. I want to run from the room as fast as I can, down the road and through the field, so fast that I can outrun the disease that is consuming me.

Then Johnny asks— "What's a sam-a-torium?"

Chapter 3

*"If difficulties were known at the onset of
a journey, most of us would never start
out at all.*

Dan Rather

Heaven: "Being your guardian angel was a lot of work at times,"
Ambriel says.

"You tested my skills. But I have to hand it to you, you kept it
interesting."

"It still gets to me that you know all these things. Millie and I
thought we were smooth, but Sister Georgiana knew exactly where
to point the finger. After all, we weren't the brightest bulbs in the
class."

Ambriel twirls her beads, when a fearsome faced angel says,
"Hello, Ambriel!"

She smiles and waves to him. He looks about 10 feet tall to
me, and seems to be walking on the river water. He holds a staff
in his hand, and carrying a young boy on his shoulder. His robe
is a brilliant red. He looks my way and says, "How was the trip,
Francie?"

I recognize him from my metals the nuns handed out in
school. He's the patron saint of travelers. "Interesting," I say back. I
can't believe I just spoke to St. Christopher.

As we walk along, Ambriel asks, "Do you know where we are
going?"

The smell of exhaust triggers my memory, and I see that I'm
on the bus headed to the sanatorium.

—⁓—

I take the first seat next to the window, and Pa slides in next to me. I brush my hands across my lap to smooth out the wrinkles on my skirt. It isn't my best skirt, just a pink and gray cotton plaid that I had hanging in my closet. I pull it down over my knees as far as I can. I always do things like that when I don't know what to do with my hands. I notice a smudge on the toe of my new pumps, so I dab my finger to my tongue and rub the spot until it disappears. "You keep rubbing that way you'll make a hole and your toe will pop out," Pa says.

I meet his mischievous blue eyes. "I know what you're trying to do". I lift my feet so he can see both shoes. "I just bought these last week, and I don't want them ruined. But I guess where I'm going I probably won't have much use for them, huh, Pa?"

"Well, Francie, we won't know until we get there. Those shoes still have a lot of walking in them."

It's hot on the bus. When I look out the window, I see the heat shimmering off the highway. It makes the air look all wavy. I keep my eyes fixed on the window, and watch telephone poles flash by, but that only makes me dizzy. Soon, everything that is familiar is behind us, and all there is to look at are billboards. There is one where a young girl is dressed in a white ruffled dress, sitting on a carousel horse. The sign reads, always Buy Chesterfield, and there she is, all dressed up, riding the carousel smoking a cigarette. When I was little, I would ask Pa, "What does that sign say," and he would answer in a serious voice, "It doesn't say anything—you have to read it."

The bus stops at almost every small town, making the time pass as slow as the clouds drifting overhead. I'm really not anxious to get to where I'm going, but all the hours on the bus gives me too much time to think, mostly about Ma, and the sadness in her eyes when we hugged and said goodbye—just like the day Tom got shipped off to Okinawa. Thinking about Tom just then sends a pang of loneliness through me. It's funny how one minute you're not really feeling lonely, and then a thing pops in your head, and that feeling climbs right inside of you. The Greyhound finally pulls into the bus station. It smells as if the inside of an oil can. Everyone on the bus scrambles to get his or her bags. Pa and I get off first. Behind us is a young woman my older brothers would call a real dish. When she steps off the bus, she walks past some army boys who are loitering outside the station. They whistle and make catcalls. One of them shouts, "Hi sugar, are you rationed?" I can tell she likes the attention.

Pa pulls his timepiece out of his breast pocket, and says "It's 8:05."

Once we get our luggage, he calls a taxicab to take us to the sanatorium.

"Where to Mister?" says the taxicab driver.

"Glen Lake Sanatorium," Pa says.

I thought I saw the man wince.

I have never been in a taxicab in my life. The man drives swiftly through the busy streets, slamming on his brakes and blasting his horn. I can't tell if I'm scared or excited. I've never seen this much traffic.

The taxicab driver is a small, intense-looking man, who hunches forward in his seat, gripping the steering wheel. He has beady little eyes that keep peering at me in the rearview mirror. It's making me uncomfortable, so I sink down in my seat, out of view of his disapproving scowl.

Once we are out of the heavy traffic, we travel some distance into a rural area.

The sanatorium comes into view. I see a towering smokestack looming in the distance. My heart pounds. My eyes drink in the scenery. We're surrounded by rolling hills and forest. Next to the building with the smokestack, there are three stucco cottages scattered along the slopes, that are built into the hillside. Just beyond the buildings, is a wooded area of birch and evergreens that lead down to a lake. Pa tells me It's called Birch Island. The view is spectacular, but it doesn't comfort me. I want to go home.

The taxicab drives into a u-shaped driveway, where a massive red brick building towers in front of me. I turn my head from side to side to see it all. The buildings on each side remind me of brick arms, waiting to wrap themselves around me, taking me captive. I tilt my head back so I can see the top, and count five floors. In the center is a peaked roof with large, triple-hung windows and a veranda. Little do I know, this is where I'll be spending the next two years of my life.

After Pa pays the driver, the man speeds away as if the place is haunted. I'm glad to see him go. Pa helps me with my things, and we go inside.

In the admitting office, a silver-haired woman, dressed in a starched white uniform, hands Pa forms to fill out.

I sit in a chair outside the admitting office, but I can hear every word they say.

Pa catches his breath when one of the questions on the form asks for permission to perform an autopsy. The clerk then asks Pa for an advance payment on the hospital stay for the return ticket home. She tells Pa this is all just a formality. She explains the ticket home is to cover the cost of transporting the corpse back to the family in the event the patient dies. Pa doesn't react. The woman goes on to tell Pa it will cost $26.95 a week for me to stay at the sanatorium. She says the county where we live will pay a portion of the bill, but Pa will have to pay the rest. He agrees and signs the papers.

After the paperwork is accomplished, Pa steps out of the admitting office. The clerk snaps an identification bracelet around my wrist, and tells Pa it's time to take me to the floor. The lady goes for a wheelchair.

Pa pulls me close, kissing the top of my head. "Your hair smells good," he whispers.

"It's Halo shampoo," I say. I'm trying to stay strong too, but my throat gets tight, and I struggle to hold back tears. "Bye, Pa. You have a safe trip back home, okay?"

He takes me by my arms, gently pushing me from him. "You take care now, Francie Girl, and do what these nice people tell you. I don't want you wearing out those new shoes just yet. The Good Lord has a plan for you sweetheart—you're His unfinished business."

The clerk comes around the corner with the wheelchair, holding it steady for me. I get in, and lean back against the wooden slats. As she wheels the chair down the hall, Pa stands with his hat in his hand. Only then does he cry, as the elevator swallows me.

—⁂—

Because there is no bed available for me this night, she takes me to the second floor where they put me on a cot in the hallway, with a screen around me. They give me a hospital gown and a bedpan. I lay there without blinking or moving a muscle and overhear two nurses talking. Their voices muffled. I strain to hear. Ma used to get after me for my eavesdropping. I can't help it—It's my nature.

"Sadie in 217 isn't going to be here much longer," says the first nurse.

The other replies, "When I was coming up the elevator, a nurse from third said they lost a patient last night and another one this afternoon."

The first nurse lets out a sigh and says, "When 217 goes, that will be four this week."

I never felt so alone in my life.

Chapter 4

*"How hard it is to escape from places.
However carefully one goes, they hold
you – you leave little bits of yourself
fluttering on the fences — little rags and
shreds of your very life."*

Katherine Mansfield

Heaven: Ambriel has me sit down next to her on a bench surrounded by white daisies and cotton-ball clouds. I hear laughter; I've heard that laugh before. "Where is it coming from?" I ask.

Ambriel says, "This is a part of Heaven I like to call Carver Heaven."

We turn another corner, and to my surprise, I see my grandfather sitting in a large chair. A little boy is sitting on my Grandpa's lap, and Grandpa is reading to him.

I hear a voice like an angel singing the sweetest lullaby I have ever heard. It's my grandmother. She stands next to the little boy. I hear my grandfather call him Joey.

"I vaguely remember Ma telling us she had a baby brother named Joey, who was run over by a car backing out of the driveway on grandpa's farm.

The driver didn't see Joey until it was too late," I say. "Ma said her parents very seldom laughed after that."

Ambriel says, "The little boy is your uncle Joey, Francie."

"Oh my goodness, he's still a toddler, and my grandparents look so young. I've seen pictures of them on their wedding day, and they look exactly now as they do in the picture."

Ambriel says, "Would you like to meet your uncle?"

"Would I!" Grandma takes my hand, and showers me with kisses. Grandpa lets out a hardy laugh.

"Come here, child," Grandpa says, hugging me. "Come and meet your uncle." The toddler squeals with joy and stretches his hands out for me to pick him up. He has a golden halo around his head. Grandma and Grandpa are beaming. I'm basking in the family reunion. It's so joyful!

Ambriel says," You must say your good byes now, Francie, it's time to go."

"We will sit here for a while and watch as you get introduced to sanatorium life," she says. Ambriel has the stem of the Christmas Lily in her teeth, while levitating on her side next to me, looking very comfortable. She tells me to close my eyes and breathe in.

—⁓—

I'm in a dark tunnel and I hear voices echoing my name. At the end of the tunnel is a bright light where my family stands huddled together waving goodbye. Ma's crying.

"Ma, Ma, where are you?" I can hear her sobbing but I can't see her. "Ma, Ma," I call out again, and wake myself up. I'm in a fog, for a moment I panic thinking I'm late for work, and then I notice the bedpan! It all comes flooding back with a hot sinking feeling— I'm not dreaming.

Outside the window, streaks of red and gold gouge the sky, and the sun is making its way above the skyline. Ma would be in the kitchen soon getting breakfast ready for Pa when he comes in from milking.

I stretch my arms over my head to pull the kinks out that have taken root in my back. I need a bathroom, but I just lay here looking at the silver odd-shaped bedpan. It looks like something Ma would put flowers in and set outside on the porch step. I have no choice. It's either that or wet myself. So, with one hand I struggle to pull my bloomers down and with the other, I shove the cold metal pan underneath me. After a second or two, I realize lying flat on my back isn't going to work. So, I push myself onto my elbows for a better seat, so to speak. I look at the screen between the open hallway and me and do my duty into the pan as fast as I can before anyone hears me. When I finish, I lift my butt and pull the pan out from under me, holding my breath to steady myself so I won't spill.

Just then, a nurse pokes her head around the screen and says, "Well, hello there. Have you been awake long?" When she sees what I'm doing, she scrambles to help me with the pan. Thank goodness, because I have no idea what to do with it. She takes it from me and disappears across the hall, but before I can get my bloomers back on, she is back and hands me some toilet paper, a washcloth, a toothbrush, and some water in a basin. When I finish, she tells me to leave everything and an aide will take care of it.

"I'm Nurse Kirschner, and I'll be taking care of you today. How are you feeling this morning?"

She has blonde hair that falls in waves around her shoulders beneath her nurse's cap. She has a warm smile.

"I'm okay," I say, rubbing some gunk from the corner of my eye. I'm still sleepy and my manners aren't the best.

"I imagine you must feel a little lost waking up in such a strange place. Was the cot very uncomfortable?"

"Oh no, it was swell." I lie.

"Your name is Francine Carver, is that right?"

"Yes."

"Well, I'm very glad to meet you, Miss Carver. I'm personally going to do everything I can to help you feel at home here."

Her voice is comforting, like a mother's lullaby. "Thank you. That's very kind of you." What I really want is a comb for my hair. I try weaving my fingers through my tangled mess, but it's too full of knots, so I have to scrap that idea and keep my bird's-nest look.

"We have a bed ready for you up on 5-Main, so come with me and we'll get you settled," she says while helping me into the wheelchair. "The other girls will be having their breakfast soon. Are you hungry?"

"Not really." I can never eat when I'm nervous. That's probably why I am so skinny.

"Well, maybe once you smell the food it will help get your appetite back," she says, as she places a blanket across my lap. We start our journey down a long hall.

I am now officially a sanatorium patient—just another name on a chart. How quickly life can change. The day before I was at home with hardly a care in the world, and now here I am in a strange place, treated like an invalid where everything is unfamiliar. All my senses are on high alert.

The overhead paging system announces Dr. Ganzer to call extension 4823. Somewhere a phone is ringing, and a cart with perfectly folded linens sits idle against a wall. Down the hall, two young girls are pushing a food cart into a patient's room leaving behind the aroma of freshly brewed coffee and the salty tang of bacon. Women in white uniforms and muffled voices are poring over charts at the nurse's stations, ignoring us as we pass by. Why shouldn't they? I am certainly no celebrity or anyone important. I am just like dozens of other patients who pass by here every day. Nevertheless, I am a little anxious. Every nerve ending in my body is standing at attention waiting for something horrible to rain down on me.

Then I notice the floor—it's made of terrazzo.

I read about terrazzo once in an encyclopedia, and the reason I remember is the bit about the goat's milk. The book said that terrazzo is made out of marble chips, clay, and get this—goat's milk, which is the sealer that preserves it and gives it that wet, marble-like look. This floor is polished to a lustrous finish, and every few feet there are circular patterns of gold and brown that swirl around. In the center of the swirls is a bright gold star-shaped sun. It's spectacular and looks like a floor that should be in a palace, but here it is in a sanatorium full of sick people. For some reason that calms me down a little. If something so beautiful could be in a place like this, maybe things won't be so bad after all. Uh—clueless, right?

When we get to the elevator, a middle-age man wearing a black uniform standing by the open doors approaches us.

"Where to, Nurse Kirschner?" he asks.

"Good morning, Mr. Clark—five please."

He helps her with my wheelchair and pulls the doors of the elevator shut. He turns the crank and the elevator is set for the fifth floor. The cage jolts once and then I feel the vibrations as it begins its journey upward.

"How've you been, Mr. Clark?" the nurse asks.

"I feel as light as air, Ma'am. Doctor said I'm good as new and get to go home in two more weeks. It's been nearly a year since I've been home with my wife and kids, and I can't wait to get back," he says grinning from ear to ear.

"That's so wonderful, but we're definitely going to miss you around here."

The elevator comes to a stop, springing up and down like the old tire swing hanging from our oak tree, causing my nervous stomach to spring with it. When we get off the elevator, I have to ask, "Is that elevator operator a patient here?"

"He is," she says as we ramble down the hall. "Some of the patients who have ambulatory privileges work here. There are patients who work in the bakery, the shoe shop, the print shop and even as elevator operators until they're ready for discharge. Mr.

Clark has been an operator for about six months now."

The wooden chair creaks as we make our way around one side of the nurses' station to my room while she explains to me that the fifth floor is specifically for patients who have tuberculosis in their bones. "You'll be in room 530," she said. "It's a ward with seven other teenage girls. You'll be in a corner bed with nice big windows on both sides of you."

When we enter the room, I am blinded by white—white metal-framed beds, white sheets and white walls. The beds are lined up against the walls on either sides of the room. At the far end of the room are two more beds facing in the direction of the door. One of the beds is vacant. This is it—my new home.

Girls my age are sitting with breakfast trays propped in front of them. Nurse Kirschner pushes my wheelchair across the room. I feel all eyes on me, like wild animal eyes gleaming in the dark sizing up the intruder.

She helps me onto the bed and says, "There you go, Miss Carver, right on time. I see your breakfast tray is here."

She smoothes the sheets around me and says, "We're going to keep you pretty busy today. Dr Wagner has ordered a lot of tests for you. I'll be back to get you after you've had a chance to eat. We'll have you stay in the hospital gown for now until after the tests. Once you're done, you can slip into something of your own."

"Okay." I sound as meek as a mouse in a room full of stray cats.

"But first maybe you'd like to meet everyone."

There is a full-length window separating my bed from the girl next to me.

"Good morning Miss Popke," says the nurse. "How are you this morning?"

The round-faced girl is finishing her breakfast. "I just came back from a five-mile run, and now I'm famished." "Thanks for asking."

"Well, well," says the nurse. No wonder you finished so quickly. But maybe you should hold off on the running until further notice."

"Now, Nurse Kirschner, you know I would never disobey the rules."

"That's good to hear. Besides, I need you to set a good example for your new roommate."

I have a habit of tampering with the rules myself. Of course, that was mostly when I was with Millie. We couldn't help it; trouble always had a way of finding us. But things will probably be different here. Miss Popke seems like an obeyer of rules.

Nurse Kirschner says, "Would you be kind enough to introduce our new patient to the rest of the girls?" She tells Miss Popke my name, and then says she will be back for me in an hour.

The round-faced girl leans in my direction and says, "Hi, Francine, the nurses here are so formal—you can call me Poppy." She smiles when she talks. Her round cheeks bunch up making her eyes look squinty.

I feel a gush of relief; she seems nice.

"Poppy…I like that." I say. "Everyone calls me Francie."

Poppy starts at her side of the room with the introductions. "Francie, meet Agnes Gardner," pointing to a small girl with wild red hair that spirals in tangles and curls around her freckled face. Poppy says, "She's the baby of our group."

Before I have a chance to say anything, Agnes rattles off, "Hi Francie, nice to meet you. I'm 15 and I've been here eight months—I have TB in my left hip—the doctors say it's getting better and I should be able to get up with privileges real soon—this isn't such a bad place—I'm sure you're going to like it here—where is your TB?"

She is a real fast talker. She almost sounds like Millie and me when we pretended to talk with a French accent around strangers to make them think we were exotic. I would be Monique and she would be Sophia. Crazy, I know, but we were much younger then. We gave that up once we got to high school.

"It's in my foot and ankle and my lungs," I answer.
Poppy doesn't give Agnes a chance to rip loose again. Next to Agnes is Izzy Kress, short for Isabelle. "Welcome to the insane asylum, Francie. Don't believe Poppy when she says she was out running. I know for a fact she would rather lie on her back and eat bonbons all day."

" Hey," says Poppy.

Izzy reminds me of the dolls Sarah and I got once when we sent in box tops from the Tide detergent boxes. Izzy's white-blonde hair is long and silky like that. She wears it in a ponytail twirling it through her fingers. I notice a combination-phonograph-radio on her nightstand with a bunch of records stacked next to it.
The next girl I meet is Lucy Marshall. "She's the married lady of our group and lets us drool over Sam whenever he comes to visit," says Poppy. "She also had a birthday a few days back and is officially no longer a teenager."

"Hi-de-ho, Francie," says Lucy.

"Happy belated birthday, Lucy." I say.

"And at the end of the room on your side is Helen Coalwell," says Poppy pointing.

Helen is pale as water-and-flour paste, and blends with the sheets, making her look half-dead. In fact, if it wasn't for the occasional rise and fall of her chest, I would have thought she was dead. It sounded like she said it was nice to meet me, but her voice is too weak to tell.

"Beatrice Lund is up next," says, Poppy, "Nickname Bea."

She gives me the biggest welcome of all.

"What's buzzin', cousin? Where ya' from?"

Bea seems a little older than the rest of the girls; maybe it's the way she wears her hair. It's dark brown and cut straight across just below her ear making her nose look pointy. I've never been a fan of that style.

"Fawn Oakes, about 200 miles west of here," I say.

"Hey, I have a cousin who lives in Lakefield. Maybe you know her…name's Katherine Atwood."

"I don't, but we play Lakefield in basketball and I've been there a lot; maybe I've seen her."

"Well, I'll have to introduce you the next time she comes to visit. You might know some of the same people."

"I'd like that."

"And last but not least is Margaret," says Poppy.

Her bed is to the left and perpendicular to mine. I say "Hello, Margaret," But she doesn't say anything, just nods her head without even looking in my direction.

I give Poppy a questioning look.

"Don't mind her," Poppy whispers. "She hardly talks to any of us, and if she does, look out—cuz she'll probably snap her cap. She's got a bad temper and a bad attitude."

I look up and down the room at all the girls and think TB sure does come in all shapes and personalities.

I survey the large room and can't help comparing it to my room at home with my sisters. The only comparison this room has to ours is that It's large, and we all have our own beds. But my sisters and I have colorful patchwork quilts that Ma taught us how to stitch. Our walls have lavender-flowered wallpaper and lace curtains and bookshelves full of our favorite books and dolls. Here the walls are white, and the windows have shades. Instead of books there are headphones hanging over each of our beds for listening to the radio. We get three internal radio stations KNUT, WCCO and WDAY a.m.

At home, Ma hangs the sheets on the clothesline to dry in the warm summer breeze where you can get lost in their crisp, fresh smell. Here, the sheets are stiff—probably ironed with a mangle—and smell antiseptic.

At home, we have dressers with oval mirrors and curved drawers with lace doilies. Here we have lockers.

I look down at my breakfast—It's cold and I'm not hungry. I can't help wonder how long I'll be calling this home.

Chapter 5

*"Man never made any material as
resilient as the human spirit."*

Bern William

Heaven: "It was hard for me those first days. I was so homesick;
all I did was cry. Oh by the way, will I be able to levitate once I
pass through the gate?" Ambriel grins and ignores my question.
Instead, she parts some clouds, and flocks of snow-white doves
appear, gleaming in a bright light against an azure sky. It's breath
taking. One dove in particular catches my attention. She spreads
her wings wide, floating majestically into a rainbow. The stream of
light resembles a path going upward. Inside are a million kisses and
hugs. Ambriel says, "This is more of Carver heaven."

I feel the hugs and kisses immediately. Then Ambriel says,
"Let's go back to the bench, and follow what comes next."

—⚅—

Just as promised, Nurse Kirschner comes for me and introduces
me to life at the sanatorium. On the first leg of my new adventure, I
spend the better part of the morning in x-ray. After stripping down,
taking deep breaths and holding still, I'm left in the dark where my
chest and other body parts are photographed from every direction.
I practically have to stand on my head whistling Dixie so they can
get the best possible shot. They then whisk me off to the laboratory
where I have even more fun, when technicians squeeze, poke, prod,
and use my arm for a pincushion so my blood can be sucked out
and placed into tubes for examination under a microscope.

Next, the day really gets rolling when I sit forward while they
pound on my back to loosen the phlegm in my lungs so I can cough

it up, spit it out and have it collected into a sputum cup. Tell me that wasn't fun—I almost gagged.

Finally, I fight back tears while staring at the ceiling and urinating into a bedpan. By this time, they have tapped into every one of my orifices that secrete bodily fluids. Talk about feeling violated! I could have walked into a crowded room naked singing The Star Spangled Banner and would have felt more comfortable— well—maybe not. But that's only because I can't sing. Anyway, the whole experience is humiliating.

By the time I get back to my room it's already lunchtime, and there is a tray waiting for me. I still have no appetite so my inquiring mind drifts toward Margaret. I can't help being curious about her. She has a stuck-up look on her face like the mannequins at Dalton's Department Store. But her porcelain skin, shiny eyes and long wavy hair flows like satin ribbons. Hers seem to be very neat for someone who has to lie in bed all day. Mine is flat as a pancake on one side and has a million snarls that will take half a day to untangle. Everything about her is prim and proper, like she is a cut above the rest of us. Now here's how my mind works; I have a fleeting urge to jump out of bed, bend her arms like a mannequin's and, just for fun, twist her head on backwards. I swear there is something drastically wrong with me.

I shake the urge and go back to watching her. She is toying with her soup, knocking it around with her spoon and does the darndest thing—she smashes her bread and tucks it underneath her plate, making it look like she ate it. What the heck. Who does she think she's fooling?

If Millie were here, we would have come up with some juicy stuff about Margaret. Millie would have said something like old Margaret probably hopped a boat and came here from another country. I would have added that she was an international jewel thief who was rendezvousing with a secret organization to pull off a heist in New Your City at a famous museum where the biggest ruby in the world was on display. Then Millie would have come up with the real zinger—that she was really a man disguised as a woman—and then we would have laughed until our sides split. Where is Millie when I need her?

I am busy ignoring my own food, conjuring up thoughts about Margaret, when all of a sudden she shoots me a threatening glance. For an instant our eyes lock, but I quickly look away. She then lays down into her pillow, just staring up at the ceiling. Okay, so much for pleasant conversation.

By late afternoon, I am feeling homesick and wishing I can call Ma. It hasn't even been 24 hours, and already my family and the room I shared with Lily and Sarah consume my thoughts. All I want is to go home. I jump when I hear a man's voice next to me.

"Good afternoon", he says. He is wearing a white doctor's coat with a stethoscope slung around his neck. The name stitched on the pocket reads Carl Wagner, M.D. His face is somewhat pudgy like he just popped a handful of jelly beans his mouth, but rather handsome, and he smells good—like Old Spice. When he sees me jump he says, "Sorry—didn't mean to startle you."

"Oh, that's okay. I guess I'm just a little nervous." I try to compose myself. "It's very nice to meet you. Are you here with my test results?" I'm anxious as all get out to find out how long I'll have to be here.

Dr. Wagner pulls the chair close to my bed. He crosses his ankle over his knee and lays the chart in his lap. He is a snappy dresser, wearing loafers with buckles and perfectly creased trousers—very uptown.

He slides back in the chair and eyes me with a serious demeanor. "Yes, I have them all right here," he says, rifling through the chart. "I see here you're 17. You'll be 18 in December, December 25th?"

Here we go—everyone is always curious about my birthday being on Christmas Day. I pull myself up onto my elbows. My hair still looks like a tumbleweed. "Yes, that's right," I say.

"Well how about that. How is it having a birthday on the biggest day of the year?"

"It's pretty fun actually. My presents usually say, Happy Birthday and Merry Christmas."

"That sounds like you get duped out of birthday presents."

"Maybe, but no one ever forgets my birthday!"

He then changes the conversation. "How has it been for you since you've been here?"

Aside from all the tests, everything's been swell."

He's very young looking. As far back as I can remember Doc Carlson was old.

Dr. Wagner says, "You have a good attitude, I like that. That's actually something that can help you get better. A positive attitude can help with recovery."

"That's what I've wanted to know," I say. "How long will it take?"

Dr. Wagner flips through the pages. "Well, let's look at the results, and then we can determine that." When he gets to what he's looking for, he stops and reads for a moment. "Tubercle bacilli were found in the material aspirated from your ankle, and your chest x-ray shows fibroid, exudative, pulmonary tuberculosis. It involves both upper lobes, and there is a question of a small cavity of your first rib anteriorly."

I must have had a dumb look on my face.

"What that means, Miss Carver, you have TB in your lungs and possibly in one of your ribs in the front of your chest and in your ankle. You're in second stage of the disease, which means you can infect other people. The diagnosis is that it's moderately advanced." He pauses, then his voice lifts. "But your prognosis is considered very favorable."

I heard favorable but could only think of advanced and infecting other people. My throat feels like sandpaper and my eyes start to burn. I'm not sure if I am getting good news or bad news. I want more than anything to talk to Ma. Instead, I say, "tuberculosis in my rib too? I thought you just got TB in your lungs?" I have been curious about TB in my bones."

"That's a common misconception, but I'm sorry to say that this bacterium is a real parasite. It can attack any part of the body, not just the lungs. Most patients usually get pulmonary tuberculosis, or TB of the lungs, because it's the easiest to get. But the bacteria can be carried from the lungs through the blood vessels to other parts of the body."

Then he slows down. He probably doesn't want to scare me. "We're going to do everything we can to help you get better. Starting tomorrow, we'll start penicillin injections; we're hoping that will fight other infections, though it won't stop the TB. Also, TB is a slow-growing bacterium and doesn't like the sun, so we're going to have you go out onto the veranda for some sunbathing. How would you like that?"

I don't —if he wants to know the truth! But Ma always told us kids if you can't say anything nice, don't say anything at all. So, I just smile.

"Nourishing food, plenty of rest and the sun's rays all play a big part in getting you cured. I'm sorry to say this, but you'll have to stay in bed at all costs—no getting up, not even to the bathroom. Moving around doesn't give the damaged tissue a chance to heal."

I knew it—more bad news. I should have made him stop after

he said sunbathing out on the veranda, then I could have at least pretended I was at a fancy resort somewhere on a tropical island with Millie.

"Try to keep in mind, Miss Carver; the TB has destroyed some of the tissue in your lungs and foot, so by lying still you'll give that tissue a chance to heal itself."

I think to myself, lie still all the time? How will I go to the bathroom? Some vacation.

He says, "We have nurses here around the clock to help you with anything you need, so be sure to ask. After we've observed you for a while, we can see how you respond to the treatment, and then we can get you started on carbon arc lamp therapy."

I don't know what that is, but I'm sure I'll be finding out. I can tell he has given this speech before.

"We can fight this thing, Miss Carver. Like I said earlier, your prognosis is very favorable. You're young and strong and, if you follow the rules, there's a good chance you can leave here in a year."

A year—oh my gosh! My heart is beating like a bass drum. My head feels fuzzy like a dandelion gone to seed—the slightest puff of air could blow it to kingdom come and nothing left but the stem fighting for survival. How will I survive a year lying flat on my back? It can't be done. I don't want to hear any more. The day has taken its toll on me. I am all alone in a room full of strangers, and a doctor I just met, tells me I have to stay in bed for a full year! I try to hold back, but the tears spill over onto my cheeks, and everything I've been holding in for the past couple of days' gush out like flood waters. I sob so hard I have to put my face in my hands. "I'm sorry to have to tell you all this, but you need to know exactly what we're dealing with and what it's going to take from you to get better. You need to work at it to get well."

He tries to be soothing. I want him to go away. I've heard

enough. I need to be alone for a while to let it all sink in.

He stands to leave. "I'll be back to see you in the morning when I make my rounds. Please try to get some sleep tonight."

My parents taught me not to be rude, but I can't look up or say anything to him. This is the second time this day I have not used good manners. I just keep my face buried in my hands, hidden away from the rest of the sanatorium, and cry. If I don't look up I can pretend I'm still at home where I belong. After a while, my face feels hot and slimy from tears. I need to blow my nose. I wipe my face, and my breath sucks up a couple of times. My whole body feels drained. I draw my eyes toward the window. A clump of trees tower against the red brick building that will now be home for the next year. My heart feels heavy and I want to cry again. The tree branches sway in the summer breeze. I can hear the leaves whispering, welcome to your new home, Francie. I watch a squirrel scamper up the trunk, circling around and almost meeting its tail on the other side. Then he darts up and out of sight. I want to be that squirrel scampering aimlessly without a care in the world.

I can see Birch Lake through the tangled branches and the sun making its journey to the west. I desperately need to hear Ma's voice.

Instead, I hear Nurse Jones.

—∞—

Nurse Jones is the evening nurse who comes on duty until eleven o'clock. She is perfectly polished and starched and marches in like a soldier to see me. Her nurse's cap sits square atop her head with her hair wound tightly at the nape in a bun, squeezing off any compassion that dares trickle out. Her arms are thick and round as tree limbs, offering no comfort to a scared, sick patient. Her large breasts give her lots of room for loud, authoritative bellowing. I hear Nurse Jones bark out a list of rules so fast I hardly absorb it all.

"Be sure to hold one of these cloths over your mouth when you cough. If something comes up, you need to spit it into this glass jar; it's called a sputum cup." She places the little jar and cloths on my nightstand. "Do not leave this room without these two items. Take them with you wherever you go. Do not get up for any reason. Use this bedpan." She then turns on her heels and whirls about the room like a vacuum cleaner, gathering everything in her path, making things as neat as a pin.

I clear my throat and try to speak, "Excuse me." Either she doesn't hear me or she just plain ignores me. "Excuse me, Nurse Jones?" I'm getting good at reading nametags, and this time the keeper-of-all-things tidy looks at me. "Um, I was wondering if I could call home."

"No phone calls during the first week" she says, while tossing some paper into a garbage can.

I brace up and try again. "But it's been a while since I've talked to my mother. I need to hear her voice."

"We have rules," she says sternly, "and one of those rules is NO phone calls during the first week! If you're homesick, things are only made worse if your family visits or calls. If you plan to get well, the outlined rules are no exceptions." She hands me a sheet of paper and says, "Here's the list of rules—you best learn them."

For heaven's sake, is she serious? I read the list.

7:15 – Rising bell

8:00 to 8:30 – Breakfast

8:30 to 11:00 – Rest or exercise as ordered

11:00 to 12:45 – Rest on bed

1:00 to 1:30 – Dinner

1:45 to 4:00 – Rest on bed, reading but no talking allowed, quiet hour

4:00 to 5:45 – Rest or exercise as ordered

6:00 – Supper

8:00 – Nourishment if ordered

9:00 – All patients in their rooms

9:30 – All lights out

It is futile to ask again. Nurse Jones isn't going to budge, so I have to wait a week to call home.

Out of the corner of my eye, I see Margaret smirking with her head supposedly buried in a book. I'm too tired to think or even care.

I look at the clock and realize I've been at the sanatorium almost one full day.

Chapter 6

Find people not to envy, but to admire.
Do not the profitable, but the admirable
deed, live by ideals.

Jonathan Sacks

Heaven: We come to a place where daises are in bloom. I pick a handful. I love their tender white petals and soft yellow center. I think they're one of nature's finest accomplishments. Ambriel grins and guides me to a corridor. I get another glimpse of St. Raphael. I'm still fascinated by the way his wings flutter when he walks. He's talking with two men wearing surgical gowns. "Those men seem familiar to me somehow, Oh, I know, they are the Mayo brothers from the Mayo Clinic in Rochester, Minnesota. If memory serves me right, I think their names are William and Charles. I remember hearing about them in the newspaper. They were outstanding surgeons. I hear the word tuberculosis."

"Yes," says Ambriel, "St. Raphael likes to be informed about science, and research and breakthrough medicines that come down the pike. But he also is known to say, it's God who heals."

I say, "No wonder the Mayo brothers seem excited to be talking with him." Ambriel says, "On this next part of our journey, I want you to pay close attention Dr. Wagner, a very admirable man. His words and his actions may help you understand more clearly."

"Oh, I agree!"

Ambriel says, "Your story is only just beginning. Now you can see what is going on with the people around you and how their words and actions influence others."

I hold the flowers in my lap touching the cushiony center with the tip of my finger. It's better than popcorn.

—⁂—

Just down the hall from my room, Dr. Wagner leans back in his office chair with his feet on his desk. It's almost quitting time. But his focus is on a medical journal. He's reading: "Dr. H. C. Hinshaw has collaborated with Dr. Karl H. Pfuetz, medical director of Mineral Springs Sanatorium in Cannon Falls, Minnesota, to give a drug called streptomycin to 54 patients. They found that the drug stopped the progress of TB in humans.

Just then, there is a tap on his door. "Come in." He says taking his feet off the desk.

It's Nurse Kirschner. "Do you have a minute?" she asks. I want to ask you about our new patient before you leave for the day.

"Oh, Nurse Kirschner, Yes, come in. Listen to this first. It's an article that says they've found a drug that's stopped the progress of TB in humans."

He shows her the journal and then reads from it.

She listens intently.

He goes on to read: "Three scientists, Hinshaw, Feldman, and Waksman, have convinced the Merck Company of Rahway, New Jersey, to fund experiments after explaining to George Merck that more people died of TB than were killed in action in World War I. Merck gave the 'go ahead'. Feldman and Hinshaw have been experimenting on guinea pigs at the Mayo Clinic and found sensational results."

"Did you hear that? Sensational results! A drug that could possibly cure tuberculosis! My Goodness! Do you know what this means?"

He hands her the journal so she can read for herself.

Nurse Kirschner scans through the journal. After reading the dynamics of the findings, she catches his excitement. "It's true," she says. "It says here that; George Merck has now ordered 50 scientists to work on streptomycin."

Dr. Wagner comes around his desk, speaking to Nurse Kirschner. Five million people are dying every year because of this disease, and we're practically helpless to do anything about it. I see their skeleton-like bodies with the flesh literally falling away from their bones, and there's not a damn thing I can do to stop it. His voice explodes with enthusiasm. "My God, they've possibly found a cure! This is a miracle!"

"Your dedication is admirable," she says.

"Speaking of, can we discuss Francine Carver? The new patient in 530?"

"Ah, yes, sweet little thing, isn't she?"

"Oh, so you've been to see her?"

"Yes, I got her tests back late this afternoon, so I went to meet her and gave her the results."

"That's what I want to talk to you about. How bad is it?"
"Her left foot shows a destructive lesion at the base of the first metatarsal with considerable soft tissue swelling." But her prognosis is favorable."

"That's good news. What type of treatment should we set up for her?"

"Let's start her out with general sun out on the veranda. We'll try some penicillin injections to fight off any infections. Then we'll go to the lamp therapy. I think she's going to need help adjusting. As expected, she didn't take the news very well that she might have to stay for a year."

"Oh dear, that's always such a low blow. She doesn't even know yet that staying flat in bed is going to be the real nightmare. I'll visit with her first thing in the morning to find out what her interests are, and hopefully we can keep her occupied."

"Yes, and make sure that Lydia girl takes her some books. She still works here doesn't she?"

He adds that last part a bit too sarcastically.

"Yes, Lydia Browning, and, yes, I'll see that she makes it to the ward tomorrow with the book cart."

"I don't think that girl is playing with a full deck." he jokes.

Nurse Kirschner sticks up for the aide. "She just has a unique way about her.

"Unique isn't the word for it."

"Put it this way: Miss Browning is a ray of sunshine for those girls, and knows how to lift their spirits. For that alone, I think she's worth her weight in gold."

"I stand corrected," he says. "Oh, Nurse Kirschner, before you go, in your opinion, how is Margaret Anderson getting along on the ward?"

"Oh, Margaret. She still keeps to herself a lot and isn't eating enough to keep a bird alive."

"I can't figure that girl out," he sighs. Her TB is improving, but if she doesn't eat, she won't be strong enough to get out of bed. I've told her that over and over. She could probably be up for bathroom privileges by now if she would just eat enough to regain her strength." I might have to call her father if she keeps going this way. Well, quitting time, he says.

"Enjoy your evening, Dr. Wagner."

"Good night, Nurse Kirschner.

Chapter 7

*The Journey of a thousand miles begin
with one step."*

Lao-Tse

Heaven: "I didn't know Dr. Wagner very well yet, but my instincts told me he was special. We couldn't get up and walk out, nor did he walk out on us."

"You are starting to understand. This is good," says Ambriel.

Just then, I hear music filling the air. I peek around the corner, and see a lovely woman singing and playing guitar. She is next to a group of people who are tending a garden. The workers are all singing and humming along to the music as they work. It seems to energize them.

"Hello Francie," says the woman guitarist. "Let me introduce myself. My name is Mrs. Sheela Flores. I was Carl Wagner's chemistry teacher in his senior year of high school."

I'm pleased to meet you, Mrs. Flores," I say.

She says, "Carl was a wonderful student. He had so many talents. One of them was playing guitar. He was the one who actually inspired me to take lessons.

Dr. Wagner gave you lessons?"

"Oh, no. His passion for music actually wore off on me and, sparked an interest in wanting to play myself. There is a saying around here that goes like this: music goes hand and hand with medicine. It's like praying twice. Music is helpful on the body and relieves stress. That's when I felt he might be confused about his future. So, I told him music soothes the savage soul, and nudged him on the path of medicine, subliminally. I think the more he thought about it, the more he decided he could do both. He had so much potential. It took a while, but eventually he realized his real passion was medicine."

"I'm so glad you gave him the nudge, Mrs. Flores. He is a wonderful doctor.

She goes back to her playing, to the relief of the garden workers.

Ambriel says, we are going to meet another person who has a lot of influence on people, so stay put, and enjoy.

—∿—

"Well, hallelujah, and top of the morning' to y'all! How is everyone on this magnificent day?"

It's the beginning of my second morning at the sanatorium, when this strange girl bursts into our room like a crazy person. She swoops over to the bed of Lucy Marshall, the married girl, talking in a loud and exaggerated southern drawl so the rest of us can hear.

"Why, I declare, Miss Lucy, I hear from the head honchos around here that they're giving you a reprieve and letting you out of bed today. I bet once those tender toes hit the ground you'll be off and running."

She swings her head from side to side, sizing up the rest of us. "Since you gals can't give a big round of applause, I would like to hear a little noise from the peanut gallery. This young lady right here is going to be the star of today's gala performance. So let's hear it for Miss Lucy-Loo Marshall, who will be making her debut walk to the bathroom today. Let's hear it for Lucy!"

I have no idea what's going on. The other girls cheer Lucy on, by saying things like, "Go, Lucy." "Yay, Lucy!" "Way to go, Lucy!"

I can't take my eyes off the new girl in the room. Her performance demands my attention as she prances around the room. She has dramatic brown eyes and matching spiral curls that bounce off her shoulders. I whisper to Poppy, "What a way to start the day. Who is she?"

"Her name is Lydia. Just wait. You're going to love her. She's in one of her I'm-practicing-to-be-an-actress modes, and the room is her stage," says Poppy.

"Okay, okay, ladies, let's not bring the house down just yet," she says, motioning for them to be quiet. Then she saunters over to my bed. "Well, well, you must be the new girl, Francie, I've been hearing so much about. It's very nice to meet you. My name is Lydia Browning—that's L-Y-D-I-A B-R-O-W-N-I-N-G." She spells it out as if she were talking to a reporter making certain he gets it right. "Now, don't ever forget it. You might see it up on a marquis one of these days. Isn't that right, girls?" She waits for validation. "Isn't that right girls?"

A collective, "Yes, oh of course, yes, yes," rings throughout the room.

"I'm here to jeer you and cheer you and make your life total chaos for the next eight hours. By the way, the jeering is rare, but sometimes necessary. Like with Margaret over there when she doesn't eat. But that's a subject we can save for another time. For now, I'm pleased to meet you, Francie."

She lights up the room, making me giggle. "It's very nice to meet you too, Lydia. You make quite an entrance."

Poppy chimes in. "You should see her on a good day when she really gets going. She's just being modest today because she wants to make a good impression on you, isn't that right, Lydia?"

"Now, Poppy, haven't I told you time and time again? Always leave them wanting more. If I give too much of a performance up front, there'll be nothing left."

"And I told you, I'm a slow study", says Poppy.

"That's okay. We'll work on that. I'll call that boyfriend of yours to come by, and we'll gang up on you. But right now, I have a little housewarming present for Francie." She reaches into the large pocket of her pink smock and hands me a small package.

Its a beautiful brown leather book with a metal clasp.

"What's this?" I ask.

"It's a diary. I know you'll probably be here for a while, and sometimes it's a good idea to write down how you're feeling." Then, in an over-expressive voice and touching the back of her hand to her forehead, she drawls, "Memory is fleeting, and you need to capture it!"

I don't know what to say. No one has ever given me anything like it before.

"This is so nice of you. Thank you."

Lydia closes her eyes and shakes her head, as if to say, it's nothing. "Other than that, I'm here to help you with anything that you need: shampooing your hair, taking you to the veranda, eating your chocolates—you name it. I'm at your beck and call. But first Nurse Kirschner and I are going to help Lucy over there make her debut walk on the red carpet."

Right on cue, Nurse Kirschner enters the room. "Good morning, everyone. I suppose you've heard by now that Lucy gets out of bed today."

I can feel the anticipation in the room. The girls get caught up in the antics by giggling and chanting, "Go, Lucy!" They're very excited for Lucy.

Poppy tells me, "Lucy's feet haven't touched the floor in nine months. Today is a big deal for her. The TB in her knee is improving, and now she has bathroom privileges. If that goes well, and keeps improving, then she will be able to take her meals in the main dining hall. Once a patient has permission to use the main dining hall, the other residents throw a big party. They have balloons and cake and it's a real celebration".

"I never thought in a million years I'd be celebrating a walk to the bathroom", I say back.

"Okay, I'm ready," says Lucy.

Nurse Kirschner peels back the sheets, while Lydia grabs Lucy's feet and moves them to the side where she slips them into a pair of hard-soled slippers. They hold onto Lucy's arms and ease her out of bed, tightening their grip when her feet touch the floor. All eyes are on Lucy. You could hear a pin drop.

Her legs are weak and wobbly and she says, "I feel like a baby taking my first steps."

"That's exactly what you're doing, Lucy," says Nurse Kirschner. "It's like learning all over again, and you're going to feel weak in your legs or maybe not even feel them at all. But don't worry about that; it's normal, and we're not letting go. Try lifting one foot now and put it in front of the other."

"My legs feel tingly."

Little by little, she wobbles down the center of the room. The rest of the girls are excited for her, but they aren't clapping and moving their arms too much. The rules forbid it. Therefore, they keep their arms tight to their sides and clap hands softly, as long as they don't tear healing tissue. This is just one of many times being reminded how much we have to keep our movements to a minimum. Any strenuous activity, even moving our arms to clap, is counterproductive to our recovery, so mostly they make fun of her.

Little Agnes says, "You look like a fledgling that's fallen out of its nest."

Izzy says, "Look at those bird legs go."

Bea says, "Hey, Luce, at this pace you'll wet yourself before you get to the bathroom."

Stop, you kids, don't make me laugh. This is hard enough."

Poppy says, "Don't stop now, Hon. One foot in front of the other."

During all the excitement, Dr. Stone enters the room. Poppy says he is Lucy's doctor. "Well, well, I guess I timed my visit just right. I see you're already up and at it. "How does it feel, Miss Marshall?"

"Hi, Dr. Stone. My legs are starting to get a little tired, but otherwise it feels great," she says with a smile as big as Christmas; but her voice sounds like she is getting out of breath.

"It's been about ten minutes, Dr. Stone, but she's still doing pretty well," says Nurse Kirschner.

"I see that," he says. "We don't want you to overdo it, Miss Marshall, so maybe that's enough for now."

She finished the length of the room, and then Nurse Kirschner and Lydia helped her back into bed. Nurse Kirschner told her they would do more later on in the day. "Baby steps" is what she said.

The next person to walk through the door is Dr. Wagner. "What's all the commotion in here? We can hear you gals clear out at the nurses' station."

Poppy whispers to me, "When someone is well enough to get out of bed after such a long time, it's the buzz of the sanatorium. Dr. Wagner knows exactly what's going on—he just wants in on the excitement."

Dr. Wagner asks Miss Marshall, "Don't tell me you got your walking papers today?"

"I sure did, Dr. Wagner. I practically ran up and down this hall. They had to hold me back."

"You keep that up, and I'm sure they'll be seeing you down at the mess hall, uh, I mean the dining room, before too long.

"That would be a nice surprise for Sam, wouldn't it," says

Lucy.

After Dr. Wagner paid his morning visit to Poppy and me, he turns his attention to Margaret.

"Margaret, did you watch Lucy get out of bed and walk?" She only nods her head.

"You know, if you start eating a little more, that could be you in a week or so. Your last x-ray and sputum culture shows very good results. There's no reason you can't get out of bed for short periods. But right now your weight is low making you too weak to be up and walking around on your own. It would be hard for your body to adjust to the extra work and you'd end up falling. But it doesn't have to be that way." He looks concerned.

"I'm not hungry," she says in a meek voice.

"Maybe you have a favorite food that we've overlooked. Is there anything special you like to eat?"

"No."

Margaret isn't making this easy for him, but he isn't giving up on her.

"How about cheeseburgers and French fries? That's my favorite, as you can see."

He is grinning and rubbing his belly pretending to be proud of the part that sags over his belt. I can't get over him. He is so unlike Doc Carlson.

Margaret just turns her head.

"I'm just kidding about the greasy, fatty foods, but you do need more nourishment than you're getting. I'm going to have Dietary start you on a special diet to help you gain some weight, but you have to work with us here, Miss Anderson. Just bringing it to you won't do the trick. You actually have to eat what's put in front of you. That's how it works."

The latter he said more firmly.

"That's my lecture for the day. Just remember, you're coming along nicely, and you could be up and out of here if you just work a little harder. Ok? I'll keep checking on you and I hope next time I see some change."

He pats her shoulder and then left to see his next patient.

I heard what Dr. Wagner said to her. I didn't mean to eavesdrop, but like Ma says, I guess I'm just a natural born busy body, and besides with close quarters I can't help it. I secretly wish It's me he's talking to, and all I have to do is eat more, and I could go home. But that isn't the case today, so instead I decide to talk to Margaret.

"Boy, that's sure good news that you're improving."

Margaret rolls her eyes.

I try to sound excited. "If that's all I had to do to get out of here is eat, I'd be pigging out every day. I'd be asking for seconds on everything and probably stealing from Poppy's plate."

"You don't know what you're talking about," Margaret hisses, without even looking at me.

Her anger surprises me, but I keep talking to her anyway. "Maybe I don't, but the doctor said your TB has improved to the point where you could be getting out of bed. Don't you want to get up and walk?"

I can't believe that someone in this situation wouldn't want to eat and get better. Who would purposely want to stay here for heaven's sake?

"It's none of your business. You've only been here two days, so don't be trying to tell me what to do. Why do you care anyway?"

By now we have locked eyes once again, but this time I don't look away.

"I care, because the way I see it, we're all in this together. If one of us gets better and can do little things like a walk to the bathroom, that just gives the rest of us hope. Didn't you see how excited everyone got excited for Lucy?"

"Oh, so I'm supposed to eat so you'll feel better, is that it, Francine?"

What is this girl's problem? "I just don't see why you don't want to get better, that's all."

"What I do or don't do is my business. If I want to starve myself—it's my business, not yours. Now leave me alone; I want to read, and I don't want you flapping your lips at me."

"Okay, it's your business then. But, all you have to do is eat and you could be walking around before I do."

Seems our little chat is over. Margaret rolls over onto her side with her book in her hand. Instead of reading, she just stares out the window. Poppy is right. Margaret Anderson isn't the friendliest girl on the ward, and she is indeed a little strange. All she has to do is eat, and she can get up and walk out of here.

It's a journey that is a whole year away for me, and I don't even know how I am going to get through one more day.

Chapter 8

Yesterday is history, tomorrow is a
mystery. Today is a gift of God, which
is why we call the it the present.

Bil Keane

Heaven: Ambriel wants us to walk again. As we move around heaven, it becomes clear to me that everything in heaven is so glorious. All the colors, the doves, the music and the rainbows. All of it! Children running about with halos surrounding their heads, gloriously happy. There is no war, no violence, no hatred, and no prejudice. Just deep contentment and pure happiness. After a while of silent serenity, Ambriel says, "I am sorry to have to spoil your contemplation again, I can only give you snippets of what is to come.

"Ambriel, I can never see enough."

"I know, dear. All in good time."

Now the path feels different. It smells of pine trees and tamaracks, and wheat fields. I feel a warm tingly sensation in my belly that reminds me of home. I think of running down our driveway after school and smelling Ma's cinnamon rolls the minute I round the corner. Sarah and Lily and I used to race through the kitchen door to see who would be first to pop the warm gooey delights into our mouths. Just thinking about them makes me delirious. I see the reason for the tingling in my belly. Ambriel has taken me to a part of heaven where I can look down and see my family. It feels glorious. I can see everyone clearly, like watching my favorite picture show.

—⟋⟍—

Ten days have passed since I left for the sanatorium. Sarah is getting the mail. She strolls down the driveway with her head tilted back, letting the morning sunshine on her face. The gravel crunches under her shoes. The driveway is lined with lilacs Pa planted years ago that have grown into gigantic bushes of pale, purple flowers. Sarah and I used to love to breathe in the fresh sweetness of the lilacs. It was our favorite part of spring. I think we smelled them dry. It's already the end of June and their little petals have almost all disappeared, but there is still a faint scent in the air.

Sarah reaches in and grabs the mail flipping through it as she walks back to the house. The first piece of mail is an advertisement with the Elsie Borden cow dressed in a frilly apron. The next letter is post marked Okinawa, Japan. It's a letter from our brother, Tom. She clutches the letter with excitement and runs as fast as she can to show Ma.

Inside the house, Ma and Lily are busy baking, and have pans of bread dough covered with flour-sack towels rising in the sun on the windowsill. Cinnamon rolls are already in the oven. Ma likes to get the baking done early before the heat of the day makes the house too warm. My sisters and I always help.

Music floats from our old Motorola that stands in the parlor, and Pa is at the kitchen table sorting through bills that are piling up faster than he can pay them.

Most of the money he earns comes from delivering milk to our neighbors and people in town. In the old days, the milk sold for five cents a quart and delivered warm right after milking. Then it became law, and the milk had to be cooled and bottled before delivery. So these days Pa has to charge a little more. More than half of our income comes from Pa's delivery service, and the other half from our farm crops.

Today has not been a good day. Pa found out he has to destroy

the cows, because they are infected with the same bacteria that caused my TB. He can't even have them butchered for the meat, and is beside himself on what to do next. The gardening and vegetables he sells won't be enough to pay the bills, and there isn't enough money right now to purchase more dairy cows.

Pa lets out a sigh and pushes the bills aside. He picks up the newspaper and leans back in his chair balancing on the back legs. He scans the pages when one particular article catches his eye. A mother was heralding her excitement over the cure of her nine-year-old daughter, Elizabeth Rae Mitchell. The girl has miraculously recovered from months of illness with TB after receiving experimental drug therapy at the Mayo Clinic.

Pa jerks the chair upright onto all four legs. "Mary, listen to this." He holds the paper stiffly and begins to read. "We had almost given up hope when doctors approached us asking if we would be willing to have Elizabeth start treatment on a drug undergoing testing at the Mayo Clinic. We had nowhere else to turn. We had no choice. We put our faith in the doctors and gave permission. Within weeks of giving her the drug streptomycin, her temperature dropped and she began getting her strength back. Her appetite improved and, after two months of treatment, she was well enough to undergo surgery to remove one of her ribs, which would help her mend. Her body had now built up its own defenses to bring the remaining disease under control."

Ma stops what she is doing and looks to Pa. "What does that mean, Joe? Have they found a cure?"

"I don't know, but it sounds like they're getting close." Pa continues. "It says here that since the girl's surgery, she's been able to get out of bed and walk around, something she hadn't been able to do in months. Her temperature has remained normal, and she's eating regular meals and they're expecting…, Mary, get this—a full recovery!" "They're expecting a full recovery!"

Just then, the screen door flies open and Sarah comes running in. "Ma, a letter came from Tom!"

The letter Sarah is waving in the air like a maniac interrupts ma's attention to the newspaper article. She hands it to Ma, who quickly tears it open and begins reading aloud.

At our house, Ma always reads letters aloud so we all can hear.

"It's dated June 16th." She stops and glances at Pa. "That's the day you took Francie to Glen Lake."

Pa avoids answering, and calmly says, "Go ahead, Mary, read the letter from our son."

Ma begins:

"Dear Family,

It's been a while since I've had a chance to write, and I miss you all terribly. I'm doing okay, so please, try not to worry. We heard the good news that the Germans surrendered to Eisenhower. We're hoping soon we will fully take over Okinawa and this can all be over, but the Japanese continue to resist. I'm keeping my wits about me and staying safe. I know your prayers, Ma, will get me home soon.

It's monsoon over here at Peleliu, and we are in mud most of the time. It's rumored that we will be going further south to Kunishi Ridge next. We have broken through most enemy lines, but in Kunishi some of the heaviest resistance still remains. The Japanese would rather commit suicide than surrender. We heard that General Ushijima himself committed hari-kari.

There are times, though; I actually find parts of Okinawa quite beautiful. The areas that haven't been destroyed by the war have Ferns growing on the banks, and the scent of pine trees and wild flowers remind me of home and your greenhouses, Pa; so you see, it's not all bad. And I've made many friends in my squad. One of my buddies, Alex, happens to be from Minneapolis. We made a pact: I watch his back and he watches mine. Our sergeant is the best there is, and he does what he can to keep us out of harm's way.

What are the boys up to since school has gotten out? I suppose, Pa, you've given them a lot of chores to keep them out of trouble. Tell Francie to write and let me know how her job at Sears is going, and say hello to Sarah and Lily and tell them to write. I hope everyone is doing well. I've gotten letters from some of the older kids; it sure is great to hear from them. Pa, when you talk to them, will you tell them that I'm fine and will be home soon? I'll write more when I can, but the conditions here make it hard to write much.

Ma, I can almost smell your hot cinnamon rolls.

My love to all of you,

Tom."

Ma folds the letter and slides it into her apron pocket.

"He doesn't even know about Francie," says Lily. "He thinks she's still at home."

"My letter hasn't reached him yet, but he'll know soon enough," says Ma.

"Well, it sounds like the Japanese are retreating, and it will all be over before too long," says Pa. "I know we'll have our boy back on American soil safe and sound."

Chapter 9

*"Oh God let this horrible war quickly
come to an end, that we may all return
home and engage in the only work that
is worthwhile, and is the salvation of
men."*

Thomas Jonathan Stonewall Jackson

Heaven: Ambriel takes me to a place in heaven where she
says this is winter, even though we are still in the daisy field and I
don't feel the cold. I can hear the wind but don't feel the breeze that
should accompany it. The trees are sparkling with beautiful crystals
lights of frozen snow of every color of the rainbow on the branches,
and the air is soft and light. In the distance, children are making
a snowman, but the snow is not even sticky, and the children are
wearing shorts. All around there is merriment and excitement and
everything is beautiful with rainbows, and doves and butterflies.
For some reason it makes me laugh.

Ambriel says, "What is so funny?"

I say, "Have you ever witnessed a Minnesota storm snow
storm?"

Ambriel says, "No, but I have heard tales of them."

"Well, that's why I'm laughing, because this is nothing like the
storms we have on our farm in the winter."

Ambriel says "Come along, time to leave.

I walk along behind her, as she puts the Christmas Lily
behind her right ear. We leave the daisy field and winter, and we
come to a clearing. The feeling I have here is nothing I've ever had
before. It's a strange thing being in heaven, looking down at Earth.

The familiar places stir up old feelings, and the sounds and smells bring back wonderful memories. But none of my senses can explain this place. I feel like I've been spinning in a circle and can't tell up from down. I look at Ambriel for the answer.

"You don't remember this place because you have never been here. It's June 26, 1945, and you are looking down on Okinawa.

—⁓—

At the same time, my family is reading Tom's letter, Tom hunches to the ground, creeping through the darkness. He holds his gun ready and prays—something Ma taught us before we could even walk. Rifles pop and machine guns rattle in the distance. The artillery shells whistle over Kunishi Ridge, as the soldiers move into position in the dark. Tom looks to his left and sees Alex, his good friend, creeping along in silence over the dry rice paddies. They are to seize the remaining ridge at daybreak.

"Hey, Alex, see anything?" Tom whispers in a hushed voice.

"No. They must be hiding in their caves. As soon as it's daylight, all hell's gonna break loose," Alex whispers back.

"Take your positions!" the gunnery sergeant shouts. Then it happens. The Navy blasts gunfire from their battleships into the enemy caves making it possible for our soldiers to move forward. In Okinawa, they call it 'tetsu no bow,' which means 'storm of steel.'

The enemy comes out of the caves near the crest of the coral ridge and opens fire. Bullets snap and pop overhead. Tom draws his Tommy and fires into their lines. Shell blasts blowholes in the ground. Black smoke and whining artillery fill the air, and then there is shouting and chaos everywhere.

Another company of Marines is swarming the ridge above Tom's company. The Japanese have deeply rooted themselves in the caves, fighting to the end. One of their soldiers rushes into full view of our attacking men. Instantly, bullets rip through his belly, spilling his blood and intestines onto the ground. Tom watches him fall over the ridge with the upper half of his body hanging in midair and his arms dangling loosely over his head.

The marines are aggressive. They clamber up the slopes toward the enemy while bullets whiz all around. Tom notices a sniper in the brush and like a robot programmed to obey, takes aim and opens fire. In an instant, the enemy falls forward onto the ground with his limbs spread eagle. Tom's eyes dart from side to side as sweat trickles at his temples. Fear has fueled him. It runs through his veins and heightens his awareness of danger, but he never looses his courage.

His friend, Alex, comes from behind and scurries to Tom's side. "Holy shit, I didn't even see that one. God, Tom, this is hell. If we make it out of here alive, I swear I'm never picking up another gun as long as I live."

Tom shakes off his anxiety and regains his composure. His voice is dry and scratches the air. "Yeah, I hear ya, buddy. We've seen enough bloodshed, that's for sure."

"This war better end pretty damn soon," whispers Alex. They are Marines and they are comrades serving their country and doing whatever it takes to make it out alive.

The rattle of gunfire brakes out again, and in an instant, the men are sprawled flat against the ground to avoid flying bullets. They scramble for cover, but one soldier just lays there. He is mumbling and rambling incoherently with his head rolling from side to side. Suddenly, he jumps to his feet and heads toward enemy fire. He is talking gibberish as the bullets roar around him.

"Bulldog, get down!" yells Alex. Tom reaches to pull him down but the soldier slips through his fingers. "Bulldog!" he yells, but the soldier just keeps walking into enemy fire until a bullet explodes into the side of his head. He stands upright for a few

seconds and then drops to the ground in a crumpled pile.

Tom and Alex lay motionless on their bellies in the dirt. Everything is spinning out of control. Tears well up and burn Tom's eyes. He struggles to hold back from releasing the rage boiling inside of him, but the tears come anyway and spill to the ground, muddying his face in the dirt. He pounds his fist and sobs, "Damn the Japanese! Damn Bulldog! Damn the war!"

Alex is already up and running and shouts back at Tom. "Get up, Tom! Get up. They're on the run! Look! We can take 'em! Let's go! Let's go!"

Tom struggles to his knees and wipes his eyes with his sleeve streaking mud across his face. He stays crouched watching the enemy fall back, and then orders come down the line for the men to advance toward the caves. Tom holds his gun tight and moves quickly across the rice paddies, keeping his head and shoulders down. The excitement in the air is electric and victory is just within their reach. The Marines overhead on the ridge have already moved in and are taking prisoners. Tom's unit is right behind them.

Once they reach the caves, most of the Japanese have been killed or imprisoned. The marines have been waiting for this break. It's finally over.

The tanks eventually make it to the crest of the ridge with water and ammunition and rations, and along with the supplies comes the mail. The men are battle worn. Nevertheless, the arrival of the tanks brings screams of joy. For Tom and the other men the mail is the one thing that keeps them going. It gives them reason to stay focused, not to take chances. It holds their sanity together. The mail brings them back to a time that makes sense—where bullets, noise, and death have no place. Soldiers clamber around the Marine as he holds the letters and shouts out names. One by one, they grab their mail and go off into their own little worlds.

Tom sits on his helmet to read his letter from Ma, but what he reads makes him shiver.

"What's up buddy, bad news?" Alex asks him.

Tom stares at the letter from Ma and says, "My little sister has tuberculosis. She's in a sanatorium."

Chapter 10

*"What one has not experienced, one will
not understand in print."*

Isadora Duncan

Heaven: Ambriel takes my hand as we enter another part
of Heaven. What I see is staggering. Young men and boys in dirty
clothes with mud stained faces, some in wheelchairs, and others
with crutches, some missing limbs carried on gurneys and others
bloodstained shirts. Weary faces of war wearing dirty combat attire
and muddy boots, and so much blood, all lining up in droves to
get into Heaven. St. Peter's assistant is busy welcoming every one of
them, telling them how courageous they are.

"Welcome," says the assistant, "Come in, there's room for
everyone! Welcome."

It seems the line will never end. "Welcome," he says again, and
again.

The assistant and the men keep on coming, and the assistant
keeps on welcoming them until finally, the line dwindles, until all
are welcomed.

Once the last man entered heaven, I say to Ambriel "It was
shocking seeing so many soldiers going to heaven. But, seeing
Tom fighting to stay alive was also devastating to see. It was odd
seeing him under those conditions. What he must have endured.
Although, in heaven, I feel a calm understanding about these
things. War and illness and death are things from Earth and aren't a
part of heaven in that way."

Ambriel twirls around with a smile, "You are learning."

We come to a waterfall where we sit in the grass, and Ambriel says, "Tell me how it was being a patient at the sanatorium.

I say in two words. "A struggle! Some days are a real effort just to keep our sanity, especially in hot weather. Tempers fly! One of the problems is the close quarters, which means seeing the same faces and hearing the same voices day in and day out, and how, after a while, that can really grind on a person's nerves."

"Let's have a look see, shall we?" says Ambriel, grinning.

At this moment, Agnes and Izzy are having a catfight. They are the worst.

—ɯ—

"Agnes, if you'd just shut up and quit running off at the mouth all the time maybe you wouldn't flunk ninth grade again!"

"Thanks a lot Izzy. You know darn well I was held back because of whooping cough! At least I never got caught shoplifting like you—that's probably how you got all those records!"

"That's a lie! I never stole anything!"

"Oh yeah? Well then how come when your friends were here they said no one can five-finger discount like Izzy can? Then you all laughed! Huh? What was that all about?"

"You better shut your mouth, Agnes, before I come over there and shut it for you!"

Before they have a chance to shout any more obscenities at each other, Father Alphonse pops in to give us Holy Communion, for the Catholics on the unit. In addition, unwittingly preventing a huge catfight from breaking out, fur balls and all. With nostrils flaring, red hair flying and steam sizzling between them, Agnes and Izzy are ready to go to blows, but instead are forced to play nice—at least while Father is in the room.

When Father gives us communion, we don't kneel at a communion rail like church. Instead, Father just comes to our beds, places the Host in our mouth. Then we make the sign of the cross while he says a little prayer, and gives us his blessing. That's it. When Father isn't hearing our confessions or giving us his blessing, he is a real hoot. He loves telling us lame-o jokes like the one, "What do you call a nun who sleepwalks—a Roman Catholic." Or the one where a drunken man staggers into a Catholic Church and sits down in a confession box and says nothing. The priest then knocks on the wall three times in a final attempt to get the man to speak. Finally, the drunk replies: 'No use knockin' mate, there's no paper in this one either.' That one really cracks me up. Moreover, coming from a priest! Sometimes he forgets he told it, but we don't mind, and by the time Father leaves, Agnes and Izzy have forgotten all about tearing each other's heads off. I love it when Father comes to visit.

Next on the agenda at the sanatorium is when Lydia shampoos my hair—We have a system. I lean over the edge of my bed with my head in a basin while she lathers my hair. I hate when the soap sometimes stings my eyes and the water trickles into my ears and runs down my neck getting my bed jacket wet. It isn't exactly a luxurious soak in a bubble bath in the privacy of my own bathroom, but it gets the job done, and when all is said and done, it feels good to have clean, fresh-smelling hair. A few times Lydia will braid it for me, which the other girls say they like. It's cooler too and keeps the coarse strands from sticking to the back of my neck.

By late afternoon, the heat in the room is stifling with the humidity making everything sticky, and bugs are constantly bumping against the screens trying to get in. I move around trying to find a cool spot on my sheet, but the heat from my body just warms it up again. I can hardly get comfortable no matter what I do. The fans help somewhat, but the long, scorching days feel like they'll never end. If I were home, these dog days of summer would be fantastic weather for swimming or walking along the lake in the evening listening to the loon's call— that is if you don't have to spend all your time in bed with tuberculosis as your sidekick.

Now I'm not complaining about my situation, really, I'm not. After all, it's the hand God dealt me, so who am I to criticize His Plan? It may sound like whining, but I'm just telling you what it was like at the sanatorium and how drastically my life has changed.

So, here's where I'm going to share with you a real stinker that makes life miserable—the dreaded bedpan. Out of everything that frazzles my nerves at the sanatorium, the bedpan takes the prize. Talk about an adjustment—it is the worst!

Imagine yourself needing to use the bathroom for a bowel movement but instead of privacy, you have to perform your job in the company of seven other girls, and God only knows whose boyfriend might pop in in the middle of it from the confines of your bed! It's grueling; trust me when I tell you this. Sometimes I have to go so bad I will hold it just because the whole experience is just so embarrassing. Think of it—a room full of girls can hear and smell everything you do for crying outloud!

My little brothers think passing gas and saying the word fart is funny—that is until Pa intervenes and tells them to mind their manners before Ma gets wind of it—pardon the pun.

There are a couple of aides that don't respect what we have to go through. Once Agnes had a sore on her backside and the aide pulled the cold pan out from under her and tore the wound open. It took a week for the wound to heal. The same aide was helping Poppy, and spilled urine on her, and she didn't even make sure the sheet was dry and Poppy ended up getting a rash. It was awful. But the worst yet was when Bea had an embarrassing and painful encounter with one of those aides. The aide flipped the sheet back, exposing Bea completely, all the while cranking up the head of Bea's bed. When the aide came back, she made sure everyone heard

when she screeched, "Oh, my goodness! What on earth did you have for lunch today Miss Lund?" Then she yanked the curtain open and scrunched her face in disapproval, and held her nose while handing Bea toilet paper. To make things worse, she then went about the room spraying some ungodly smelling spray for fumigating. Bea was mortified. The aide was so rude!

I believe those aides are not here anymore. But all the other nurses, like Nurse Kirschner and Nurse Jones do what's called "pillow fluffing." They always do the nice extras to make it more humane, like putting powder on the bedpan so it won't stick to our skin or warming it under hot water before we use it, and allow us privacy to clean ourselves afterward and never ever make us feel ashamed if it smelled.

The thing is, we all have to stay in bed to relieve ourselves— that's just how it is. But the bedpan adventure isn't the only thing in close quarters that we share. We struggle with our periods, having baths, privacy, loneliness and our emotions. Many nights you can hear poor Helen crying into her pillow. Sometimes in the middle of the day for no apparent reason, she will break down. We try to console her, but there are just some things we go through that can't be fixed. There are times I want to jump into her bed and cry right along with her.

Privacy is one commodity that doesn't exist at the sanatorium, and there are just some things that should only be done behind closed doors. But when thin curtains take the place of closed doors, privacy takes center stage with an audience of innocent young girls. Let me explain.

We aren't able to go out on dates like other teenagers, but that doesn't stop our hormones from working overtime. Most of our conversations are either about boys and sex or sex and boys, which just gets everyone stirred up.

So it's late in the afternoon and Lucy's husband, Sam, is visiting. Two of the girls are napping, and some are either reading or writing letters; you know the usual amusement to help fiddle away the time. Izzy is playing records and Poppy and I are knitting and singing along. Without us noticing, Sam pulls the curtain closed around Lucy's bed, and soon we hear strange noises coming from behind Lucy's curtain. They are muffled sounds at first that grow in intensity. Sam's husky whispers followed by Lucy's whimpering, and breathy sounds intermingled with moans.

Poppy and I look at each other; our mouths drop open. We can't believe what is happening, right here in the room with all of us present and where anyone can walk in for heaven's sake!

Margaret and Helen are sleeping, but the rest of us can't help hearing what is going on. We try not to listen, but it is like a train wreck—we know we shouldn't watch but can't look away.

Bea pulls the covers over her head and, being the smart aleck she is, recites, "See no evil. Hear no evil. Speak no evil."

Oh, she is a wise little monkey.

Poppy and I cover our mouths and laugh like hyenas. At one point, we even start humming like a pair of dodo birds to distract ourselves, but that only makes it worse. Thank Goodness when it finally ends, otherwise they would have been stitching us up from the laughter that is tearing our sides apart.

Sam surfaces from behind the curtain, and we all pretended to be minding our business like good little actresses.

Yes, I will say we share a lot of things during our days at the sanatorium, whether we want to or not. But like my Pa used to say, "What doesn't kill you only makes you stronger."

Well we got stronger all right, and that's why we can't wait for Sam to leave so we can give Lucy the business.

Chapter 11

No hand can make the clock strike for
me the hours that are passed."

George Gordon Byron

Heaven: Ambriel sticks the Christmas Lily into her belt of beads, and says, "I think I got more than I bargained for when I asked you to tell me about life in the sanatorium.

"I like to be thorough, I laugh. And I'm enjoying the waterfall, almost as much as the teasing we give Lucy."

Ambriel has us walking again through the most glorious part of heaven that I've seen yet. The waterfall is spectacular and the air is warm and engaging. Strangely there is no sun, or no moon. "Again, I could stay here forever," I say to Ambriel. We then pass from the waterfall to a crystal river that flows from the throne of God. There are trees bearing every kind of fruit, and there are no annoying bugs, just dazzling beauty. A fragrance tickles my nose. The scent is indescribable. Ambriel then parts the water into a babbling brook, and says, "Time to go check in with the girls at the sanatorium.

Hey Lucy, Glad to see you came up for air kiddo! We were all gettin' kinda' worried there for a minute" says Bea.

"Hope you're all right." Says Izzy.

"Knowing CPR can really come in handy in an emergency situation—my uncle saved a woman once in a restaurant who was choking. Is that what happened to you, Luc? Were you choking? Did Sam have to save you?" says Agnes.

"Hubba-hubba!" Poppy says, grinning.

Lucy turns three shades of red and snips at us. "Ha-ha. You

kids think you're so cute."

"Ah, Luce, don't get your water hot," I say, not letting up on her. "We're just jealous. As a matter of fact, we'd all like someone to practice CPR on us, right girls?"

Poppy agrees. "Hey, maybe the next time Sam comes to visit, he can teach us the proper technique." Says Poppy.

Everyone laughs hysterically, but Lucy is a tough little soldier.

"For your information, it isn't what you think. Maybe we got a little carried away, but it is no big deal. Sam just misses me—that's all. So you can all get your dirty little minds out of the gutter!"

"Sure, Luce. Whatever you say." I lie.

When we think we tormented Lucy enough, we all get back to our crafts and listening to music on our headphones. Poppy and I pick up our knitting, because It's the one activity that seems to pass the time the most, and believe me, if it isn't for our crafts, and not to mention the little side shows like what happened with Lucy, the time can really drag. Hours turn into days, days turn into weeks and weeks turn into months. I used to look at a clock if I wanted to know the time; now I look at a calendar. Trying to lie still all the time is mind numbing, and if lying still isn't enough, the sanatorium has even more rules.

We all have bone TB, but a lot of us also have TB in our lungs; Helen's seems to be the worst. The rule is we aren't allowed to stretch our arms, laugh too loud, rest on our elbows, clap our hands strenuously or jerk. All of that can stress our chests and tear any new healing tissue. The doctors and nurses emphasize this to us daily; in other words, that doesn't leave us with a lot of options. So we read, write letters, knit, and listen to music. Those of us who have graduated from high school take college courses and others take high school courses.

Listening to the radio on our headphones also helps pass the time. There is a two-way radio switch for patients, which comes on from seven to one and three to nine. We have a choice of three stations: WCCO, WDAY and KNUT. My favorite program is *Listen to the Falcon* on KNUT on Tuesday nights. I also like Red Skelton, Danny Kaye and Molay Mystery.

"This really helps pass the time, doesn't it?" I ask Poppy.

"What, listening to *'Smoke Gets In Your Eyes'* or knitting?"

"Well both actually; but I'm talking about making things."

"I know, she says "It seems like I just get going on this darn thing and two hours have flown by."

"Yeah, if we keep this up, we'll be turning out sweaters left and right. Maybe we could sell them."

"Huh! Poppy says, I don't know about you, but I don't think I'm going to get rich from my work. I keep making mistakes and having to pull it apart. If I'm not careful, it's going to end up with one sleeve."

I laugh when she has to untangle a lap full of curly yarn.

Nurse Kirschner breezes into the room to pass out meds and takes time with each of the girls, admiring our work and asking about their families.

"Nurse Kirschner sure is pretty, isn't she? I say to Poppy, I wonder if she has a boyfriend.

Poppy always knows the gossip. "I heard through the grapevine that one of the doctors has a crush on her, but she won't date him."

"Why not?"

"Who knows, maybe she doesn't want to date someone she works with, or maybe she's just waiting for Mr. Right."

"If the chemistry isn't there, what's the use? Now Ken and I—there's chemistry! I get a rush in my chest just thinking of him," Poppy gushes while pulling out another row of stitches.

The headphones are killing my ears, so I slide them off and let them rest around my neck. "How did you and Ken meet?"

"We were high school sweethearts. I was a sophomore and he was a senior. We met during a dance in the school gym."

I see from the dazed look in her eyes how bad she has it.

"Do you know he's come to see me every weekend since I've been here? He hasn't missed one in the past eight months."
"You're very lucky."

"Sometimes I worry that he'll get tired of waiting for me, though. What if I never get better? How long do I dare ask him to wait?" Poppy's frustration is more than her raveled up yarn.

"Ken loves you—he'll wait."

"I don't know, Francie. This disease is so contagious. What if he gets scared and thinks it's just not worth it?"

"No. You don't really think that do you? He'll wait."

"Why should he? Who knows if I'll ever get well enough to leave this place? Maybe I should just cut him loose so he can live a normal life."

"Oh, Poppy, that sounds really harsh. I think you'd be making a mistake. But, I do get what you mean; tuberculosis isn't the greatest aphrodisiac. I'll probably never even get the chance to fall in love. At least you have that."

"I suppose."

I was starting to feel sorry for myself. "Do you ever wonder why—why me? Why did I have to get sick?"

"I've asked myself that a million times," she says.

"Are you afraid of death, Poppy?"

"Yes," she says in a whisper. "I think about it sometimes late at night or I'll wake up from a bad dream and find myself crying. The thought of it overwhelms me. I see myself lying in a coffin with my hands crossed over my chest; with my family gathered. Then I

picture them lowering me into the dark, cold ground, and I literally wake up and get sick to my stomach thinking about it."

We aren't t supposed to talk about death and dying; that is also against the rules, but there are times you just have to let it out.

I say, "I try not to think about it, but I do wonder what I did to deserve this and if I'm being punished for something."

"Do you think God is punishing us, Francie?"

"I don't know. Maybe, maybe not. It's just that sometimes I want answers, and it always leads back to that. Do you think He's punishing us?"

Poppy says, "I can't help it."

"I guess it's just one of those mysteries why we are chosen. Maybe we'll understand when we're dead and gone."

Poppy says "Well, I hope that's not any time soon. Do you ever wonder what people will say about you after you're gone?"

"Well I hope they say she made me laugh and made a big fat impression on me when she passed by here."

"You're a nut case, do you know that?"

"I try hard." I don't want to be sad anymore. "You know; I was just thinking about something Pa said to me the day he brought me here. He said I'm God's unfinished business."

"He told you that?"

"Mmm-hmm, just before he kissed me good bye."

"What do you suppose he meant?"

"Well, I'm not sure, maybe I'll be the one to find a cure for tuberculosis and save the world!"

"Yeah, right!"

"And by the way, I don't know what you're so worried about. You're getting better every day, and your knee is just about healed. You'll probably be up and out of here in no time, and then you and Ken can run off into the sunset together." The thought of what I just said makes me laugh.

"What—why are you laughing?" Poppy asks.

"I think I'm beginning to sound like Lydia—running off into the sunset and everything having a happy ending. But in your case, I can feel it. Ken loves you. He will wait for you as long as it takes. You are truly one of the lucky ones."

"Well ladies, it's your turn, says Nurse Kirschner. Plug your nose and swallow quickly."

She interrupts our gab session and hands a plastic cup with two red pills for Poppy. She sees the yarn in Poppy's lap and asks, Whatcha got goin' on there Miss Popke?"

"I'm really not too sure at this point," says Poppy, throwing the pills back and chasing them with a sip of water. "I keep dropping stitches and ripping it out. I think I'll just call this my master of disaster."

Nurse Kirschner smiles and hands me a cup. "And who is that adorable little sweater for, Miss Carver? It's really cute."
"Thanks. It's for my sister's new little boy, Joey. She has seven kids and Joey is the baby. I haven't gotten to see him as much as their other kids."

"Wow, seven kids! Your sister must have her hands full."

"Oh she does. I used to stay with her and help during the summers. Those boys would wear me out; they were always getting into my makeup. I miss not being with them this summer. I wish they were getting into my makeup right now."

"Well, I hope they come to visit. I would love to meet them, even if they are a handful." She puts the empty medicine containers back on the tray and says, "Okay. Lydia will be here any minute to take you and Margaret down for a lamp treatment."

So the dog days of summer drag on. Instead of helping Ma with the laundry or baking, I spend my days out on the veranda or under the carbon arc lamp. Sputum cultures, lab tests and x-rays are now my way of life. Visiting hours are the highlight of my day, and reading, knitting and writing in my diary are my pastimes. Poppy has become my new best friend, and the other seven girls on the ward are my new family.

Time is passing us by and maybe even helping us adjust whether we like it or not, but one thing is for sure—we never know from one minute to the next what the sanatorium has in store for us.

Chapter 12

"Mankind must put an end to war or,
war will put an end to mankind."

John F. Kennedy

Heaven: This time, it's St. Peter himself opening the Gates of heaven, welcoming more and more people of all nationalities. "Who are all these people going to heaven?" I ask Ambriel.

"They're victims of disasters, disease, violence, accidents, and innocent victims of war.

"Welcome," says St. Peter, "Come in, come on in, the Gates are open. He is waiting for you."

I ask, "Why are they getting into heaven and not me?" Ambriel just smiles and spins her beads. "Because I have been given a task from my supervisor to take you on this journey to help you. As of yet we still have a long way to go." Then she says, "Events that happen in your lives are sometimes the calendars that jog your memories. Years can go by, but bring up a certain event and you'll probably remember exactly what you were doing at the time."

It seems this is one of those days.

—⚶—

No sooner has Nurse Kirschner mentioned Lydia's name, she breezes into the ward wearing a bright smile and a new hairdo. Instead of her brown curls bouncing off her shoulders like coiled springs, her curly locks swept into a twist with soft tresses falling loosely down her neck. She looks like a movie star.

"Hubba, hubba! "Says Izzy, "Take a look at the model in the room girls."

Little Agnes sticks two fingers between her lips and lets out a shrill whistle and then stops just as abruptly when she realizes what she has just done.

Tom tried to teach me to whistle like that, but I could never get the hang of it. All I could muster was a lot of hot air.

The rest of the girls join in making crisp remarks to tease Lydia.

"Why thank you, ladies," she says in a slow, lazy drawl. "A girl must always look her best when out in public. You never know when a hungry photographer might be lurking around the corner, and I don't want to be caught off guard. When I get to Hollywood, I'm going to have my hair done twice a week with a different coiffure each time," she says.

"Where did you get the idea for that style, Lydia?" Bea asks.

"Well, it's sort of my own creation. When I was at the movies last night with my friend, Mark, the preview of coming attractions showed Veronica Lake with her blonde hair over one eye. She's so gorgeous and I love that look, but it seems like everyone is copying it, so I decided to do be different and put mine up. Besides, it stays out of my eyes, and I need both eyes wide open for keeping a good watch on you ladies."

Izzy twirls her ponytail through her fingers and asks, "Have you ever tried putting it in a snood?"

"Oh you mean one of those lacy little sacs? I loved the way Scarlet O'Hara looked in hers in Gone with the Wind. I'll have to get one and try it. That's a good idea, Iz." Then she goes on in her dreamy tone, "Someday, I'm going to invent my own hairdo and everyone will want to copy it. I'll be the talk of Tinsel Town. Once I'm done with my acting classes and I've saved enough money to go to Hollywood, you'll be seeing my name up in lights right along with Betty Hutton and Cyd Charisse."

"I can see it now," says Izzy. "Lydia Browning starring in Love

Me or Leave Me."

Everyone laughs. It's always fun when Lydia's in the room. I think we live vicariously through her.

"Interesting title," says Bea. "That sounds like our Lydia. She knows what she wants and she's going after it, and damn any man who gets in her way."

"Hmm. Let me think now," says Lydia, tapping her finger to her cheek. "Maybe I should change my name. Most actresses do that you know. Did you know that Cyd Charisse was born Tula Ellice Finklea? Can you imagine that on the Marquis? I read somewhere that her baby brother couldn't pronounce the word 'sister, so he called her 'Sid' instead, and I guess it stuck. Pretty catchy, huh?"

Bea says, "I think you've been reading too many of those Hollywood movie magazines, Lydia."

"Oh no, no, no, Bea. One can never get enough info on the tricks of the trade, and I need to know it all if I want to make it in Hollywood."

Just then, an announcement comes over Izzy's radio and interrupts our Hollywood banter. We all stop what we're doing to listen. "Izzy turn it up, Bea says.

We interrupt our regularly scheduled programming to bring you this message just in. It has been reported that The United States of America just dropped an atomic bomb over the city of Hiroshima, Japan, in an effort to end the war. The bomb, nicknamed Little Boy, exploded at approximately 8:15 a.m. Japan standard time. People who saw Little Boy say that it resembled another sun in the sky when it exploded and that the city was hidden by a gigantic cloud that seemed to mushroom. The strong wind that was generated by the bomb destroyed most of the houses and buildings within a 1½ mile radius. The estimated number of casualties at this time is reported to be over 100,000.

I suck in my breath when I hear the news.

I repeat. At approximately 8:15 this morning, Monday, August 6th, 1945, the United States has dropped an atomic bomb over the city of Hiroshima, Japan. We will update you later when we have more on this late-breaking news. We now take you back to our regularly scheduled program.

There is a hush on the ward and then everyone chatters at once.

"Oh, my gosh, what is this world coming to?" exclaims Bea.

"How could one bomb cause so much destruction?" asks Izzy, spinning her ponytail.

I can barely hear Helen when she says, "Just think of all those poor people who've been killed. It's awful, just awful."

Little Agnes talks faster than usual. "I'm sure President Truman knows what he's doing—this terrible war has to end soon—maybe this is the only way."

"I think you might be right, Agnes," says Lydia. "I heard on the news that the Japanese just refuse to give up and too many of our young soldiers' lives are being lost. Something drastic like this probably needed to be done."

My eyes well up with tears. "I wonder what this means for the boys still fighting across seas?"

Margaret puts her book down and makes no comment directly to anyone but says, "Maybe now the war will end."

We all look briefly in her direction. We aren't used to her joining in on any of our conversations, and to hear her voice is strange. But, then again, what is happening in the world is strange—war, bombs, illness, death. Her soft spoken-words are a whisper in the wind when you considered the big picture.

My mind races with thoughts of Tom and I wonder what he is

doing at this exact moment.

"Worried about Tom?" By now, Poppy can read my mind.

"Yes. I wish I could call home and talk to Ma. She must be worried sick. Who knows what will happen next? Tom's been in Okinawa since the early part of April and in the thick of some of the worst fighting. His letters don't get too detailed, but Pa reads the papers. I know how worried they must be. This is such big news. It's like the whole world is changing right before our eyes."

"And we're trapped in these beds," says Poppy.

We look at each other with the same understanding of our battle with TB that men fighting side by side in war have with one another. It's a feeling of camaraderie that only those who experience it can understand.

Then Lydia says, "I hate to have to do this, but, Margaret and Francie, I have to take you down for your lamp treatments. No matter what, your treatments have to go on as scheduled. Francie, I'll see what I can do about getting you to a phone so you can call home later. Maybe your parents will have more news about our boys overseas by the time you get back."

Lydia is so great. I am beginning to think she would make a better doctor than an actress.

When we get to the room where we lie under lamplight for therapy, Lydia helps us get undressed. We strip down to a G-string and wear these funny-looking goggles to protect our eyes. Margaret looks like something from outer space in hers. I can't see myself, so just for fun I imagine I must look like a pretty hip chick. Once we are in position on the table wearing nothing but the G-strings and goggles, the technician pulls down the large coach lamp that hangs from the ceiling. Then she turns on the lamp and a timer. We have to lie on our stomachs for a while and then when the timer goes off, we flip to our backs. That gives the light the best chance to penetrate and kill the bacteria.

When we are on our stomachs, I say to Margaret, "I wish you could walk down to the dining area to find out if the radio has any more news on the bombing."

"Wouldn't you rather walk down there yourself?"

So much sarcasm. She never quits. "Of course I would. I'd like nothing better. But as you know, I haven't been here long enough, and I'm not ready to be up and walking. Heck, I'd run down there if I could. But you-u-u on the other hand could be walking if you wanted to."

"I know I could. My TB isn't as bad as yours," she snaps.

She is so smug. I don't know why she always has to lash out at me; but my will is stronger than Margaret's will, so I just fire right back. "I'm not going to let anything get in the way of my recovery. When I've been here as long as you, I plan on getting up and walking."

It didn't take much to set her off. I guess I pushed her buttons a little harder than she could take, because she finally let her anger loose on me.

"Who do you think you are anyway? You haven't even been here two months, and you talk like you know it all. I've been here for nearly a year, and I know better than you what it takes to get cured. Maybe it's time to prove it to you, Miss Smarty Pants—or I mean G-string."

Wow, that almost hurt. I try not to laugh.

"I'll show you who can get up and walk and who will have to stay in bed. Maybe It's time."

I turn my head to the other side. I hope it is too. Sparring with Margaret and worrying about the war, has me worn out. I actually doze off during the lamp treatment and jump when the timer goes off, indicating we're done—just like chickens on a barbecue. I hand the goggles back to the technician, dress, and then Lydia takes us back to the ward—and back to the boredom. I can hardly stand the thought of just lying in bed again. I ache so bad to get up and walk outside. But walking isn't in the rules. I have no choice. We have to stay in bed at all costs.

Okay, so let's face it—being a teenager, some days are just harder than others to follow that rule.

Chapter 13

*Some people march to a different
drummer—and some people polka."*

Anonymous

Heaven: When we're back in the heaven of angels, I ask Ambriel, "Just what is heaven anyway, Ambriel?"

"You know what? I'm glad you asked me that. It's actually a very good question. Many people on Earth don't think it even exists. But to answer your question specifically, I will say to you, that heaven or the heavens, however you want to call them, are anything you want them to be. That is the beauty of heaven. You have seen quite a bit already, but there is an infinity, way beyond even your imagination. There is still more discovery that awaits all of us. So for now, how about listening in on the Polka Fest that is happening in music heaven?" Just then, St. Christopher asks Ambriel to polka with him. I almost split my side laughing watching her dance. Polka heaven is a real hoot, Ma and Pa would love this.

"Oh my," gasps Ambriel when St. Christopher escorts her back to me. "That was great fun!"

I try not to laugh.

"OK, back to work" Ambriel says. "You have Margaret all stirred up."

"Maybe it's the catalyst to jump start her attitude. She needs to eat." I say.

"You see? Words and actions…"

"Ok, ok, I'm learning."

Ambriel tickles me under the chin with the Christmas Lily. What is it with her and that Lily?

—⁓—

Now part of Lydia's job is to keep us busy so we aren't so bored, and also to help us follow the rules and not dwell on things that can get in the way of our recovery, which is a feat she is exceptionally good at. It's the day after the bombing of Hiroshima, when Lydia pokes her head into our room and says, "Okay, so this doctor asks this nurse: How is that little girl who swallowed 10 quarters last night?' The nurse answers: No change yet."

Groans from the peanut gallery. Okay, so it s lame, but she gets our attention.

"Good one, Lydia, got any more?" asks Poppy.

"I've got a million of them, but leave them wanting more, I always say."

Lydia is giddy. She says, "Instead of another joke, I have something more exciting I want to share with you. You girls are in for a real treat." She has something in her hand.

Bea isn't looking at her hand—she is looking at Lydia's legs. "Where on earth did you get those nylons? And seams! They're lovely."

"Hubba, hubba," says little Agnes.

"Aren't they nice?" grins Lydia, showing us her legs. "And I didn't even have to stand in line to buy them. Look closer, they're not nylons. I just took an eyebrow pencil and drew lines up my legs so that it looks like I'm wearing nylons. Isn't it a gas? Everyone's doing it."

I say, "You can't even tell."

"I'm going to get a real pair soon, though, cuz I hear Kinsley's Department Store is getting some in any day now. I plan on being first in line. I think nylons make a woman's legs look so sleek and elegant, don't you? This shortage makes me so crazy."

Lucy sits up. "Sam told me about an article in the newspaper about a woman who stood in line for three hours in Chicago to get a pair, and when she got to the counter put down $300 and ordered as many stockings as she could and didn't care what color."

"Wow, $300!" gasps Bea. "That's crazy!"

Poppy says, "Did you hear about the poll they took in Chicago where they asked women what they wanted most, and two to one said nylon hose!"

"That's not what I'd have wished for," says Helen.

"Me either," says Poppy. "A lot of good they'd do us."

"Yeah, but just think how long they'd last us—no runs!" I say. "Now the garter belt is another story; the rubber tabs would probably leave permanent dents in our thighs from being squished against the mattress. Who needs that?" I squirm at the thought of the pain. "Okay, Lydia, if it's not the nylons, what else has you so excited?"

Looking smug, Lydia dances over to Izzy's phonograph and puts a record on the turntable. It crackles when she sets the needle onto it. "Watch this," she says moving to the middle of the room.

When the song, *Beat Me Daddy Eight to the Bar* vibrates from the phonograph, she puts her hands out at her sides and starts dancing to the music. Her hips sway back and forth, as she pivots on her toes around the room.

"I went dancing with my friend, Mark, last night and he taught me how to do the Lindy Hop. It's been all the rage for a while now," she shouts above the music.

Just then, Dr. Wagner appears in the doorway. Lydia gets a glimpse of him out of the corner of her eye and dances toward him. Things are heating up. All the girls are wide-eyed and grinning. She actually dances a circle around him while clapping her hands to the beat of the music, and then gives him a sly look as if daring him to dance with her.

The nurses and aides have to be respectful and comply with the hierarchy when it comes to the rules of the sanatorium. He could be in hot water.

It would be frowned upon. I'm ready to jump out of my skin anticipating what he will do! He hesitates, but then as if a light bulb turns on, he smirks.

I wonder if he is thinking about the conversation with Nurse Kirschner about Lydia lifting our spirits. Maybe this once, he decides to ignore the rules.

He turns to face her. The piano keys tinkle in fast-paced rhythm. He takes her hand. She looks into his eyes with her head bent, grinning like a Cheshire cat. He takes her dare! The phonograph echoes, *the rhythm he beats puts the cats in a trance.* We all watch in awe as the unlikely pair boogie-woogie their way from one end of the room to the other. The piano music fills the room along with our excitement.

The couple twirl and dance in perfect harmony. The music seems to empower them. The louder it gets, the faster they swing. Dr. Wagner twirls Lydia under his arm, turns around and switches hands without missing a step. When it gets to the chorus, *And when he jams with the bass and guitar, they holler, Aw, BEAT ME, DADDY, EIGHT TO THE BAR,* It's hard for us to lie still.
Who would have guessed Dr. Wagner is such a swell dancer? He has moves just like any regular guy out on a Saturday night. I sure can't picture ole' Doc Carlson cutting a rug in front of his patients like this; the thought of it makes me cringe.

Lydia's three-minute performance of Lindy hopping with Dr. Wagner sure puts a new spin on the mood in our room. Probably why Dr. Wagner Played along. He is one dedicated doctor. But he will probably get reprimanded.

I think his dedication to us trumps the rules.

We are frozen in the moment and no thoughts of illness, or pain, or war, haunts us—we are too engrossed in what they're doing to think of anything else. Even if it's fleeting. We have this moment. Lydia spins her magic once again.

When the music ends, we are all excited. Even Margaret seems to be enjoying herself. Agnes and Poppy say encore, encore!"

The couple take a bow, and then, just as quickly drop hands.

"Miss Browning, thank you for this dance," says the out-of-breath, dancing doctor. "May I escort you back to your, ah, hmm." He can't quite figure out where to drop her off.

Good ole' Lydia lets him off the hook. "Thank you, Dr. Wagner. You cut a mean rug. But now I must be on my way; my dance card is full for the rest of the evening, but maybe we can do this again sometime."

He nods in agreement. When he looks up, Nurse Kirschner is standing in the doorway, looking flabbergasted. You can see his cheeks go red. I cover my mouth to stop myself from laughing. This is so out of character for him. But how fun.

At that moment, every female in the room have her eyes on him. And then a voice rings out over the loudspeaker. "Paging Dr. Wagner, extension 5331; Dr. Wagner, extension 5331." How lucky can he get?

He breaths a sigh of relief and says, "Sorry, ladies, I would love to continue but duty calls," and he bolts for the door.

Nurse Kirschner steps aside so he can make his escape, and he rushes to the nurses' station to take his call.

We are still giddy with excitement.

Agnes says" this was more fun than watching the Shriner's when they are here."

Izzy is twirling her ponytail, and says, "Lydia, you and

Dr. Wagner should put an act together and perform in the auditorium for the rest of the sanatorium."

Nurse Kirschner says, "You and Dr. Wagner were quite entertaining."

"We were pretty good, weren't we?" says Lydia, a little out of breath.

Bea ads, "Maybe you've got some more moves you could teach him."

"Now, now, Bea, don't be funny. Dancing and acting are the only moves I'm interested in."

"Well, that's what I meant," Bea teases.

"Ah, I think one performance is all you're going to get out of us. He was a good sport though, wasn't he?"

"He sure was," says Agnes. "Why—the way he moved—he was great! Did you see him, Nurse Kirschner?"

"I sure did, Miss Gardner. And I think you're right. I applaud his integrity. "Okay, ladies, I hate to interrupt all this fun, but it's time for you to go the veranda for some sun. Lydia, do you want to help me get the girls outside?"

The routine is the same: they line us up on gurneys side-by-side in the fresh air to lie quietly and soak up the sun, and for the rest of the afternoon, we leisurely muse over Lydia's performance with her surprise dance partner. When we finally get back to the ward, Izzy and Bea are still talking about it.

That's when I come up with a plan for some of my ever so popular rule breaking. "Hey, kids. I have an idea. Why don't we put the music on and let's get up and dance? What do you say?"

They look at me like I'm nuts.

"What are you talking about? We can't do that!" says Helen.

"Why not?" I say.

"Yeah, why not?" asks little Agnes.

Her red hair isn't the only thing that's unmanageable. I love her angst.

"Let's do it," she says.

Poppy chimes in, "Wait a sec, you kids, let's not get carried away." But she is slowly catching the fever. "Do you really think we can get out of bed and try it?"

I was luring her into my web of shenanigans. "Yes I do!" I say. "We're thinking of doing something forbidden. It will get the juices flowing won't it?" "Come on, girls." "Izzy put the music on and let's just try, " Poppy says !"

I am so caught up in the anticipation of actually getting up and dancing, I can't stand It. It's been so long, and Lydia made it look so fun. "C'mon, who's with me?"

"I guess. Well, okay, What can it hurt to give it a try?" says Izzy. She puts the record on.

The music begins. *"In a dinky honky tonky village in Texas."* We all look at each other and decide what the heck. Izzy goes first. She grips the side of the bed for dear life and slides her bony legs over the edge. It is now or never.

Helen and Lucy are too close to the door and hesitate for fear of being caught, but everyone else follows Izzy's lead.

This must have been one of those times Ambriel whispers, "beware, danger," because for a nanosecond my excitement wavers, and I hear a little voice telling me this is wrong. But do I listen? Nope! We are breaking the rules and it feels great. The whole country is rejoicing in anticipation of the war ending, and we just want to be part of it. It is a time to celebrate, I tell myself. The music speeds up and heightens the fun. I sit up and pull my legs over to the side of the bed. A stinging sensation shoots through my left foot. I try putting one leg over the side, but bring it back when the pain jolts through me again. I look down and notice a small wet spot on the sheet where some oozing from my toe. My foot and ankle throb, so I just sit for a minute to catch my breath. I am going to watch the others just until the pain goes away before I try again.

Ambriel is good.

There is no stopping Poppy. She swings her legs over the side and eases her feet to the floor. She is laughing so hard she loses her balance and falls back onto the bed.

My foot is throbbing harder, but watching Poppy fall over, I laugh as hard as she does. At the other end of the room, Lucy and Helen finally let the music lure them to the dance floor. Helen is having trouble like me, but Lucy's strength is somewhat better. But not quite strong enough. She also falls back onto her bed, still smiling.

By this time, every girl in the room is either dangling her feet or trying to stand up. Once they actually try to stand, our weak bodies tremble and we fall backward onto our beds laughing hysterically. Its like we are pumped up on laughing gas. Our legs are just too weak to hold us, but we don't seem to care at the moment, and end up falling backward. Our laughter and the music fills the room. Even Margaret gets out of bed and stands like a flagpole blowing in the wind; she has gained some strength in the passing weeks. I look at her and smile in amazement. "Margaret, you're standing! How does it feel?" She grins and stands motionless for a moment to get her balance, then sways her hips back and forth and snaps her fingers. She lifts her head and actually laughs! After a few moments of gyrating, she tries to move her feet, but within a blink of an eye, her legs give out, and she instantly tumbles to the floor in a heap.

Without warning, we hear, "What on God's green earth is going on in here?" Booms the voice of Nurse Jones.

She catches us off guard. Everyone scrambles to get back into their beds, but It's too late. We're caught.

Nurse Jones runs to Margaret first, who is lying on the floor, struggling to get her breath. "What have you done child?" Nurse Jones' large arms scoops Margaret off the floor with the ease of a crane. While still lifting Margaret, she turns her head toward Izzy and snaps "Shut that blamed music off! Now!"

Izzy has just about manipulated her way back into bed, when Nurse Jones barks again. "Isabelle, I said turn that off right now—do you hear me?"

Izzy quickly picks up the needle and sets it on its holder. That's when the room falls awkwardly quiet. Everyone manages to get back into bed and are wide-eyed in fear of what will happen next.

My foot is still stinging. I lie back and keep my mouth shut, watching in fear as Nurse Jones gently lays Margaret onto her bed. Then she turns on the rest of us.

"If you girls have done any damage to your bodies from this disgusting performance, I swear I'm going to rap each and every one of you along side the head for good measure. What in tar nation are you thinking?"

No one says a word. All of a sudden, I'm not so brave anymore.

Nurse Jones goes to each bedside to making sure no one is hurt, scolding as she goes. When she gets to me, she notices the oozing coming from my foot onto the sheets. "Well now look what you've gone and done. You've probably torn perfectly good tissue that should have been still so it can heal, and now the TB bugs have burst out and are running free again. You girls just don't get it, do you?" Without waiting for an answer, she rages on. "Now I'm going to have to call Dr. Wagner in and have him take a look at your foot. What on earth were you thinking trying to get out of bed in your condition?"

For some reason, she was focusing all her anger on me; not that I didn't deserve it, mind you. Better me than the rest of the girls—it was my brainchild after all. So I tried to apologize. "I-I'm sorry. I didn't mean to..."

"Oh, sorry. That's a pretty empty word if you ask me."

She turns to all the other girls. "You've probably set yourselves back months now because of this pitiful display, and I won't feel one bit sorry for any of you either, do you hear?"

Oh yes, we hear her. Then—I had to hand it to Poppy—she was brave for speaking up. I wanted to scream at her to shut up, but she didn't catch the warning.

"Nurse Jones, Poppy says. We just wanted to have a little fun. It's hard to just lie here all the time."

Nurse Jones spins around placing her hands on her hips and eyes Poppy until she squirms. Poppy pulls the sheet up a little closer to her body. I knew she should have been quiet. Nurse Jones is on the warpath.

"We're not here to have fun, Miss Ann Popke.

Wow, her full name!

"You better keep that in mind the next time you decide to pull something like this." Her large bosoms are heaving.

Margaret stifles a giggle.

Nurse Jones looks like she's ready to pop a cork.

Poppy and I look at each other at the same time. Our eyes dart back and forth from Nurse Jones to each other like nervous little chicks in a hen house.

"To make up for the damage you've done to yourselves, there will be no movie tonight." A collective moan among the girls. We didn't want to draw too much attention to ourselves, but movie night in the auditorium is our get-out-of-jail-free pass. We all look forward to it. Patients who have privileges are able to walk to the theater, while others go in wheelchairs or on gurneys. Tonight the movie is *Anchors Aweigh* starring Frank Sinatra and Gene Kelly. It's supposed to have lots of singing and dancing and romance. Our favorite! Now we have to miss it.

"I will not have you moving about any more today than you already have. That's it—no movie, and it will be lights out early tonight. Now all of you—lie back and rest until supper."

The warden had spoken, and we aren't about to argue with her. We know we did wrong and feel relief that the punishment for our crime isn't any worse than missing a movie.

When Nurse Jones leaves the room, the giggling starts up again.

"Well, I don't care what ole' Nurse Hitler says, it was fun," says Izzy. "I haven't laughed that hard in months."

"She can punish us all she wants," says Bea. "We still had a great time."

"Yeah," says Poppy. "We deserve a little free for all. Who cares about ole' Nurse Jones? It was great!"

Agnes says, "We can't dance like Lydia, but we sure had fun trying."

She looks like a freckled-face little rag doll sitting in her bed with her hair all scattered, grinning from ear to ear. The dancing hadn't hurt her one bit.

Only Helen and I lay quietly in our beds. I wasn't so convinced this was such a good idea after all. Helen has some pain in her chest, and I am a little scared about my foot. It has been hurting for a while, and now the pus oozing from my toe has me worried. I lift the sheet to take another look. My ankle is swollen and my toe is throbbing. The open sore oozes yellow pus onto the sheets. It's gross and actually scares me.

Dr. Wagner comes into the room just then. He seems to brace himself for some teasing, but no one says a word. He looks around like he has the wrong room. He walks to my bed, shrugging his shoulders and says, "Miss Carver, that call that I got earlier was from a colleague of mine. His name is Dr. Charles Evans. He's an orthopedic surgeon who's just came home from the Army."
And he's telling me this why?

"The last time I examined you, I noticed swelling again around your foot and ankle. I've been a little concerned about it, and that's why I contacted Dr. Evans. He's going to be here next week, and I've asked him to come and take a look at you." He goes on to say, I see oozing on the sheet. I will ask Lydia to take you to the lab. I want the open sore aspirated and cultured." Then he stops. "Is something wrong? You don't seem yourself. I sense something in the room."

Nurse Jones hasn't gotten to him yet.

I can't help looking over at Poppy and struggle to keep a straight face. I say the first thing that pops out of my mouth. "Oh no, nothing's wrong. Uh-It's just my foot—I've been wondering about it too. It hurts a lot." "yes, I'm not surprised; it's pretty swollen and oozing. We'll shoot an x-ray of it while we're at it. In the meantime, try not to worry and keep doing what you're doing."

He has no clue what he just said.

"Oh, I will," I say. "I feel fine. Today's been a swell day."

Some of the girls snicker.

Dr. Wagner shakes his head. Under his breath, I hear him say, "Teenagers!"

Chapter 14

*God gives every bird its food, but he does
not throw it into the nest.*

J. G. Holland

Heaven: "It was fun watching our pathetic attempt at dancing, but I see now I should have listened to your warning."

"Yes you should have. That's why they call them rules. I will admit I rather enjoyed the antics," she says.

Ambriel has us back at the waterfall. She asks me, "How much do you know about the Virgin Mary?"

It takes me a minute to think of something smart to say. "Hmm, from my storybooks as a child, I learned that she was a pious woman and she knew poverty. She also tried to protect Jesus."

"Does that remind you of anyone else?"

"She reminds me of Ma."

Through a window into heaven, I see Mary next to Jesus. I smile.

"We're going to stay here awhile and have another look in on Fawn Oakes. The Christmas Lily is behind her right ear.

Pa sits in one of the stuffed chairs in Costello's Barbershop waiting for a haircut. It's a one-man shop owned by Bernie Costello. The steady stream of customers over the years proves it's a gathering ground for the locals. The tattered chairs are mute testimony of its popularity. You needn't be in a hurry when calling on Bernie. Customers usually read the paper, catch up on gossip with neighbors, and even engage in a casual game of checkers while waiting turn for Bernie's clippers.

Besides known for the best haircut for miles around, his shop contains the warmth of the town. Memorabilia decorate the walls from pictures of the old one-room schoolhouse that burned down in the '20s to championship basketball and football teams from earlier years. A picture of the pavilion, which was located on the beach of Crystal Lake, hangs in the center of the wall. The picture was taken in the early '20s and is a reminder of all the dances held there. It is still one of the best spots in town for kicking up your heels on a Saturday night.

In a corner of the shop is an old-fashioned barber's chair and beside it a hand-carved oak stand draped in white linen displaying the tools of his trade and the pride of its owner. Costello's Barber Shop is a haven for old memories and friendly conversation; getting a trim is secondary.

While waiting, Pa skims through the pages of Life Magazine. In large bold print, he reads— *JAPAN SIGNS THE SURRENDER: World War II formally ended at 9:08 on Sunday morning, September 2, 1945."* Pa's chest heaves a sigh of relief. He goes on to read, *"When the last signature had been affixed to Japan's unconditional surrender, Douglas MacArthur declared with the accent of history 'These proceedings are closed.*

"Okay, Joe, you're up," announces Bernie, who stands more than six feet tall. Black hair covers his arms and knuckles and sprouts through the top of his shirt. If he were to dress in a shiny black suit with wide lapels, he'd look like a gangster.

Bernie shakes the cape and fastens it around Pa's neck. "I suppose your boy will be coming home from the war soon."

"He sure is, Bernie. We heard from him last week. He'll be landing on American soil in another week and hopefully back in Minnesota by Christmas. His Ma and I can't wait—it's been six months since we've seen him."

"Okinawa, isn't he?"

"Yup, right in the thick of the worst fighting. Mary and I thank the Lord that he'll be coming home in one piece."

"That's sure good news. Wasn't it a shame about Jake Mitchell's boy? Only 20 years old. His funeral was over in Jackson County. I guess darn near the whole town showed for it."

"I read about that in the newspaper. I don't know Jake very well, but I watched his boy play basketball against Fawn Oakes High. He was a real good athlete."

Bernie takes the razor to Pa's sideburns. "They brought him home in a casket. Jake and Alice still haven't gotten over the shock."

"I don't know how a parent could. All of those boys have been in our prayers since this darned war started. I'm not sure yet where Tom will be stationed after this, but anywhere will be better than where he's been. Yup, Mary and I have a lot to be thankful for."

"Say, Joe, how's Francie doing over there at Glen Lake? I hear that's a real good place for curin' tuberculosis."

"We get to talk to her once a week on the telephone, and she and her Ma write back and forth a lot. The doctors tell us her lungs are doing okay, but now they found TB in her left foot that's spreading to her knee."

"In her foot and knee? Well I'll be doggoned. I didn't know tuberculosis spread like that."

"The doctors tell us that it can attack any part of the body."

"That's a darn shame, Joe—it sure is. What are they doin' for her?"

"They had an orthopedic surgeon take a look at her knee, a pretty good fellow—just home from the Army. That's when they discovered her TB has spread. They're watching it for now, but they might have to do surgery if it gets worse. I guess it's a procedure called an arthrodesis."

Bernie combs through Pa's hair and buzzes up the back of his neck with the clippers "Poor thing. She must be scared."

"Francie has a lot of faith; she's coping pretty well. I'm not sure I can say the same for her Ma.

"Well, you tell Mary we're thinkin' about her, and we'll keep Francie in our prayers. I sure hope they find a cure soon."

"That's what we're hoping for, Bernie. Dr Wagner told us researchers are working on an antibiotic that slows it down, and they've even been testing it out on some patients at Mayo Clinic. It's still pretty new, and they don't know all the side effects yet, but I guess most of those patients are already doing better."

"Can't they try it on Francie?"

"Not yet. The War Production Board has stepped in and taken over handing out the drug."

"Why's that?"

"Because there's a world-wide outcry for it, and I guess there just isn't enough of it to go around. Dr. Wagner told us they appointed one of the scientists to decide who gets it and who doesn't, a guy named Hinshaw. Mary and I have written letters to him and Mayo Clinic and the Merck Company to see if they can help our girl too. I feel like we're running out of time, Bernie. We just can't sit back and wait for the doctors to do it all. We have to get involved, because we need that cure now."

Bernie sweeps his little brush up and down Pa's neck and across his shoulders. "I hear ya, Joe—it must be rough. I know if it was my kid, I'd be doin' the same thing. It doesn't seem fair; you and Mary are such good people. You hang in there, ya hear?" With that he loosens the cape from around Pa's shoulders and says, "That'll be two bits, Joe."

Chapter 15

*"What a wee little part of a person's life
Are in his head and known to none but
himself"*

Mark Twain

Heaven: "Our stay in Fawn Oakes is brief," Ambriel says. But that one tiny glimpse at the barber shop speaks volumes, hopefully showing you the affect you have on your family, and why they keep marching on."

"I'm at peace watching Pa, even though he's hurting. I understand now that my parents are following the road mapped out for them."

I follow Ambriel as she takes me to see more of heaven. I'm surprised when I see people in heaven praying for people on earth. Butterflies flutter around heaven everywhere. One lands on my hand. The touch is tingling. I don't see her, but I hear Margaret's grandmother praying, asking God's help for Margaret. After some time, the butterfly takes flight. Ambriel says, "It's time to go."

"I think Heaven is transforming me," I say. There is so much goodness."

Ambriel fusses with the Christmas Lily but leaves it behind her left ear and says, "We still have a lot of work to do. Time to look down on the sanatorium again, where things are getting interesting.

———

I'm tossing and turning in my sleep, dreaming about bugs coming for me, moving slowly past the meadow, toward the farmhouse. I turn away to avoid their stench, and my hair tangles across my forehead, sticking to my skin. They're getting closer inching their way up the stairway to my room on the second floor. I try to scream. Nothing! I try to run. My legs won't move! A stabbing pain shoots through my knee and jolts me awake. I gasp for air, coughing until I catch my breath. My nightgown is soaked in sweat. I lay terrified looking around the room, and then I let out a sigh of relief. It's just another bad dream. I try to sit up but that makes the pain in my knee worse. All I can do is lay here. A sliver of moonlight streams through the window onto my sheet. I stare at the light and try to will my knee to stop hurting—it feels like a branding iron pressing into my flesh. Tears sting my eyes. I put my hand underneath my leg to try to stop the pain, and then I hear a noise. I look over at Poppy, but she's sleeping, as are the rest of the girls. Something moves. I try focusing my eyes in the dark, and see a shadow moving awkwardly in the center of the room. I squint, but I can't quite make it out.

Margaret?

Yes, yes. Its Margaret! But what is she doing? I blink hard, and through a salty haze, I can see Margaret pushing a chair and walking behind it. When she gets to the far end of the room, she turns around and walks back toward her bed. As she gets closer, I ease my head back onto my pillow, pretending to be sleeping. I don't move a muscle, but keep my eyes on her. I can't believe it— there in the middle of the night is ole Margaret out of bed pushing a chair and walking up and down the center of the room while everyone else is asleep.

She is not as weak as she has been pretending. That little fake! Why would she do that? I watch her walk back to her bed and push the chair up against the wall where it normally stands. Then she climbs back into bed, and I don't hear another peep out of her the rest of the night. She has obviously gotten stronger, but why is she hiding it? What is she up to? That girl has too many secrets.

I try to relax and get back to sleep, but as hard I try, the night drags on. I can't get the image of Margaret out of my mind. Then other thoughts creep in and haunt me. Thoughts of dying and never seeing my family again. The talk I had with Poppy about never getting better and lying in a coffin creeps in and won't let go. Lying alone in the dark, I feel abandoned, and tears once again well up. I pray to God for a cure and cry myself to sleep in my lonely nighttime pillow, like I've done so many times before.

—⚬⚬⚬—

Morning brings bad news for Helen. Dr. Stone pays her a visit.

"Good morning Miss Coalwell. How are you feeling this morning?"

It's hard to breathe, Doctor, she pants.

"Yes, your temperature is elevated and your sputum culture has grown out more tubercle bacilli, which means your TB is worsening. It's, not responding to the treatment. He hesitates. "I have decided it is time to perform surgery. I'm sure by the way you've been feeling, this is no surprise to you.

Helen looks too ill to say much, she merely nods her head.

"We need to try and give your lung a rest so it can heal. We've decided the best way to do this is with a procedure called a pneumothorax. It's a fairly simple operation where we make a small incision in your chest and pump air into the space around your lung. This will cause your lung to collapse so it can relax. Think of it like a balloon lying quietly in your chest. Resting the lung like this will give it a chance to heal. We'll give you Novocain for the procedure, but there still may be some discomfort from the collapse of the lung."

Helen is short of breath, so speaking is hard for her. "I-I trust you, Dr. Stone," she says. "Do my parents know?"

"Yes. I was in contact with them earlier today. They're coming to my office and then they'll be up to visit with you. We're also going to do a fluoroscopy before each air-injection treatment to see how your lungs are doing."

"What's that?"

"It's like an x-ray but without film. We'll do this every other day, gradually collapsing more of your lung. Eventually we'll inflate it again and you'll be able to breathe as you did before. We're hoping this procedure will allow the holes in your lung to close up and cure you of the disease."

"When?"

"I have you on the schedule for 8 o'clock tomorrow morning if your parents agree. After the first treatment, we'll move you to 4-East to a private room for awhile so you can get as much rest as possible. Eventually, when things are looking better, you can come back to the ward. Well that's all for now. I will see you tomorrow morning."

Helen closes her eyes and Dr. Stone leaves the room.

I keep my eyes on Margaret, who is eating breakfast. Instead of twisting and mangling the food with her fork and hiding it under her tray, she is actually eating. Eating. Walking in the night, breaking the rules, eating her food— this is unlike Margaret. Is she actually trying to get her strength back? I can't help thinking that Margaret is up to something. She seems different somehow, almost smug. Margaret looks in my direction and smirks.

"Okay Margaret, this is your big day," Nurse Kirschner says as she enters the room. "Lydia is on her way, and once she gets here, you, my dear, are going for a walk." The other girls are surprised at the sudden turn of events. No one had any idea Margaret was anywhere near ready to be up and moving about.

"Do you really think I'm ready?" Margaret acts surprised.

I roll my eyes and wait to see what her next move will be.

"Dr. Wagner is quite pleased with your last test results and doesn't want to waste any more time moving you on to the next level of your recovery. We'll take it nice and slow and let it all depend on you, just like we did with Lucy. How does that sound?" Before Margaret has a chance to resist, Lydia bounces into the room bursting with energy. "Well, well, well. Look who's next on the list to try the famous ward-530 tap dance. Up and atem young lady; time's a wastin', and you ain't getting any younger. We're not wasting one more minute watching you lie around all day," Lydia teases.

All the attention is on Margaret. There is no way she can get out of it. She has to go along with the doctor's orders and let them help her try to walk. The routine is the same as with Lucy, Nurse Kirschner on one side and Lydia supporting her on the other, and the girls coaching her on. The walk down the center of the room is slow. Margaret seems to be in pain and struggles to put her weight on her long, lean legs, whining the whole while. At one point, her legs buckle, and Lydia and Nurse Kirschner have to hold on tight to keep her from falling. I watch in amazement. Margaret is a good little actress, no doubt about it.

By the end of the week, Dr. Wagner tells us Helen has had two pneumothorax procedures and is fine, but she still has a way to go before she'd be able to come back to the ward. As for Margaret, every day Lydia and Nurse Kirschner walk her, and every day she struggles and pleads with them to quit before her time is up.

Then something very strange happens.

Chapter 16

"For the times they are a-changin'."

Bob Dylan

Heaven: I'm basking in the beauty of the waterfall, when I say to Ambriel, "I can't imagine what it will be like when I enter the gates." We turn a corner of heaven, and I see the most beautiful woman garbed in a simple blue robe and white turban covering her hair. Her face seems sad. "Who is she?" I ask.

"She's St. Veronica, Patron Saint of photographers and laundry workers. She is known for her compassion when she wiped the face of Jesus with a cloth at His Crucifixion."

"No wonder she looks so sad."

Ambriel says, "It's known through the ages, when she wiped His face, it left an imprint on the cloth." Let's see what kind of compassion awaits you at the sanatorium."

When I look down, I see some of the girls going to the movies.

—⁂—

It's Wednesday evening, and the girls on the ward are at the movies except for me. Dr. Wagner has ordered an infrared lamp treatment for my knee. Nurse Jones is just bringing me back from the treatment when she realizes she doesn't have my chart. When we get to the elevator doors, she tells me not to go anywhere and that she will be right back. She even smiles. I guess that is her attempt at humor. She does that sometimes. There is another side to her. I see it. She just doesn't share it with us too much. But It's there.

Pa used to tell us kids that sometimes we have to look past what's on the outside of people and be patient for the good stuff that's on the inside, something about not judging a book by its cover.

I lay on the gurney watching Nurse Jones walk down the hall and out of sight. All of a sudden, someone comes up behind me and presses the elevator button. There isn't an attendant on duty tonight. Before I have a chance to see what is happening, I'm being pushed onto the elevator and heading for the basement. When I finally get turned around, I see the culprit.

"Oh, my gosh! Margaret! What do you think you're doing?"

"Hello, Francine Rose. I'm just taking you for a little joy ride."

"What do you mean a joy ride? Nurse Jones will throw a fit if she comes back and I'm gone. What do you think you're doing? I thought you couldn't walk by yourself."

She doesn't answer.

"You can't do this."

"Well I'm doing it, aren't I?"

"I knew it. I knew you could walk." My temper flares.

"Ah, did you figure that out all on your own?"

"What's with you? Why do you always act like this—and where are you taking me?"

"My, my, you ask a lot of questions for someone who thinks she knows it all."

"I don't think I know it all. What are you doing? Where are we going?" I was getting frantic.

"You'll find out soon enough."

The elevator comes to a stop, and the doors open. Margaret pushes the gurney out into a dimly lit hall and moves along like nobody's business.

"I've seen you at night, Margaret."

"Why whatever do you mean, Francine Rose?" and keeps walking.

"I've seen you when you thought everyone was sleeping. I've seen you walk."

"How do you know it was me?"

"Oh, it was you all right. No one else would hide the fact that they can walk. I saw you walking around the room pushing a chair, and I saw you faking it when Nurse Kirschner and Lydia were helping you."

"If you're so sure about that, why didn't you say something?"

"I don't rat on people, and besides, I figure what you do is your business."

"Well, for once I agree with you," she says, getting closer to the end of the hall.

"But why keep it a secret? It seems to me hiding it just takes a lot of energy."

She laughs that smug little laugh of hers and says, "As you can see I have a lot of energy."

"Yes, I do see that, and I'm glad for you, and I'm sure everyone else would be too. But why have you been pretending otherwise?"

"Okay, okay. Enough chitchat. It's time I drop you off and say goodnight."

"What do you mean, drop me off? This is the tunnel to the morgue! Why are we going to the tunnel?"

"Oh, we're not—you are."

"What? Cut it out, Margaret. This has gone far enough. You take me back right now." I was frantic but then backed off in case she meant it. "I promise I won't say a word. You can keep your little secrets for all I care. Just take me back before Nurse Jones comes looking for me." I plead.

"So sorry, Francine Rose."

I hate when she says my name like that.

"I don't have time to take you back. I need to get back to the theatre before the movie lets out," and then she opens the door and pushes the gurney into the dark tunnel.

"You've got to be kidding me! You can't just leave me here for heaven sake!"

"I can and I am. Have a good night, and don't let the bed bugs bite," she says, taunting me. Before I can even blink, Margaret pulls the doors shut, leaving me in the dark tunnel.

The tunnel is black. I can't see a thing. "Margaret, wait. Come back!" I panic. "Margaret, don't do this. Please! Come back and let me out of here! Are you crazy? Get back here right this minute! You can't just leave me here!" I hold my breath and listen, hoping she is still out there. The only sound I hear is my anxious breathing in and out of my lungs. There is nothing but emptiness. Just a dark hollow feeling in the pit of my stomach. I don't like this—I don't like this one bit. Oh that Margaret! Why is she doing this?

I look around. The tunnel is cold and dark and the thought of what is on the other side gives me goose bumps—it is where they perform autopsies. An aide told Poppy and me all about it. She could have been fired for telling us, but we were so curious we promised not to tell. She told us she has been in there once and said it is a tiny little room with a steel table and two refrigerator boxes that are encased in solid oak cabinets. I picture it in my mind and get nauseous.

I lay on the gurney without moving a muscle trying to calm my stomach. The air is so black I can't see my hand in front of my face. My other senses come alive in the murkiness forcing me to smell, feel, and taste. A faint odor of formaldehyde burns my nostrils, and a bitter taste regurgitates into my mouth. I wince and swallow it back down. My stomach is percolating. The damp air wraps itself around me forcing the cold into my bones causing my body to tremble—or maybe it is just my nerves making me shake, I don't know. The only thing I know for sure is the people who came through this tunnel on a gurney are dead people—and I want out!

I try to take my mind off my situation and think of the tunnel at Catholic School. This tunnel is nothing like the tunnel at school. In grade school, the tunnel connected Sacred Heart Catholic School to the Church. It was warm and well lit, and the cement walls painted green. In winter, instead of going outside to get to the lunchroom that was in the church basement we lined up single file and walked through the tunnel. When I was in that tunnel, I could hear the glorious sounds of the church bells ringing out the Angelus during the noon hour and laughter from the kids eating in the lunchroom.

Once when the nuns weren't around, Millie and I ran from one end of the tunnel to the other making screeching sounds listening to hear our echoes. Ambriel must have been nearby, because we soon got bored and left before the nuns came back to catch us. That tunnel was fun.

I close my eyes and take a deep cleansing breath to try and relax so I can think. What to do, what to do. Think, Francie, think. I am pretty sure Margaret is just trying to scare me and will be coming back. Well, somewhat sure. She isn't really planning to leave me here all night—is she? It's so quiet. A chill runs through me, and makes the hair on my arms stand up. "Get a grip, Francie," I tell myself in a low whisper. "Don't be scared. Don't be scared." I swallow hard.

Minutes tick by and I don't know what to do. I can't take it anymore, so I take a deep breath and cry out, "Help! Help me! Someone, anybody! Please help me!"

I am literally on the verge of tears, when I think I hear footsteps.

Chapter 17

*"You don't have to go looking for love
when it's where you come from."*

Werner Erhard

Heaven: "Oh, that Margaret," I say to Ambriel.

"Do you know the meaning of the word serendipity?" asks Ambriel.

"Is that something like two people meeting up at the same place and time and find their soulmates or maybe call it fate?" Ambriel twirls around spinning her beads and says, "Very good, now follow me."

"I have a feeling this is going to be good." I say following her through a maze of rose petals, getting another glimpse of heaven. The petals are everywhere: in trees, flowing in rivers, in bird nests, and scattered on paths. I follow Ambriel on one path leading to a meeting of a round table. All of the people at the table wear a bright golden halo and a few have wings. "What is this?" I ask.

It's a meeting of Patron Saints of love." Ambriel says, "Let me introduce you. At the head of the table is Saint Monica, Patron saint of wives and mothers." "Nice to meet you." She says to me.

'Next is St. Jude, Patron Saint of lost causes. "Hello, Francie." He says with a smile. "And this is Saint Raphael, who stands at the throne of the Lord. He is one of the three archangels. His name means God has healed. He heals their love and drives out demons. He nods. Next to him is Saint Alice or Adelaide. She is the patron saint of second marriages and widows. "Nice meeting you, Francie, Ambriel is a thorough guide. You are in good hands."

"Yes she is, thank you," I say.

"You might recognize this next saint from your Bible studies, says Ambriel"

The saint looks my way, "Yes, I do recognize you from my books, I say with a smile. You are Saint Joseph, patron saint of fathers and spouse of the Blessed Virgin Mary."

"Have a chair and join us," he says to me.

"Thank you, Joseph," says Ambriel, "but we can't stay."

Next, Ambriel says, "I'm positive you know this last saint but certainly not the least."

I muffle a squeal and say, "It's Santa Claus!" He turns and says, "Ho, ho, ho, Francie."

Ambriel says, "His given name is Nicholas of Myra, he is an ideal saint to seek, assistance for matters of the heart. He helps the needy and the suffering, and known for his generosity. Besides, matters of the heart, he is patron saint of poets.

Ambriel thanks the panel for letting us interrupt their proceedings. We leave the rose petal path and Ambriel says, "Let's see what in store for you next, shall we?"

—⁓—

The footsteps are getting closer. Thank goodness. Margaret must have reconsidered, and decided to come back for me. She has left me long enough. I know she is just trying to throw a scare into me. Well, it worked. "Margaret? Is that you?" No one answers. The footsteps stop, and I hear someone outside the tunnel doors. "Margaret? I can hear you. For heaven sake, let me out of here!" The door opens. My heart races. "I knew you wouldn't leave me here. What a relief you came back...Margaret?"

The door opens wider, and the light filters into the tunnel, forcing me to squint. "Margaret?" I want to read her the riot act, but just as quickly I think better of it, for fear she will leave me again.

I get a whiff of aftershave. The light is too bright for my eyes.

All I see is a shadow—It's too large to be Margaret.

"No, I'm not Margaret. I'm Jonah."

It's a man's voice…

"Looks like you could use some help."

I let out my breath cautiously. "Ye…yes, I sure do."

The young man standing in front of me takes hold of the gurney and pulls it out into the hall. "What are you doing in here?"

"I…I'm not sure."

"You're not sure?"

"Uh, uh, I mean, it's just a mistake."

"Do you know how you got here?"

"It was an accident."

"Well if this is an accident, then lucky for you I punched the wrong number. I thought I heard someone calling for help. It's a good thing I came looking. How did you get in here anyway?"

In the dim light, I find myself gazing up into smoky, brown eyes and a face so handsome, I blush. His voice is deep and vibrates through me. All of a sudden I can't speak.

He repeats. "Don't you know how you got here?"

Oh jeez, he must think I am some kind of crazy person who talks to voices in her head and drools on herself. I try to collect my thoughts, but for the life of me, I can't think straight. All that comes out is, "Margaret."

"Margaret? Your name is Margaret?"

The fog starts to lift, allowing my tongue to form a coherent sentence. "No. Margaret is my roommate. She's playing a joke on me."

"A joke?"

"Oh, you know how girls are. She's just trying to scare me."

What I didn't tell him is that I think Margaret is a raving lunatic who needs to be put into a straight jacket and hung out of a ten-story window dangling by her heels.

Instead, I just say, "thank you for coming to my rescue and ruining her prank."

"My pleasure," he says with an impish grin that sends a blood-rush through my chest.

"What's your name?"

A wisp of black hair tumbles in a curl down his forehead. Oh my!

"Francie Carver," I say shyly. "And you're Jonah?"

"Yes. Jonah, like in the Bible. Jonah Fischer to be exact."

"Umm, the Bible? I'm not sure..."

"You know, Jonah and the whale? Big fish—swallows a kid named Jonah—spits him out three days later?" He smiles, and huge dimples dent his cheeks.

I practically melt into oblivion trying to find my voice. "Oh, sure, I've heard the story. Jonah's a nice name."

"I think my parents were trying to be clever."

"I think it has character." I say.

"In the story, God must have had other plans for Jonah, like rescuing young damsels in distress." He's grinning again, and there come those dimples.

I divert the conversation back to our names. "My parents named me Francine Rose. Francine after my grandmother and Rose because my mother likes them. They already had five kids, so my father was willing to go along with whatever my mother came up with."

"Francine Rose. That suits you. I'm glad your father didn't object. Well, Miss Carver, where to?"

He is easy to talk to, but I don't want to spend one more second so close to the morgue. So I say, "That would be room 530," and then I ask, "Are you a patient here?"

"I am. I've been on 3-main for the past year. They say I should be ready to go home by the first of the year."

"That's wonderful. You must be thrilled."

"I can't wait. A year's an awful long time…" He stops abruptly. "That was insensitive of me. I'm sorry."

"Oh, please, don't be sorry. I know it takes a long time. I think everyone who comes through the doors of the sanatorium knows that. I've only been here three months, and I know I still have a long way to go."

"I've seen a lot of people come and go in the year that I've been here. It's a good place, and the doctors are the best. I know they'll find a cure soon."

I suppose he was wondering the same thing as me, if a cure will ever come, because we both get quiet. He breaks the silence. "So tell me, Francie, why aren't you at the movies tonight?"

I was glad he changed the subject. "I wanted to go, but Dr. Wagner ordered some extra lamp treatments for me, so I had to miss. How about you, I thought all the boys would be clamoring to see Incendiary Blonde. Betty Hutton is so beautiful."

"I'm kind of partial to brunettes, myself."

I feel my cheeks flush. His eyes roam over my face. I lower my eyes and fumble with the ties on my sweater. I wish I would've put the matching ribbon in my hair.

Things like that always happen to me. Some days I get all dressed up and look great, and nothing special happens. Then I will have a day like this where I'm stranded in a tunnel and the cutest boy I've ever seen rescues me, and I don't even have on the matching ribbon that goes with my sweater, for heaven sake.

He is standing at the side of the gurney with his arms outstretched on the rails, and bends his body low to meet my gaze. He is so close I can feel the warmth of his breath on my cheek. His stare sends shivers through me.

"I-I suppose I should be getting back. Nurse Jones will be wondering where I am." What is wrong with me? I sound like I'm ten.

For the longest time, he doesn't move, but his eyes search my face.

I hold my breath—paralyzed.

"I'll tell you what. I'll take you back to your room if you say you'll go to the movies with me next Wednesday."

I think my heart is going to pound out of my chest. My voice is stuck somewhere in my throat, and I can only manage a nod.

"Okay then, it's a date. I'll come to your room and pick you up."

When he finally stands up, I let my breath out and swallow hard, hoping he doesn't notice. Somehow, I manage to mutter, "All right."

Cool, Francie, real cool.

We are the only two people in the basement, and the sound of the gurney rolling on the glassy Terrazzo hallway echoes along with the click of his heels. My head is whirling. I can't believe what is happening. A few minutes ago I was trapped in the tunnel leading to the morgue, scared out of my wits, and now I am being whisked away by the cutest boy I've ever seen, who just asked me for a date. What is this world coming to? Then Margaret creeps across my mind.

The elevator doors open to the fifth floor and Jonah escorts me to my room. When we round the corner, I hear Nurse Jones talking to the girls who've just gotten back from the movies. When she sees us coming, she blocks the doorway. Hands on hips. She looks ready to explode.

"Well it's about time. Where have you been, or need I ask?"

If looks could kill, Jonah would be laid out on the floor.

She doesn't wait for a reply.

"I guess it's pretty clear what you've been up to."

"I'm sorry, Nurse Jones, but I can explain." I look past Nurse Jones and shoot daggers at Margaret.

Nurse Jones fixes on Jonah. "You, young man, have some explaining to do, and it had better be good. I can have you arrested you know."

"Arrested! Ah, c'mon on," he teases.

However, Nurse Jones isn't having any of it.

"Nurse Jones, this is all quite innocent, honest," he says.

"When it comes to teenage boys, there is no such thing as innocent," she fumes. "Miss Carver, I have a good mind to call your parents and tell them exactly what you've been up to."

I turn away from Margaret, who is still looking smug, and I say, "I haven't been up to anything. Jonah found me and was kind enough to bring me back to my room."

Now if you think I was about to rat on ole Margaret, you are clueless in the ways of teenage high jinks. There's an unspoken code among teenage girls—a loyalty, if you will. 'You don't rat on me, and I won't rat on you.' Well, maybe it's just my unspoken code, but nonetheless, I need to play it cool with ole Margaret and twist the knife a little.

Margaret squirms and looks out the window.

"While you were gone, someone moved me so they could get another cot onto the elevator," I lie.

Margaret doesn't move a muscle, as if she is waiting for the bomb to drop.

"Without realizing it, they pushed me too close to the ramp, and after a few moments my gurney rolled backward down the other hall. I was scared to death until Jonah came to my rescue."

Another look toward Margaret. Good, she looks confused.

While Margaret and I are playing let's-see-who-can-kill-who-with-looks, Nurse Jones still fixates on Jonah, who gives her one of his sultry smiles. It seems to have almost the same effect on her as it does on me. She clears her throat and quickly looks away.

I continue. "When Jonah found me, I had rolled halfway down the other hall. It took us this long to get back because of everyone coming from the movies. We had to wait our turn at the elevators because the line was so long."

I was surprised how easy the fib poured from my lying mouth. Ambriel must have been hard at work, because I secretly promised myself I would go to confession first thing in the morning.

"Really, Nurse Jones, Jonah was just looking out for me. That's all there is to it."

She starts to soften, but she isn't quite done scolding. "Young men his age cannot be trusted, and it would be wise for you to remember that, Miss Carver." Then she says to Jonah. "Next time something like this happens, you come and find me and I will escort her back. Now step aside while I get my patient into bed where she belongs."

"Yes ma'am, I'm truly sorry we worried you. It won't happen again." He is grinning from ear to ear at her, but she is trying not to notice. He winks at me and mouths the words, "See you at the movies."

By this time, Margaret's mouth is hanging open. I smile sweetly at her, like a Cheshire cat, and get into bed. I am sure she didn't expect her prank to end up this way.

When all the dust finally settles, and Nurse Jones goes back to the nurses' station, I decide to twist the knife a little further into ole Margaret's gut. "I suppose I should thank you for the wonderful time I had this evening."

"Oh? Did you enjoy your outing?"

There is that sarcasm again. That girl never quits.

"It was very interesting. Quite ironic, wouldn't you say, and I only have you to thank for it." I can sling it as well as she can spew it.

"Oh, I don't think it was all fun and games," she says.

"Okay, I'll admit, it was a bit of a struggle at first, but like my Pa always says, struggle is nature's way of strengthening. I think at this moment I could lift the world with one hand."

Her innocent act quickly turns to agitation.

"Oh your Pa—your Pa. You think he knows everything. Well, he doesn't!"

Her temper explodes into the air like waves crashing against a rock. Her sudden mood change surprises me. "No, he doesn't, but he speaks what's in his heart, and I want to be just like him when I grow up." Without realizing it, I hit a nerve with Margaret. She starts to cry. "Okay, Margaret, what gives? Why did you do that to me tonight and why are you crying?"

"Mind your own business, Francie. Go be with your old boyfriend and forget about me." Her words vibrate with self-pity, and she rolls over and pulls the covers over her head.

I don't want to forget about it. What gives with her? An hour ago, she was being as mean and spiteful as she can, and now this. I don't know whether to be angry or feel sorry for her. Whatever it is—it can't go on much longer. I decide for tonight not to upset her any more. It can wait another day. Besides, I am still reeling from the events of the evening. Something else Margaret said. She called Jonah my boyfriend. Another blood rush!

"Pssst, Francie," Poppy whispers. "What happened to you tonight? Nurse Jones almost snapped her cap looking for you. Who was that dreamboat who brought you back? Hubba, hubba!"

"Oh, Poppy," I almost squealed. "Isn't he cute? His name is Jonah Fischer. He's a patient here, and he asked me out to the movies for next Wednesday."

"What? He asked you out on a date. Okay girl, I want details, and don't you leave out a single word."

Poppy and I whisper back and forth for the next hour. I tell her about seeing Margaret walking at night, and how she pushed me into the tunnel. Then I tell her about Jonah rescuing me.

Poppy is on pins and needles, drinking in every detail. "What are you going to do about ole Margaret over there?"

"I really don't know, Poppy. As dumb as this might sound, I think tonight she might have been reaching out to me."

"Well I think she's a horrible person and should be reported. You can't let her get away with this."

"When you think about it, Poppy, she kind of did me a favor. I probably wouldn't have met Jonah if it wasn't for her."

"Well, I'll give her that, but she's just plain weird. Who knows what she'll try to pull next?"

Just then, Nurse Jones comes in and announces, "Lights out."

Chapter 18

"Not everything that is faced can be changed, but nothing can be changed until it is faced."

James A. Baldwin

Heaven: We're sitting by the waterfall, and Ambriel is twirling her beads, probably contemplating my punishment for lying, when she says, "Lying to Nurse Jones was wrong, but I have to give you a pass since you were protecting Margaret. That was even kind-hearted. You did make a good choice by not reporting her. Your words and actions prove to Margaret that she can trust you."

A man comes running toward us. He's wearing an orange and gold frock, and a dove hovers over his head. One side of his face is clean-shaven, and the other side has a full beard. It looks weird. In his hands, he's holding a bible.

"Hey there, Ambriel," says the saint. "This must be your protégé."

"She sure is," says Ambriel. "Francie, this is the one and only, Philip Neri. He's the patron saint of comedians and practical jokes." "Philip, do you have any words of wisdom that you would like to bestow upon Francie?"

He laughs. "Don't take yourself too seriously." He says. Wait a minute, I see an aura about you that tells me you already have mischievous tendencies," and one day, a relative will tell your story, and it will be on the best sellers list of your family." He laughs and says," No time to waste, I am off to laughter convention. Nice meeting you, Kiddo."

"That was fun," I say to Ambriel. Before she says it, I say "I know, I know, time to go back to the sanatorium."

She says, "What happens next is one of those times you have another positive effect on someone.

—⁓—

I like all the quirky girls on the ward, but Margaret is really a mystery to me. Now I know she has played a nasty and mean-spirited trick on me, and it scared the daylights out of me. But, for the life of me, I can't stay mad at her. I'm starting to realize more and more how lonely Margaret must be. Nevertheless, she won't let any of us in. I think if she would just open up and talk, maybe whatever has her knickers in a bunch won't seem so bad. Just then, Lydia bursts into the room as bubbly as ever. "Okay, Francie and Margaret, it's out to the veranda with you for fresh air and sunshine." Margaret tries to protest but Lydia is stronger and more experienced, and has her on the gurney and out the door before Margaret has a chance to complain. However, we can hear her whining all the way down the hall.

"That Lydia sure knows how to handle Margaret," says Poppy. I like the way she trotted out of here before ole Margaret had a chance to weasel her way out of going for therapy. But now you have to put up with her hostility for the next hour. Poor kid!"

"Poppy, have you ever noticed that no one ever comes to visit her?"

"Now that you mention it, I have," says Poppy. That is strange."

"She must be so lonely." I'm starting to feel sorry for her.

"Did you forget what she did to you yesterday?"

"No, but I am kind of seeing her in a different light."

Before we have a chance to pursue our discussion any further, Lydia is back and says, "Hop on, Francie ole gal, and I'll take you away to Never-Never Land."

I love being around Lydia. It's as if every day is a party with

her. She is like a magician performing magic, making my illness disappear—or at least helps me forget about it. Whenever Lydia is in the room, everyone has a smile on their face.

"Lydia?"

"Yes?"

"I think you should forget about being an actress and become a doctor instead," I say, while getting on the gurney. "You already know how to make people feel better."

Lydia throws her head back and lets out a screech. "Ewe! Are you kiddin'? I could never do that!"

"Why not?"

"Because doctors have to wear surgical masks."

"So?"

"Wear a mask and cover up this beautiful face?" She lifts her chin into one of her movie star poses. "No way! I want to be seen on the big screen not in an emergency room. Now let's stop this insanity and get you outside. You're going to give me a heart attack talking like that!"

I let out an exaggerated sigh, and in a singsong voice, I tell her, "Okay, whatever you say; but I think you could be missing your true calling," then out the door we go with Lydia exclaiming that is the most absurd and outlandish thing she's ever heard.

It's nearing the end of September, but the air feels unseasonably warm and dry. When I look across the veranda, I see rolling hills and fields marking the change of the season, with yellow and gold maples, red sumac and rust-colored field grasses. I just love fall— It's so beautiful. I love the dried cornstalks in a farmer's field, and in another direction the stillness of Birch Lake is mesmerizing. The lake is one of my favorite things to look at. I love when the water is calm and mirrors the trees. The baby loons haven't flown south yet and call out to each other. There is not a more beautiful sound in the world to me than the call of the loon— it's another one of nature's little pleasures.

I put my head back, close my eyes, and breathe in the aromas. The sun on my face feels heavenly. The wall next to the veranda blocks any breeze, letting the warmth of the sun's rays wash over me in a refreshing bath of sunshine. It feels good to be breathing the crisp fresh air, thick with the scent of dried leaves and fresh mowed grass. It reminds me of home.

On our farm, Pa has a greenhouse behind one of the machine sheds, and every spring, he plants seeds for flowers that flourish under the heat of the hothouse during the early spring months. He tends them like newborn babies. The seedlings spring into brilliant-colored geraniums, impatience, petunias, and marigolds. Then my sisters and I help Ma plant them in the flowerbeds and clay pots around our house. Their pungent fragrance gets thicker in the fall long after most perennials have lost their blooms.

Margaret is lying on her gurney with her head turned away from me. Lydia leaves in a streak telling us to play nice. I open my eyes and say, "That Lydia sure is a character, isn't she?"

Silence.

The warmth of the sun makes me feel good all over, and I close my eyes and concentrate on that feeling, to help overcome the annoyance that is building up in me toward Margaret again. With my eyes still closed I say, "Do you want to talk about what's happened between us?"

No answer.

The silence finally gets to me. Enough is enough. I want to jump off the gurney and choke the truth out of her. How would she like that? However, not being a person who is prone to violence, I decide instead to play it cool. Margaret can't keep this innocent act up forever. Something has to give.

I decide to try another approach. Maybe if I keep talking, Margaret will forget herself and open up. So I prop myself up on my pillow and grab my stationery.

"I'm writing a letter to my niece, Patty. She's the oldest of my sister Dorothy's seven kids. Little Joey is their baby. I've been working on a blue sweater and cap for him so I can give it to him for Christmas."

Margaret remains quiet.

"They have one other girl named Donna and the rest are boys. Would you like to hear my letter to Patty?"

Margaret glances at me, then immediately looks away. I seize the moment and begin to read aloud, whether she wants me to or not.

September 20, 1945

Dear Patty,

I guess it's about time I answer your letter, don't you think? Gosh, Patty, I really was surprised to receive your letter, and I think that you write very well. I was also very happy to hear that you are all feeling fine. Tell Mommy and Daddy that I really enjoyed their visit and that I wish they could have stayed longer.

The next time you write, have Jim, Donna, and Dick put in a few lines. Oh, by the way, Jack and Ronny too. You know, I was so happy to hear that you are all praying for me. I just know that is what is getting me well, so keep it up; maybe I'll be home soon. I sure miss you all. I bet you have grown so that I won't know you when I do get home. I was glad to hear that you all like school and are getting along so well. I can't imagine Dick being so shy though.

I'm sure you've been having fun outside running and playing and jumping in the leaves. The leaves started to fall here too. Of course, I don't get to go out and walk in them because I have to stay in bed all the time. I suppose you can't imagine staying in bed for a whole year

*at a time, can you? So, Patty, I hope you and all the other kids eat all
the food Mommy gives you so you don't get sick and have to stay in
bed like this.*

*I'm sending you a picture of me so you can put it in your
scrapbook. This is the place where I am staying. There are seven
other girls in the same room with me, and I have a corner bed with
windows on all sides of me; but of course, you can't see it very well on
this picture.*

*Well Patty, write again and I will try to answer your letter
sooner than I did this time. Goodbye again and keep up the prayers.*

Love to all,

Aunt Francie

I can tell Margaret is listening, so I just keep talking. "I used
to stay with my sister in the summertime, helping her with the
children. I would get so darned mad at those little boys because
they would mess with my things and get into my makeup." I pause
for a sec and then say, "I'd give anything to have those days again.
I think that's the hardest part about being here, really missing the
ones, you love. How about you, Margaret, who do you miss?" I hold
my breath and hope for an answer.

Margaret doesn't look at me, but after a long moment says,
"My mother died giving birth to me," after that it was just my
brother Frank, my father and me."

I can hardly believe my ears—an actual sentence without
sarcasm. Like walking on slippery rocks, I choose my words
carefully. "I'm sorry to hear that."

She continues, "We had an aunt who came to stay with us to
help take care of Frank and me. When I turned eight, my father
figured I was old enough, and no need for my aunt anymore."
"That summer, my father hired a man to help with some of the
farm work. My brother, Frank, helped too, but he really wasn't big

enough. He was only ten."

I'm glued to the sound of her voice, as she gazes toward the sky, almost in a trance, not hearing or seeing anything but the summer she was eight.

"The man's name was Mr. Gunderson. He smelled bad, and always stared at me. I didn't like it when he stared at me."

A faint breeze blows a wisp of Margaret's hair across her face, but she doesn't seem to notice.

"One day, when my dad was out in the field, I made him some lunch and went looking for Frank to take it to him. Mr. Gunderson was in one of the buildings working on a tractor."

Suddenly, she stops talking. I wait. Finally, I say, "What happened? Did you find Frank?"

She doesn't answer, and her breathing quickens.

"Are you okay Margaret?"

Her chest heaves, and she gulps for air. She tries to sit up but she is having too much trouble getting her breath.

"It's okay, Margaret, I say, we don't have to talk anymore. Just relax and take a deep breath."

Her anxiety increases, and her breaths come in short gasps.

"Margaret, can you hear me? Take a deep breath and let it out slowly."

She starts coughing and bright red blood shoots out of her mouth.

"Nurse, Nurse! I call out. "Help, we need help!"

In a flash, a nurse is at her side. She has a paper bag, and cups it over Margaret's mouth and tells her to breathe into it. Margaret's eyes are wild with panic, as she tries breathing in and out of the bag. Another nurse comes with an oxygen tank and puts the mask on Margaret, and says, "It's gonna be okay, Margaret, this is oxygen. Just breathe slowly, Hon. That's it, that's it, go slow. You're okay, you're okay. There you go."

After a few moments, her breathing calms, and the two nurses wheel her from the veranda and out of sight.

An icy breeze comes out of nowhere and gets into my bones. I pull a blanket around my neck. I am scared for Margaret. Seeing her spit blood like that really flipped my lid. We came so close.

After that episode, there is one thing I know for sure— Margaret is carrying around a suitcase of regrets, but it will be two more weeks before I find out what is really tucked away at the bottom.

Chapter 19

*"Woman was taken out of man; not out
of his head to top him, nor out of his feet
to be trampled underfoot; but out of his
side to be equal to him, under his arm
to be protected, and near his heart to be
loved."*

Matthew Henry

Heaven: "Margaret came so close to opening up to me."
"Yes she did."
I follow Ambriel through a dark path. "It's hard to see," I complain. Within a blink of an eye, there is light. I see every kind of animal that has ever walked the earth.

There are birds from all creations producing offspring of every kind. There's oceans, seas, and babbling brooks. Rivers flow pure gold. There is an aromatic resin and onyx in the river. Waters swarm with fish. We pass through an orchard and then we come to a garden. There are beautiful fruit-bearing trees of all sorts. In the middle of the garden in the east is the most stunning tree I have ever seen. Ambriel says, "This is the tree of knowledge. A woman stands near the tree wearing a fig leaf while a serpent tangles through the branches.

"Are we in the garden of Eden, "I ask?
"Francie, this is Eve."
"Welcome to my garden, Francie, just be careful not to pick any fruit from this tree," she says.
I nod my head.
"Ambriel tells me you have a beau."

"Well, I just met him."

"Just remember, out of his side, woman compliments man, and to be equal to him."

"I will remember that."

"Thank you, Eve," says Ambriel. "Let's do lunch soon."

"I will bring Adam." Eve says.

We leave the garden and Ambriel says, "Do you remember when I told you that you will have an influence on someone else?"

"Yes."

"Care to make a guess?" She swings her beads.

"Lydia?"

"You planted a seed."

"Really?"

"We'll address that another time. For now, do you know what day it is?"

"How can I forget?"

—⚹—

Time passes at a snails pace at the sanatorium, but these past seven days, I think the clock actually stopped. It's finally Wednesday and time for my date with Jonah. Meeting him has been like a breath of fresh air in my suffocating world of tuberculosis. He dropped into my life without any warning, catching me completely off guard. He's breathed new life into my lungs, and this past week has helped me forget the pain, the loneliness, the needles, the bedpans and the constant struggle of trying to lie flat on my back for hours on end. As bad as things are all around me, I'm on top of the world, spinning right along with it, and never want to come back down. For one brief moment in my little corner of space, meeting Jonah is my time out.

Life is like that sometimes—a reprieve so to speak. The warden opens the jail cell and lets you run free for a while.

Lydia has been helping me get ready for my date. She shampooed my hair and rinsed it with a jazzy smelling conditioner, and now she's styling it. She takes the bobby pins out and combs it into soft waves, and sweeps my bangs across my forehead and fastens a pearled barrette at my temple. I'm wearing my favorite green sweater, the same color as my eyes. Lydia says "It gives your olive complexion a healthy glow.

"There you go kid. You look just like Jinx Falkenburg."

"Who?"

"Jinx Falkenburg. You know, she was in The Gay Senorita. She's gorgeous."

"I've never heard of her."

"I'm sure you'd recognize her if you saw her picture. I just saw her in a magazine modeling in an ad for Lipton Tea. You look a lot like her with your hair like this."

"I agree," says Jonah.

I don't see him at first because Lydia is in front of me, but the sound of his voice washes through me. His hands are shoved into his pockets and he's leaning against the doorframe, watching.

"Now ya see," says Lydia. "Here's a guy who knows what he's talking about. Doesn't she look just like Jinx? I told you, Francie, just like a movie star." Then she turns her attention to Jonah. "You must be the infamous Jonah I've been hearing about. I'm Lydia." She extends her hand as he walks toward us.

I'm glad Lydia is doing all the talking, because the moment I see him, my blood rushes through my chest like hot lava.

"I hear you're quite the hero," Lydia says, while shaking his hand.

"Hero!" That'll ruin my bad reputation, he chuckles. "If you're referring to the night I met Francie, I was just in the right place at the right time." He looks at me with an impish grin that shows off his dimples, giving him a little-boy-like quality. "We meet again, Francie."

I try to appear demure, but instead my cheeks get hot and my palms get sweaty. I'm such an amateur!

"If you're ready, the movie starts in half an hour. Oh, by the way, do we have the blessing of Nurse Jones tonight? For a while there, I thought I might have to fight my way out of here with you."

"See, I knew you were a hero," says Lydia. "Already willing to fight for her."

"Hey, I only sound tough. Nurse Jones scares the heck out of me."

I let out the breath I've been holding for the last five minutes and say, "You're safe. She's on a break."

"In that case, we should get going before she comes back. I don't want to have to arm wrestle her to see which one of us gets to push you to the theatre."

"That's one match I'd pay to see," says Lydia.

For a first date, instead of Jonah sitting in our family parlor in Fawn Oakes under the watchful eye of my Pa, we're part of a weird and wacky scene with me on a gurney and him pushing me down the hall. However, in our world it's as natural as taking our first car ride together. People meet and date at the sanatorium all the time. Poppy says there are even weddings held in the chapel on the main campus. I guess there is no stopping affairs of the heart.

When we get to the theatre, Jonah pushes the gurney to a dark corner in the back and grabs one of the easy chairs, and sits along side of me. The room quickly fills with other patients who come on cots, in wheelchairs and the stronger patients, like Jonah, walk on their own. Jonah goes to get us some refreshments before the lights dim, and when he comes back, we munch popcorn and talk easily together.

I'm captivated by the sound of his voice. When he smiles, his eyes dance, and every time my name passes through his lips, it stirs warm feelings through me. He opens his heart to me, and I feel safe. When the music starts, the lights dim, and the movie screen comes alive. The muffled voices in the theatre fade, and the only sounds heard above the speakers are occasional coughing, and the whir of the movie projector. Jonah leans closer to me, and gently slides his hand around mine. The tenderness of his touch makes my flesh go tingly.

When the movie ends, we don't move. We stay in the theatre until every person is gone. Still holding my hand, he looks at me and pulls me closer to him.

"I suppose I should take you back to your room," he whispers.

"I suppose you should."

"I don't want to," he says

"I don't want you to." I counter.

"Do we dare cross Nurse Jones twice?"

I sigh. "No, we better not."

His face is close to mine. I wait in anticipation. He cups my cheeks in his hands and presses his lips to mine—sweet and gentle like his touch. In that moment, our worlds collide, with the stars and the moon in perfect harmony. Jonah tenderly moves his lips on mine. They're soft and exciting. When our lips finally part, our eyes stay locked, and there is a sweet silence between us, that is intimate.

Nurse Jones is at the nurses' station doing some last minute charting before she makes her rounds to the ward. Her final round involves making sure we're in our beds, passing out evening meds, and attending to any needs before we retire for the night. However, on movie night, we're allowed an extra hour before lights out. That rule usually annoys Nurse Jones—it somehow seems to throw her off balance like the only person on a teeter-totter.

The other girls return in small groups, as the evening aide's transport them back to their beds. Like a hen to her chicks, Nurse Jones scurries into the room. She makes it known that she doesn't want anyone wasting time dilly dallying, and jibber-jabbing about the movie. The hour is getting late, and she wants things in their proper order. Without missing a beat, her eagle eyes detected I wasn't in my bed. I guess she he heard the rumor of my so-called date with that rude young man who was responsible for keeping me out the week before— the one with the dark brown eyes and dimples the size of canyons. I think her blood pressure rises when we appear in the doorway. Nurse Jones looks at us, then at her watch, and a puff of air sizzles through her, lips making known her agitation.

Jonah stops and gives her one of his heart-melting smiles and says, "Hello Nurse Jones. How's my favorite nurse tonight?"

"The clock's ticking, Mr. Fischer."

"I know; that's why we got here as fast as we could. I didn't want to miss seeing you before saying good night to Francie. I was hoping you'd still be here. I enjoyed talking with you at our last visit, and just wanted to say hello again."

He's really laying it on thick. I roll my eyes.

"Save the flatter. I'm glad to see you can tell time; now if you don't mind, I have work to do."

"Oh yes, of course you do—and from what I hear, you're the best. We sure could use a few more good nurses like you around here, "he teases. Also knowing it to be true.

"Mr. Fischer."

"Okay, okay I'm going." He turns and winks at me. "I had a great time tonight. I better run, but I'll talk to you tomorrow, okay?"

"I'll be here", I say

—⟋⟍—

It's 11:15 when Nurse Jones leaves the sanatorium for the evening. She's had a long day and looks tired. She sits at the bus stop waiting for the last bus to take her home when a car engine backfires, causing her to jump—her nerves are tight. The bus pulls to the curb, and she drops some tokens into the coin machine. She leans her head against the window and stares into the darkness. The ride home is her time to think and unwind, giving her a chance to rebuild her strength, because God only knows she might need it when she gets home. It's rumored around the sanatorium that she and her husband, Roy, are going through hard times. Life has changed him, and his escape is at the bottom of a bottle.

The bus pulls to a stop. Before standing to leave, Nurse Jones sucks in her breath before releasing a long, tired sigh.

Chapter 20

*"Life belongs to the living, and he who
lives must be prepared for changes."*

Johann Wolfgang von Goethe

Heaven: I didn't know much about Nurse Jones's private life, only from the rumors around the sanatorium. I do know she is a very private person."

"Most lonely people usually are private, "says Ambriel. "This next part of heaven goes even further than being lonely.

We are walking on a suspended bridge damaged from war. Once we step off the bridge, I see millions of Jewish men, woman, and children. Their bodies look like skeletons. Their clothes are in rags. I say, "Despite their condition, they seem actually happy."

"Of course they are. Some of them were survivors of the war, others weren't so lucky, but now they will all get their just rewards.

"For now, let's have a change scenery. It's good for a person every now and then. It gives a person new perspective." She twirls around on her toes, and her Muumuu billows out, making her point. I have to laugh.

"Maybe that will happen for Nurse Jones," says Ambriel "In the meantime, it seems young Mr. Fisher has quite an influence on you".

I blush.

"Let's see just how strong an influence you have on him."

—⚬—

For the first time in weeks, I wake up actually looking forward to a new day. Jonah has asked me for another date, and got permission from Dr. Wagner to take me outside on campus. Instead of my usual lineup on the veranda, with the other girls for fresh air and heliotherapy, we are going on a picnic instead.

Lydia helps me pick out what I will wear. Even though my options are limited, when I see my reflection in the mirror with my red cotton dress, matching red ribbon for my hair, and black cardigan sweater, I feel like I'm going to the prom. Ma sent me ribbons of every color that I usually just match up with my bed jackets. However, today I will not dress like a sick person.

Most of the other girls are already out on the veranda when Jonah comes for me, except for Agnes, who has been teasing me about my date with Jonah. We always get excited for each other when something good happens, and teasing comes with the territory. She is still in a joking mood as Jonah and I go out the door.

"Don't do anything I wouldn't do," she calls after us.

I'll get back at her for trying to embarrass me when she least expects it. For now I just say, "Have a good day, Agnes."

When we are outside, he pushes the gurney to the back of the building leading to the hillside, just beyond the sanatorium. The terrain slopes down to Birch Island Lake. He knows where there is a small grove of trees where we can picnic by ourselves. It's the end of September and feels like Indian summer—a perfect day for a picnic. I've never been outside the sanatorium before, nor have I seen it from this angle. It's amazing how small my world has gotten in the past few months. I have forgotten how huge the sanatorium is. Looking at it now, it doesn't look as terrifying as it did the first time I saw it. In addition, the beauty of the countryside takes my breath away, unlike the first time.

He struggles with pushing the gurney over grass, but once we get behind the grove of trees, we are out of sight from the rest of the sanatorium, and in a matter of seconds, his lips are on mine. His breath is sweet, and his kisses are soft. I'm floating. When we come up for air, he says, "I've been waiting all morning to do that."

My heart is pirouetting in my chest. "Is it worth the wait?" I whisper.

"Well let me see—I think I need another sample," he mumbles while pressing his lips against mine. He smoothes the hair from my cheek and, gently lets his fingers trace the line of my jaw that sends the blood rushing straight to my chest. "Your face is so soft," he whispers, with his lips still against mine. Then he slides his hand behind my head and pulls me closer to him, kissing me harder. I think my heart will beat right out of my body. I'm sure he can feel it when he leans against me. I close my eyes and responds to his kisses. It's magical.

Just then, we hear voices. There is a group of ambulatory patients out for an afternoon stroll, heading in our direction. I pull away quickly, and Jonah groans.

"Uh, maybe we should eat." I say.

Jonah forces a greeting when the walkers pass by. I thought I heard one of them snicker.

"So," Jonah says, regaining control. "I went to the kitchen this morning and charmed the help into throwing together this picnic lunch for us."

"And just how charming were you?" I ask.

"Enough to score us some turkey sandwiches on fresh-baked bread, carrot sticks, and strawberries. And even charming enough to have them throw in a couple a bottles of soda pop instead of milk."

"Sodas," I gush, "You must have really poured it on to get them to break the nutrition rule—it's not even Saturday night."

"I just flashed them a smile, and told them I have a date with the prettiest gal in the San, and they were putty in my hands. So, are you still hungry or would you rather…"

I cut him off and pat the space next to me on the gurney, and I say, I'm famished. He looks disappointed, like a little boy who lost his lunch money, but gives in and scrambles beside me. We eat our lunches under the trees with the sun filtering through the branches. We talk, and laugh, and, when I had a crumb of bread that stayed on my lip, he brushes it away with his fingertip.

A dopey little thing like that touch makes my skin prickle.

It's amazing the effect he has on me.

I am only allowed an hour, so our date has to be short—but I don't care. Just being near him again gives me goose bumps. I love looking at him and the sound of his voice. I love his dimples when he smiles, and I love the feeling that washes through me when he says my name. We talk openly about almost anything and everything. It isn't awkward when we are silent—it all feels so right.

When we finish eating, we sip our sodas, and he holds my hand. I feel warm, safe, and excited. I guess you can say, I'm smitten with him. When our time is up, he takes me back to my room and asks to see me again. I accept.

After he leaves, I can't stop thinking of him, when my eyes land on Margaret's empty bed. Despite wrapped up in my own goofy feelings, her empty bed has a weird effect on me. Suddenly guilt rears its ugly head. I realize that in all the time I have been at the sanatorium, I don't know one thing about Margaret. None of us does. Day after day, week after week, she shares space with the seven of us, and none of us knows who Margaret Anderson is. I just had the most exciting lunch ever, but guilt over Margaret takes over and gnaws at me.

Now, I'm not saying that Margaret doesn't have faults—we all know she can be a royal pain in the butt. Nevertheless, that doesn't mean we should ignore her or leave her out of things.

Like my sixth grade teacher, Sister Georgiana, used to say, "Let those of you without sin cast the first stone."

Now God only knows that I can't cast any stones—I have a checkered past myself. So I decide I want to do something nice for Margaret. She needs a friend, and I am sure she needs her family.

I mean no harm.

"Psst! Lydia," I whisper, Can I ask a favor?"

"Yes? What can I do for you?"

"It's a big favor."

"Shoot."

"Well, I want to make a phone call, and I was wondering if you will take me to the phone in the nurses' lounge where it's private."

"Do I detect a secret rendezvous with a certain someone?" she says, in a singsong voice.

"No. It's nothing like that. I really do want to make a call. It's something kind of personal, and I really don't want anyone to overhear. Do you think you can help me out? Oh—and I'll need a phone book too."

"You don't ask for much, do you? Yeah, I suppose I can finagle it, and I do love a good mystery. However, I have a few things I need to do first. How about I get the phone book, and then come back in half an hour to get you?"

"You're the best, thanks."

"No problem, be back in a shake."

Once she comes with the phone book, I frantically page through the A's and find there are a gazillion Andersons. Then I remember once overhearing Dr. Wagner talking to Nurse Kirschner about speaking with Margaret's dad. I remember him saying his name was—something like Orville or Oscar. No wait—It's Owen. He had said, "I just got off the phone with Owen Anderson...," and then their voices trailed off as they walked away.

Ma says when she wants me to do something, I never hear, but when there is something, I'm not supposed to hear, I pick right up on it. Why is that?"

Pa says, if you want someone to hear, whisper. I smile. He is so wise.

I run my finger down the list of Andersons until I come to one Owen Anderson at 642 Cedar Lane. I quickly jot down the phone number on a piece of paper and wait for Lydia. I have no idea what I am going to say to Mr. Anderson or even if I dare go through with it—but I need to try. Margaret needs him.

As promised, Lydia shows up to take me for my secret phone call. She has checked out the lounge to make sure It's empty.

"I' can only give you five minutes, then I'll come to get you before anyone sees us."

"Thanks so much, Lydia. I owe you big time for this."

"I'll think of something and collect later; now hurry before someone comes and catches us."

I give the number to the operator at the sanatorium switchboard, and wait. I swear I can hear my heart pounding in my ears, I'm so nervous. I calm my breathing. Mr. Anderson needs to hear me out.

"Hello?" Answers a deep voice.

"Hello. Is this Mr. Owen Anderson?"

"Yes. Who's this?"

I swallow. "Hello, Mr. Anderson. You don't know me. My name is Francie. I'm a friend of your daughter, Margaret."

There is a silence on the other end—it must run in the family.

"Mr. Anderson, the reason I'm calling is…" Before I can say another word, he interrupts.

"What did you say your name is, and where are you calling

from?" He sounds irritated.

"My name is Francie Carver. I'm a patient at the Glen Lake Sanatorium. Margaret and I share a room together."

"What's she done now?"

"Oh, no sir. It's nothing like that. She hasn't done anything. It's just that, well… you see, Mr. Anderson, I think Margaret might be, um…lonely." I blurt it out and hold my breath. The moment is awkward. Then he speaks.

"Listen, I don't know who you are or what you're up to, so I'm not gonna stand here and listen to something that is none of your business. I'm busy!"

Slam! The phone goes dead and I am too numb to move.

I feel just awful. He didn't even give me a chance to talk. Why didn't he want to know about Margaret?

I wait for Lydia.

"So," she says when she comes for me. "Were you able to get through to your mystery call?"

"No…but I want to try again tomorrow. Will you help me?"

"The plot thickens. Sure. What do I have to lose—besides my job, my income, and my reputation—minor details. You just say when and where and I'm on it."

"Thanks, Lydia. You're the best."

"Haven't I been trying to tell you kids that for months now? It's about time someone figures it out."

When I get back to the ward, Poppy is getting ready to go down to the main dining hall for the first time. When she gets to the dining room, she will be eating her meal sitting at a table for the first time in a year-and-a-half. I'm excited for her. Lucky kid. I don't tell her about calling Mr. Anderson. I don't want anything to spoil this day for her. She has been working so hard to get to this point. The first two weeks of work-up, they allowed her to get up once a day to use the bathroom. She told me that her arches had fallen and after she walked for the first time, the pain was excruciating, and her neck muscles ached from the strain. The second two weeks bathroom privileges were twice a day and the pain in her feet and neck went away. The third two weeks, three times a day, and the last two weeks, four times a day. After eight weeks, she's finally ready to leave the room on her own. I am thrilled for her. "Lucky kid!" I say to her.

"This can't have come at a better time for me, Francie."

"You're not worried about Ken again are you?"

"I've been in here too long. I can't expect him to wait forever."

"Well, at the rate you're going, you'll be up and out of here in no time. How many people have you seen get out of here within months of getting dining room privileges? You know Ken isn't going anywhere, and besides, absence makes the heart grows fonder."

"I hope you're right."

"I know I'm right—now get out of here and go have your supper like a real person."

Poppy walks over to my bed, and plants a big fat kiss on the top of my head.

"Hey, what was that for?"

"For giving me confidence. I love you, ya know."

"Me too. "When you come back, I want to hear every little detail. Don't leave anything out."

Little does Poppy know that big things lay in store for her down in the dining hall. The workers and other residents often surprise a first timer to the dining room with a party. I can't wait to hear all about it.

—◊—

When supper is over, Poppy enters the room. She is gleaming

from ear to ear. I say, "By the look on your face, things went well?"

Without a word, she extends her hand, showing off the ring. I almost fall over. "A ring? Now It's your turn, and don't leave anything out."

"When I got to the dining room, she says, there were streamers and balloons and they all yelled "Surprise!" Then I see Ken standing in the middle of the room, with a huge grin on his face, motioning me to come closer. When I did, he dropped down on one knee.

I almost squeal excitement for her.

"My legs got wobbly for the first time in six weeks, and I almost fainted. Everyone in the room was watching.

"Oh, Poppy." Then she tells me how he proposed. She remembered every word.

"He said, "I have loved you since our first dance in high school. You're my best friend, and when we're apart you're all I think about. I know I will love and cherish you forever. Will you make me the happiest guy on the planet and marry me?" Then he reaches into his pocket and pulls out a ring. The room was so quiet you could hear a pin drop. All eyes were on me. You bet I will, I said! Then he threw his arms around me, and the room exploded into cheers."

I say, "I would have given anything to have been there to see the look on your face when he proposed".

Life at the sanatorium sure is full of surprises. We never know what a day holds for any of us.

Chapter 21

"The face is the mirror of the mind, and
eyes without speaking confess the secrets
of the heart. "Much God loved little
children

Saint Jerome 374 AD-419 AD

Heaven: "I was so glad for Poppy," I say to Ambriel, but I know it won't be long before she gets discharged, and I will lose my best friend. How selfish of me for thinking that."

"You can't change the way you feel. It's in humans nature to be selfish once in a while. Come along to see more of heaven."

I cough a little when dust gets into my lungs. There is a little boy wearing chaps, riding a Unicorn. The unicorn is in full gallop. Beside the seashore waves splash toward them as they gallop. I get a glimpse of Jesus watching the little boy. "I can't believe I just saw Jesus." I say, He looks so pleased." Ambriel says, "God loves all the little children. We sit quietly in the sand watching the boy ride. It seems we watch for hours, or even days, it's hard to say. It could be months. I finally say, "The beach is so grand, and the warm sand tickles my feet."

"It is lovely isn't it?" says Ambriel. But as the poets say, all good things must come to an end." She puts the Christmas Lily behind her right ear.

Let's see what's waiting for you at the sanatorium, shall we?

—⁗—

It's late one afternoon, and Lydia has taken me for another lamp treatment. I am feeling a little anxious because I know Margaret is going to be there. I hadn't seen or talked to her in over two weeks. When Lydia wheels me into the room, I am surprised to see Margaret is already there. I am anxious to tell her about Poppy—but either our last encounter or the passing of the last two weeks, has mellowed her, because she is first to talk.

"Hi, Francie."

"Margaret, it's good to see you. How are you feeling?"

I really am glad to see her.

"I'm doing a lot better."

"What happened to you?"

"The doctors told me that my coughing spell tore some tissue in my lung—that's why there was blood on my hanky that day on the veranda."

"Where did they take you?"

"They had me go to a quiet room on 4th where I couldn't talk to anyone. They said the tissue needed to heal itself again, and, in order for that to happen, I had to lie perfectly still and quiet for two weeks."

"How awful for you."

"I get to come back to the ward today."

I want to keep the conversation light, so I don't tell her I tried talking to her dad. Instead I say, "You look great, kid." We've all been wondering about you. It'll be nice to have you back."

"Do you really mean that?"

"Of course I do. We all want you back. And guess who got engaged?"

"Don't tell me. Ken proposed to Poppy."

"How did you guess that?"

"I know I don't talk much, but I hear things."

"Well, you're right on. She is on cloud nine! He popped the question in the dining room with half the sanatorium watching."

Margaret gets quiet again, so I change the subject to keep the momentum. "I finished the sweater I was making for my nephew Joey. If you want, I'll show it to you when we get back to the room. I want to give it to him for Christmas."

"Francie, remember that day on the veranda when I started to tell you about Mr. Gunderson?"

How could I forget? So much for keeping the conversation light. "Yes, I remember."

"I've never told anyone about what happened in my family that summer."

"Do you want to talk about it?"

"I think so. Uh—I mean, yes. I think I need to tell someone, and I want to tell you. I trust you."

She trusts me. Now I wish I hadn't thought about hanging her upside down out the window in a straight jacket.

"Okay. If you want, I'm listening."

"It was horrible, and it changed our lives. I did something awful. I committed a bad sin and I can't go back and make it right."

"Didn't you say you were only eight years old? How bad could it have been?"

"Bad." My father said it was."

I don't know what to say, so I keep quiet.

Margaret takes a deep breath and begins her story where she left off two weeks earlier. "I wanted Frank to take the lunch I made out to dad, who was in the field. Frank was in the barn cleaning stalls, so I went to find him. When I got to the barn, I could hear Mr. Gunderson's voice. I stopped dead in my tracks, because sometimes he scared me."

She stops, and I think she's going to cry. "Margaret, are you okay?"

She clears her throat, and continues.

"I can hear his voice and I got scared. I didn't want to talk to him if dad or Frank weren't there. He always had dirty fingernails and his breath smelled. I don't know why my dad hired him. Something about how good he was fixing machinery. Anyway, I think Mr. Gunderson knew I was scared of him."

I'm looking at her, and tears are trickling down her cheeks. The secrets of the past came calling.

"Did he hurt you?"

Margaret puts her hands over her face, as if she is trying to hide. I get terrified she might start hyperventilating again. I keep my voice gentle. "What did he do to you, Margaret?"

She wipes the tears from her face, keeping her breathing under control. "No, no, not me. It was Frank."

"He hurt Frank?"

"When I heard his voice, I moved closer to the barn. I didn't want him to see me, but I wanted to see who he was talking to. As I got closer, I could hear it was Frank, and it sounded like he was crying. I could see Mr. Gunderson, but I couldn't see Frank—I could just hear him. I wanted to get closer to see why Frank was crying, and that's when I tripped over a pitchfork. Before I knew what was happening, Mr. Gunderson fumbled around and jumped to his feet. Then he came after me. I didn't know what to do—I just froze. He grabbed me by the collar and I started to scream. He told me to shut up if I knew what was good for me. I yelled at him, 'What's wrong with Frank? Why is he crying?' He just kept yelling at me to shut up. He told us both to be quiet and that if we told anyone we'd be sorry. I didn't even know what he was talking about, but I was afraid of him so I said I wouldn't tell, and Frank said he wouldn't tell."

My blood rose up hot through my chest and my heart sank. I can't believe what she's telling me.

"At supper that night, our father could see something wasn't right with Frank and me. When he asked us what was wrong, Frank shot me a look that said 'you better not tell,' so I didn't tell. The next day, I couldn't find our cat Cocoa, so I asked Frank to help me look for her. We went out to the barn, and there she was hanging from a rope tied around her neck."

I drew a breath when she said that.

"Mr. Gunderson stepped out of nowhere and almost scared us half to death. He said, 'Ya see your cat over there? You say anything, and that's what I'll do to your Pa. Now get outta here and take that cat with ya'!'

Frank and I were crying so hard, we could hardly see what we were doing when we took Cocoa down. We put her in a shoebox and buried her behind the barn. We never told our father."

I hardly knew what to say. "Oh, Margaret, I'm so sorry that happened to you." I feel sick to my stomach. I can't imagine a person so insane to do such a thing to two small children. Then I remember something Margaret said earlier. "I hope you know, you didn't commit any sin. Mr. Gunderson is the one who sinned. You were only eight years old and terrified. He's the one to blame, not you. He was a very sick, pathetic, human being, and you didn't do anything wrong."

The color has drained from Margaret's face, and she looks like she could have been that eight-year-old child all over again. "Yes I did, Francie, yes I did. I should have told. I should have told."
"No. It wasn't you—it was him. He manipulated you. He made you too scared to tell. It's not your fault."

She has her hands over her face again and says, "Wait. There's more."

My heart sinks a second time. How could there be more? How could this get any worse?

She braces herself and continues with her story. "Mr.

Gunderson came after Frank again when my father went to town for supplies. I was in the kitchen standing on a chair at the sink doing dishes after breakfast. It was the same as the last time. Mr. Gunderson trapped him in the barn. This time Frank screamed for help. I thought I heard something, but the radio was on and I was running water for dishes. Frank kept screaming this time. Apparently, Mr. Gunderson couldn't make him shut up. No one really knows for sure. That's what the authorities said later."

"What do you mean later?" I knew I didn't want to hear the answer. My heart was breaking for Margaret. I looked at her and saw that small child who was afraid of a crazy man, a child who should have been running and playing without a worry in the world. A child who had no mother and whose father was so caught up in his own grief that he was blinded by another tragedy going on right under his nose—and now there is more.

Life can be so cruel.

"When Mr. Gunderson couldn't get Frank to be quiet, he put a horse blanket over his face and held it until Frank quit struggling. He held it, held it, and held it until Frank had no air to breathe… and… and he killed him. He killed my 10-year-old brother."

Margaret's voice trails off. I try to shield against the horror that washes over me. Then she says, "You're right about one thing, Francie. Mr. Gunderson was sick. When he realized what he had done, he took my father's shotgun, and ran into the woods and put it to his head, and that was the end of it. Do you see now? I should have told my father. He said that I if had told, Frank would still be alive today. I was bad, I should have told. All these years my father has blamed me. He hardly ever talks to me. That's why he doesn't come to visit. That's why it doesn't matter if I live or die."

Painfully, everything about Margaret has becomes all too clear.

Chapter 22

*"You can clutch the past so tightly to
your chest that it leaves your arms to full
to embrace the present."*

Jan Glidewell

Heaven: Ambriel takes me to the part of heaven where we see the little boy riding the unicorn again. But someone else is watching.

"Do you know the little boy and the woman watching?"

"No I don't, do you? What am I saying? Of course you do."

"She's Margaret's mother and brother Frank."

"Oh… I feel like crying, yet no tears fall. "I know, I know, there are no tears in heaven."

Ambriel does a cartwheel on the beach. Then she says, "Good afternoon, Missus Anderson, "

"Hello, Ambriel, nice day for a walk. Who is your friend? "

"Where are my manners, says Ambriel, this is Francie, a friend of Margaret's.

"Oh how wonderful. I'm praying for Margaret and her father."

"A person can't have enough prayers." I stumble on my words. Ambriel comes to my rescue.

"Have a good day Missus Anderson; we have more left on our journey."

"Let's go back to your story", she says to me.

—◊◊◊—

After hearing Margaret's story, I feel just awful for every mean-spirited thought I ever had about her. "I see why she shuts herself off from the world, and why she doesn't let any of us in. She's probably bitter, and lonely and afraid. The one person in the world, who should be here for her, has let her down. He turns his back and blames her, when she is just an innocent victim. No wonder she doesn't trust anyone. Things have to change for Margaret before it's too late.

—⟋⟍—

Once I got back to the room, the day started to look a little brighter. Earlier, I convinced everyone we should make Margaret's return to the ward special. Little Agnes and Izzy construct a banner where Lydia places it over the head of Margaret's bed. They decorate it with all the fall colors by drawing falling leaves, acorns and a horn of plenty filled with gourds and cattails, trimmed with an auburn ribbon. Large blocked letters announce 'Welcome Back, Margaret!' It is a masterpiece.

Bea, Helen and Lucy all chipped in and got her a vase with a single red rose; they bought at the gift shop in the sanatorium, and placed it on the side table next to her bed. Poppy and I get her a cupcake decorated with purple frosting and candy sprinkles set on a lace doily next to the rose. Overall, we are quite pleased with ourselves.

The mood on the ward is changing right along with the colors of the leaves on the trees. The war is over, Poppy's engaged, and Lucy has gotten word of discharge at Christmas. As for me, well, I am in love. All this good news is catchy, giving us hope—and with hope comes good cheer and camaraderie. Even towards Margaret.

We hear Lydia's voice coming down the hall. It takes longer than usual to bring Margaret back, because we hear Lydia stopping everyone she meets to welcome Margaret back from "solitary", as she puts it. When they finally come through the door, Lydia helps Margaret into bed. Margaret sees the banner and her face seems to brighten for a moment.

Talking as fast as she can, Agnes says, nice to see you, Margaret, sorry you had to be gone so long. Hope you're feeling better."

Izzy says "Agnes slow the heck down. Then she says to Margaret, "Are you sure you want to come back to this?" Izzy looks at Agnes.

Poppy says, "Glad you're back, hasn't been the same without you."
Not sure Poppy meant that in a good way or not.

Bea says, "Two weeks is a long time to be in bed without talking. How did you manage?"

Margaret answers, "I read a lot and listened to programs on the radio. Lydia visited me every day, even though she was the only one talking, since I was restricted."

Izzy says," Maybe you should be shipped to solitary Agnes. I wonder how long you could survive. You'd probably go stir crazy if you couldn't talk.

"Very funny, says Agnes.

Margaret chokes up when she sees the rest of the party favors, and says, "You went to a lot of trouble just for me. Thank you. This is very nice of all of you."

Margaret's lip is quivering and she struggles to hold back tears.

For a time, I think we lifted Margaret's spirits. Like a breeze catching a leaf letting it flutter in the air, only to watch it drop again. I decide I will try calling Mr. Anderson again, but this time I know what I will say to him.

—⁂—

The next day, Lydia once again works her magic and sneaks me to the nurses' lounge to use the phone. She is so clever—she hands Nurse Jones a message asking her to come to the lab—something to do with sputum culture reports, and that she, Lydia, says she will keep an eye on things on the ward while Nurse Jones is gone. Lydia knows the other nurses are either delivering meds or on their afternoon breaks in the cafeteria and won't be back for a while. Her timing is impeccable. Lydia is excited about our secret rendezvous, because she likes the idea of doing something forbidden without getting caught. She says, "A little adventure is good once in a while—it gets the juices flowing."

Nevertheless, I am nervous—not because I was afraid of getting caught sneaking into the nurses' lounge—heck, Millie and I used to do much worse, but because of what I am going to say to Mr. Anderson. I know more this time than I did before—a family secret. Something so horrible and disgusting, a father has kept it locked away for years, blaming his only daughter, so he could hide from the truth and wallow in his own grief. I would be treading into murky waters where I'd probably get stuck in the muck, but Margaret's well-being seems to be at stake. She is sinking deeper into a black hole, and no matter what we do or say, she still needs her family. The switchboard operator rings the number.

Again, I wait. The phone rings twice.

"Hello?"

"Hello, Mr. Anderson? This is Francie Carver again."

"Who?"

"Francie Carver—from the sanatorium."

"Oh, for crying out loud. What do you want now? I thought I told you not to bother me."

"Mr. Anderson, please don't hang up. The only reason I'm calling you is because I know Margaret would love to talk to you, but I think she's too afraid."

"Is that so?"

"Yes… it is. I know she would like to see you."

"Did she put you up to this?"

"Oh—no, sir. She doesn't even know I'm calling you. She'd probably be upset if she found out."

"Well then why don't you just mind your own business and leave us be?"

"Mr. Anderson, please. Margaret is so lonely. Can't you just come for a visit? I know it would mean the world to her."

"What do you know about anything?"

"I know firsthand how hard it's being sick and away from home, Mr. Anderson, and Margaret doesn't have anyone who comes to visit her. I know she's lonely."

"Listen. I don't know who you think you are, and why you need to poke your nose into our business, but I'm telling you for the last time to butt out and leave us be!"

"Mr. Anderson, if you don't let go of the past and reach out to her, you could lose her forever. Are you willing to let that happen? Margaret is wallowing in guilt she didn't earn! She needs to hear it from you that things aren't her fault. She thinks you don't love her Mr. Anderson."

He hangs up. Lydia opens the door. "It's time to go. Nurse Jones could come back any minute."

"Are you ready to go?

"Sure, let's go."

She maneuvers me out the door and into the hall, but she can tell something is off. There doesn't seem to be anyone around, so we talk openly. "What is it, kiddo?"

"I feel like crying.

"Why, what's wrong? Is it the phone call?"

"Ah, Lydia, I did a dumb thing. It's Margaret."

"What to do you mean? What's happened?"

"Nothing's happened really. I just feel so bad for Margaret. No one ever comes to visit her. She never gets any calls or letters or anything."

"Yeah, I know. I've seen the look in her eyes when the rest of you get visitors or gifts in the mail. She looks like someone slapped her in the face."

"I know she's lonely." I say.

"But what does that have to do with right now?"

"I called her dad."

"You did what? Oh my gosh!"

"I thought I was doing the right thing. I tried to convince him to come and see Margaret.

"Oh, Francie! I don't know. I'm pretty sure that is for the doctors to decide. What did he say?"

"He told me to mind my own business, and then he hung up on me again."

"Again?"

"Yeah, that was him I called before, and he didn't want to hear anything about Margaret then either."

"Oh that awful man says Lydia. Poor Margaret."

Lydia and I look at each other in that knowing way people have when they're thinking the same thing—Margaret has no one.

We thought we heard Nurse Jones, so Lydia jumps to attention and jogs back to the ward before we get caught, and have to make up a story as to why Lydia has me out in the hallway.

Little did we know Margaret was parked around the corner in a wheelchair and overheard everything.

I meant no harm.

Chapter 23

*To run away from trouble is a form of
cowardice and, while it is true that the
suicide braves death, he does it not for
some noble object but to escape ill."*

Aristotle

Heaven: Ambriel says, "Even though your intentions
are good—some things are out of our hands. We walk until
the waterfall is out of sight. The atmosphere turns somewhat
depressing. It's not like on Earth when the clouds move around and
block the sun or when it's twilight time. This place has no color, just
a pasty, ashen, unhallowed tone.

"Hello, Ambriel"

"Hello Luke, how is the painting coming along?"

The man is sitting at an easel with tripods surrounding him,
with all colors of the rainbow.

"Not so good. As hard as I try, I cant seem to brighten the
atmosphere here, "says the painter.

"Francie, this wonderful painter is St. Luke the evangelist. He's
the patron saint of painters.

"Do you paint, Francie?"

"Once in kindergarten, but all the kids laughed, so I gave it
up. His wings go up and down when he lets out a booming laugh.

"You have a spitfire here, Ambriel," says St. Luke. "Don't I
know it," says Ambriel. When the prayers start flooding in, I'm sure
your paintings will brighten. For now, we will have bid you ado.

"Time to peak into the sanatorium", says Ambriel."

Halloween and Thanksgiving have come and gone, and Margaret is sinking deeper into depression. We all try to cheer her up, but she is even more withdrawn than ever, and isn't talking to anyone again. Once again, she just plays with the food on her plate knocking it around with her fork. She doesn't want to get out of bed and rejects lamp treatments and crafts. The staff is concerned and hold a meeting to discuss her treatment.

Dr. Wagner calls Mr. Anderson to update him regarding his daughter's condition and his concerns regarding her mental status. He tells Mr. Anderson Margaret is growing weaker every day, and her mental status is hurting her recovery. "If she keeps going like this, she will become too weak, and the tuberculosis will worsen. I want you to be aware of what were facing. I don't want to see her condition take a turn if there is something we can do to prevent it."

"I will come tomorrow morning", says Mr. Anderson.

Dr. Wagner may have just gotten through to Margaret's Dad.

That evening, Nurse Jones has announced lights out. I am teetering in and out of sleep—the pain in my foot and knee makes sure of that. I am exhausted. Normally, I would have been all over Margaret about her not eating and skipping lamp treatments, but right now, I just want to close my eyes and have it all go away. I will get on Margaret tomorrow—when I feel better, and then I drift into a fitful sleep.

The room is quiet. The only sounds are heavy breathing and an occasional cough. In the darkness, Margaret lays flat on her back staring into space. Tears slide along her cheeks, tumbling under her chin and down her neck. Seemingly, in a trance, she gets out of bed; her nightgown falls about her ankles when she stands. She walks past my bed until she is in front of our window. She pushes the window open. The cold November chill rushes into the room.

Poppy moans a little and pulls her blanket up around her.

Margaret makes her way through the open window, and lets her long legs guide her out onto the ledge and braces herself against the cold, hard bricks of the building. The icy breeze has her shivering.

The cold air sweeps through the room, forcing Poppy to sit up and notice the open window. "Who opened the window?" She catches a glimpse of Margaret's nightgown billowing from the breeze in and out of the window. Poppy snaps her head in the direction of Margaret's bed. It's empty! Springing to her feet she yells, "Margaret!"

It doesn't take much to bring me out of my tortured sleep. "What are you doing, Poppy? It's freezing in here!" I groan.

The other girls began to stir, and their voices rumble up and down the rows. "What's going on? Why is it so cold in here?" asks Bea. Why's that window open?"

"I think Margaret's out on the ledge," says Poppy.

"Oh my gosh", I gasp!" I have a better view of the ledge from my side of the room. Panic rushes through me.

Poppy gasps, and says, "Oh my God, Margaret, what are you doing?"

By this time, the other girls are awake, and it doesn't take long for everyone to realize that Margaret is out on the ledge.

"Oh, God, Margaret, no," I whisper. A jolt of pain burns its way into my foot forcing me to grab my leg to stop the fire. "Lucy, get Nurse Jones." I can barely get the words out my pain is so intense.

Even though running is not allowed, Lucy goes as quickly as she can to the nurses' station, even though running is not allowed. "Nurse Jones! Come quick!" she exclaims.

Nurse Jones looks up from what she is doing and says, "Lucy, what are you doing out of bed?"

"It's Margaret—she's out on the ledge. I think she's going to jump!"

Nurse Jones is aware of Margaret's declining condition, and doesn't waste a moment to spring into action. "Nurse Clara, "she shouts to another nurse, "Call the fire department. Margaret is out on the ledge threatening to jump. Call Dr. Wagner! And you better get a hold of Mr. Anderson—tell him it's his daughter. Hurry!" She shouts the orders while on the dead run to ward 530.

When she gets to our room, the girls with privileges are on their feet with blankets wrapped around them huddled together in fear. The rest of us sit up in our beds and don't know what to do. Panic sweeps through the room. What if Margaret jumps?

"Okay everyone, calm down and be quiet."

Nurse Jones has dealt with many depressed patients, but has never faced a situation as urgent as this one. Poppy steps back, allowing Nurse Jones to approach the window where Margaret stands just beyond her reach. She leans out into the night air and says, "Listen to me child. Come in here now before you catch your death of cold."

Margaret's back is flat against the building with her arms at her sides, shivering and crying.

In a tender voice, Nurse Jones's says, "Margaret, honey, come inside now won't you? Please?"

Margaret just keeps crying and doesn't speak.

"Margaret, can you hear me? Please, honey, please —give me your hand."

"I just want it all to be over." Margaret's voice is strained.

"Oh, no Baby, please. Come back inside."

Margaret doesn't move.

"Here, Margaret, take my hand."

Nurse Jones must have been freezing, but she keeps her hand as steady as a rock as, she holds it out to Margaret. I can hear Margaret sniffling.

"I want the hurting to stop."

Nurse Jones takes a deep breath, but keeps her voice smooth and firm. "This isn't the way, Margaret. Just give me your hand, and everything will be all right. I promise."

Margaret flinches and slides sideways when Nurse Jones reaches for her.

"Please, Margaret, don't move. I'm right here. Let me help you, sweetheart."

"It's all my fault." she whimpers.

"No, Margaret. Just come in and we can talk this out. None of this is your fault.

"This is the only way." Margaret says.

"No! Please, Margaret, come inside."

"L-leave me alone. I j-just want to die."

Inside the room, we were on pins and needles holding our breaths, and expecting the worst will happen. By now, all the girls are shivering and weeping into their blankets, so scared for Margaret. I'm praying as hard as I can.

I remember something Sister Jane Frances told us in Catechism class. She said God shows us other people's sufferings to let us know that ours aren't so bad and, that if we're ever in pain we should offer it up to God like Christ did for us. So, I offer my pain up to God. I know the fire in my foot can't be as bad as the pain Margaret must have been feeling. No matter how bad my pain gets, I want to live and get better, but Margaret's pain must be so bad, that all she wants is to die.

The room is freezing cold by this time. Then it happens.

Chapter 24

*"The person who completes suicide dies
once. Those left behind die a thousand
deaths, trying to relive those terrible
moments and understand..."*

Unknown

Heaven: we are still in the dark and stormy part of heaven. Before we start walking, Ambriel says, "You did the right thing, offering your pain up to God. That was the best you could do." "That was Margaret's preordained future. It was inevitable.

"This is a very strange part of heaven," I say. As we walk, I see crowds of people gathered in what looks like holding stations.

"It is a crucial part of heaven, she says.

"Why is that?"

It is a place to decide the next chapter of another person's destiny." "Only God decides who goes to heaven and who does not." "Oh".

"Let's go back to the sanatorium and watch the fallout."

—∽∞∽—

Everything happening is a blur. Within moments, sirens are whaling, and workers rush around in a frenzy. Nurses and doctors that are on duty, huddle outside our room talking over strategy to help us get through the night.

Shivering from the cold, I pull the blankets close to my face and cry as if I have never cried before. Poppy almost trips on her blankets, when she gets out of bed and stumbles across the room to my bed. We reach for each other and hang on for dear life. I press my face into her shoulder, and she buries her head in my hair. Our tears soak each other. My head is spinning. I remember hearing Helen coughing, and something about blood. They take her away. Izzy and Agnes are holding on to each other, crying. Bea and Lucy are both crying in their own beds. It's madness. In the dead of night, the sanatorium has come alive. Nothing will ever be the same.

My body is too numb to feel the pain in my leg and foot anymore, but I do feel myself getting sick and have to push Poppy away so I can get my emesis basin. Poppy quickly grabs my hair out of the way while I throw up. When there is nothing left, she rubs my back, and we both cry. All the little things that I had ever been thinking about seem so insignificant at this moment. My stupid hair—my matching ribbons—my knitting—my schoolwork—everything. What does any of it matter? Her death puts it all into a deeper perspective. She had given up caring, and in the process, brought our worlds to a crashing halt. We will die a thousand deaths reliving this horrible night, and the weeks leading up to it before things will ever seem bright again.

The nurses and doctors come to spend time with each one of us, and give us sedatives to help us sleep. I dream about Mr. Anderson and Margaret. In my dream. I'm holding a large black phone. It grows too big to hold, and I end up dropping it. Lydia is there wearing red nylons, and takes the phone. Mr. Anderson is digging in his yard, and finds a cat. Nothing makes sense. Everything scrambles together.

—⚶—

The news of Margaret's suicide blazes through the sanatorium like wild fire. Jonah hears what happened, and comes to me the next day to take me away from the ward. It's Saturday, and most of the regular workers are off duty. He wants a quiet place where we can be alone, so he pushes the gurney along a deserted hallway, and finds a spot behind a portable X-ray machine, that stands against the wall. When he is sure we we're alone, he climbs onto the gurney, wrapping his body around me like a blanket, and for the longest time we don't speak. The sadness from what happened to Margaret is unrelenting, so I just let the comfort of his nearness ease my pain. I lay my head against his chest, listening to his beating heart, when tears well up again, uncontrollably. He gently strokes my hair and whispers, "Let it out, Francie, let the tears come.", and they do. I sob, and he pulls me closer. "I can't even imagine what you and the others have been through, he says, gently stroking my hair, my face, and my arms, lessening the pain, replacing it with a timid sensation, as my senses respond to his gentle touch. He strokes his hand down the curve of my back, resting it on my hip—It's electric, He runs his fingers slowly up the length of my body to my face, and, with one finger, tips my chin to meet his gaze. My pain and sorrow tangle together, as he kisses me. And just as muddled, anxiety creeps in. I pull back. Jonah senses my apprehension. He instinctively backs off, and says, "I love you.

He slides his hand around my waist as I relax, and lay my head back onto his chest surrendering, myself into the comfort of his body, and I say, I love you too, Jonah.

That's when the rest of the world fades away.

—∭—

In the days that follow, our room is like a funeral parlor. Margaret's empty bed is a constant reminder of that horrible night. The doctors and nurses work overtime trying to put things back to normal for us—whatever that is. Helen recovered from her setback and returned to the room, but she looks worse for the wear. We all do. Margaret's suicide has taken its toll, and we constantly relive that night, haunting us like a ghost in the room.

Of course we aren't allowed to go to the funeral, but Lydia

was there, and came back and shared the details of the service with us. Even though we aren't supposed to talk about morbid things that could bring us down, Margaret's death is like an open sore that needs tending. So Lydia ignores the rule and helps us make sense of things. I ask about Mr. Anderson. She says "He mostly stood with his head bent, looking quite broken." That makes me wonder if he regretted the way he treated Margaret. I can't help but feel sorry for him.

Many days pass, where we are in our own little worlds, thinking about Margaret, and what we could have done or should have done to make things different. That's when our private thoughts make us crazy, we talk long into the nights, sharing our haunts with each other. I am at loose ends, filled with guilt that is making me depressed. Then something happens that gives me some sort of closure, and soon lessens the guilt.

—⁓—

It's afternoon, and I'm reading Moby Dick. I look up from my book, and see a strange man in a black wool trench coat, hunched over in the doorway. His arms are long, dangling at his sides, hat in hand. He stands there as if he is lost, and looking for directions. A nervous feeling comes over me—there is something oddly familiar about him. He steps inside, still searching, until his eyes are on me. I see Margaret's eyes looking back at him. My blood runs cold, and I know instantly that I am looking at Mr. Anderson. I am pretty sure he knows who I am. I think my interfering is just about to catch up with me.

He walks to my bed. Since I can't run or hide, I brace up to take whatever he has in store for me. I have stuck my nose into his family business, and now it's time to pay the piper—face the music—put up or shut up. Whatever, I was running out of metaphors, and he looks determined.

"Miss Carver?"

"Mr. Anderson?" My voice is smooth, but my insides are Jell-O.

"I think It's time I pay you a visit."

Oh?" I say. The scowl on his face tells me he is serious, but when I search his eyes, I find sorrow.

"You're a very impertinent young woman."

I don't know what that word meant, but I figure by the way he said it, it isn't a compliment. He has every right to be angry with me. He has just lost his daughter and I am partially responsible—or so I think. "Mr. Anderson, I can explain…" He cuts me off.

"I've come here to have a say, and would appreciate it if you wouldn't interrupt."

I deserve that. I had no right interfering, and I owe him the chance to set me straight.

"I'm not a man of many words, so this will be short."

Oh thank you, thank you, thank you, God.

"I owe you an apology. I should have listened to what you were trying to tell me."

He is apologizing to me? No, I should be telling him how sorry I am.

"I'm not proud of the way I've treated my girl. You saw she was in trouble, and you were right to try to help her. I should have listened to you."

He stops talking, and I don't know if I should respond or not—so I just sit there like a duck in a shooting gallery.

"Well, that's all I come to say." He turns and walks toward the door.

Lydia is right. He did look broken, and nothing I can say or do, will change that. "Mr. Anderson?"

He stops, but doesn't turn around.

"I miss her a lot, and, well, I'll work on my impertinence."

As soon as he left, I grab my dictionary and rifle through the pages until I come to the word.

"Whatcha lookin' up?" Lydia asks when she comes to take me to my appointment with Dr. Evans.

"Impertinent. It means—cheeky, brazen."

"Does it also say, for a better definition look under Francie Carver?"

"Ha-ha, very funny," although I rather remember Sister Georgiana using that word once to describe Millie and me. Oh well, probably too late to do anything about it now.

While pushing me down the hall, Lydia asks, "Did you hear Dr. Evans is working here since his discharge from the Army?"

"Yeah, Dr. Wagner told me. The last time I saw him he was just home for a short while, and came to see me as a favor to Dr. Wagner. Nevertheless, my toe is still bothering me, and the pain in my knee has been getting worse. I hope he can help."

"I notice your toe oozing a little during your bath this morning, but don't you worry. Dr. Evans is one of the best there is. I'm sure he'll have a plan after looking at your test results."

"I hope you're right. It's even starting to smell bad. It would be so embarrassing if Jonah were to notice."

"I'm pretty sure you've reeled him in hook, line and sinker. I have a feeling he's not getting away."

"You make him sound like a fish."

"Honey, the way I see it, all men are like fish. You throw a little bait their way, and when they bite, you just sit back and reel 'em in."

"Well, I'm not quite sure that's how it is with Jonah and me. The first time we met, we locked eyes, and from there, everything just seemed right."

"Well, okay, maybe you didn't have to bait him and reel him in, but I do think he's a keeper."

I'm laughing out loud by this time. It feels good. "I swear, Lydia, you do have a way of painting a picture."

"That's the Hollywood in me trying to get out," she says.

"I still think you should consider medicine. You're good for what ails us."

"Okay, okay already. We've had this conversation before. It's time I drop you off before you start sounding like a broken record. I'll be back to get you after your exam. Later, my dear."

With that, she was gone, leaving me alone in the examining room, waiting for Dr. Evans. My toe is throbbing, and the pain in my knee won't let up. Five-and-a-half months have gone by since I was admitted to the sanatorium, and things haven't gotten any better. I have been following all the rules, and doing everything they tell me, except for that one silly moment when we all tried to dance. Aside from that, I'm playing by the rules. More than anything, I want to get well and go home. Since meeting Jonah, It's more important than ever. He has beaten this disease and ready for discharge. Maybe Dr. Evans will perform his magic, and things will start to turn around for me too.

The door opens, and he walks in. "Good afternoon. How are you feeling today?"

I have heard that question more times in the last five months than you can shake a stick at. I wonder if anyone really expects an answer. "My toe and knee hurt a little, but otherwise I feel swell."

"Okay then, let's have a look." He stands at the foot of the gurney and rolls the sheet up so he can examine my toe. "It's oozing quite a bit, he says, and there's marked swelling, but that much you already know."

"It smells bad too."

"Hmm, yes. That's the bacteria erupting through your skin. I know it's not very pleasant, but I'll tell you what we're going to do. We'll monitor your knee for a while, and keep up with the lamp treatments. We'll make a decision at a later date, what kind of therapy will be necessary after further evaluation. For now, we're going to focus on the toe. I'm going to schedule you for a minor procedure on Monday where we will take you to surgery and remove the toenail. That will give the lesion plenty of air and, hopefully allow it to heal on its own.

"Remove my toenail? Won't that hurt?"

"Like I said, it's minor. I'm not saying there won't be any pain, but we will give you something to help you along with that. If everything goes all right, you should be feeling better in no time."

"Wow, removing my toenail. Well, I guess it could be worse. What can I say? I guess let's do it."

"Good girl. I'll call your parents and explain it to them."

"Yes, I'm sure Ma will want to come. She'll probably worry that I might need moral support or something."

"Do you?"

"Probably."

Chapter 25

"In three words I can sum up everything
I've learned about life:
It goes on."

Robert Frost

Heaven: Ambriel and I walk through a tunnel, and when we come through the other side, everything is bright and colorful again, as if a completely new heaven just opened up. The air is lighter. I breathe easier. I say to Ambriel "I understand now what you meant by sometimes things are out of our hands. No matter how hard I tried, I guess some things were not meant to be."

"Another lesson learned."

I see Margaret again. The attendant is letting her out of the holding station. He takes her to see God. Their conversation is muffled, and then I hear God say to her," You have suffered enough, my child." It is time for your rewards."

Frank and Missus Anderson are gleaming with pride. It is a beautiful thing to behold. There is a celebration party for Margaret in the party room. Margaret sees me and says, "I'm surprised to see you here."

I'm surprised myself."

"You're wearing your poodle pajamas!"

"I didn't have time to change."

"Would you like to come to my party?"

I look toward Ambriel.

She says, "We can spare a moment."

We don't speak of what happened. That's when I see the halo around Margaret's head. She looks so happy.

It's time, Francie," says Ambriel.

"Until we meet again, Francie." Says Margaret.

We leave the celebration and walk through a grove of flowers. Ambriel tells me it's time to put the focus back on Jonah and me. I can't be happier.

—⁓—

I thought about Margaret all the time, and what I could have done differently, but Dr. Evans has scheduled surgery for me so fast, that it became my main focus—and I am anxious to see Ma and Pa. I need them more than ever to put their arms around me and tell me everything will be all right. Then Jonah enters the room.

Every girl turns her head as he walks by. He's wearing a long-sleeved black shirt that accents his dark hair and coal-black eyes, lending more maturity and mystery to his boyish good looks. He holds a bouquet of red roses, with one white rose, and a smile that tugs at the hearts of every female in the room. However, his eyes are only on one girl—and that is me. He stole my heart in a dark abandoned tunnel, and now all I can do is think about him.

The sun is setting and a yellow-orange light radiates through my window, like spun gold. When Jonah walks into the ray, our eyes meet, and the rest of the world vanishes. It's just the two of us. All our problems cease to exist, and we live only in the moment. We are in a whirlwind, and our love for each other is at the eye of the storm, and growing in intensity.

"Oh, Jonah, you brought me roses—they're beautiful." "These are for when you come back from surgery tomorrow. When you look at them, I hope they'll remind you of me, and how much I'll be thinking about you."

"I hardly need reminding."

"A guy can't take any chances."

I hold the flowers close to my face to breathe in the aroma.

"You're safe. I'm pretty sure when I look at these I'll be thinking of you." I touch the petals of the white rose.

"Your parents aren't here yet?"

"Not yet. They should be any time. Are you nervous about meeting them?"

"It shows, huh?"

"You have nothing to worry about. They're going to love you."

"That is if Nurse Jones doesn't get to them first and warn them about me."

"Oh, I think you've made quite an impression on Nurse Jones. She just tries hard not to show it."

"How about you? Worried about the surgery?"

"A little, but Dr. Evans said it's a pretty simple procedure. I just hope it works and heals the TB in my foot. The pain is even getting worse in my leg."

"He's a good surgeon. He'll make things right for you, Francie, I know he will."

"Thank you, Jonah."

"For what?"

"For loving me."

Nurse Kirschner comes into the room. "Well hello there, Mr. Fisher. What beautiful roses!"

"Only the best for my girl," he says.

"I have good news, Miss Carver. Your mom and dad are here."

"Oh good, I can't wait to see them. It's been so long."

"I had them go into the family room, and told them I will bring you there. You'll have more privacy." She looks toward Jonah and grins.

"What are you grinning at?" he says.

"You. Are you ready to meet the family?"

"The whole family's here?"

"Not the whole family, I'd need a bigger room—just half of them."

"Oh great."

Nurse Kirschner is enjoying watching him squirm. "Now, now, Mr. Fisher, just relax and be yourself. I'm sure her dad won't even be thinking you're the guy making moves on his daughter. You'll be just fine."

I butt in. "I've been trying to tell him that. Even though Pa stands over six feet tall, and is stronger than an ox, he's a very gentle man." I tease.

He gets a painful look on his face, but ignores me, and says. "How many are there?"

"I think I counted four kids, and Mom and Dad, "You do the math."

Jonah sighs. He helps Nurse Kirschner put me onto a gurney, and pushes me to the family room. As it turns out, he'd worried for nothing. My family welcomes him warmly. Pa and Jonah shake hands, and exchange the usual formalities. Pa always said you can tell a lot about a man by his handshake, and if he looks you in the eye.

Pa gives me a wink. I know he approves.

Michael and Johnny think Jonah is funny when he pulls a quarter from behind their ears. And, and of course Sarah and Lily stumble all over themselves for his attention. But most of all, I can tell Ma likes him. One side of her mouth rises up at the corner when she is pleased with something. She is doing that now.

—✲—

The next morning, Jonah sits with my family, and waits for me to get through the surgery. Outside the bare trees silhouette against the pale blue and pink layers of the morning sky. There is no wind disturbing the rolling hills and raspberry landscape. Pa has been appreciating the beauty of it all. He picks up the morning paper, and reads 100 patients a year die at the sanatorium.

When the surgery is over, Dr. Evans greets my parents in the waiting room, and tells them I am doing fine "You can see her shortly in the recovery room. She will have to spend about two days in a quiet room before she can go back to the ward." He goes on to say, removing the toenail and debriding the damaged tissue is a simple operation. She tolerated the procedure well."

Doctors have a language all their own. He told them I am strong and a real fighter. "I'm hopeful we can stop the TB from spreading any further.", he says. "

The doctors are battling this disease as best they can. Nevertheless, without a drug to cure TB, it's still a game of chance. Sometimes their efforts are successful, and other times the ferocious monster attacks and no one can stop it.

The painkillers allow me to sleep away most of the day. I open my eyes now and then, and see Ma. She strokes my cheek, and, I fall back to sleep. Can't stay awake. I dream I'm lying on the shore of the lake. The sun is warm. I let the gentle waves move over me. I open my eyes.

"There's my girl." Pa's voice. They sit with me until evening, and then Pa says, "Well Francie Girl, It's time we pack up the kids and head back home. We need to let you rest." He shakes Jonah's hand, and tells me "I think you're in good hands."

I am sad to see them leave, but Jonah stays by my bedside. I'm tired. Jonah kisses me lightly on the lips. "Rest now.

I dream about Margaret.

Chapter 26

"If you could choose one characteristic that would get you through life, choose a sense of humor."

Jennifer Jones

Heaven: Ambriel and I are still walking through the flower grove when we hear laughter. There is a group of saints sitting in comfortable swivel back chairs, telling jokes to each other. The air explodes with laughter. "St. Augustine of Hippo sees us coming and says, "Come in, come in, Ambriel, and bring your friend." Here pull up a couple of chairs and join us for some fun.

Ambriel says, "Gentlemen, I'd like you to meet Francie Carver."

"We meet again", says, St. Philip Niri of the 16th century. "You're just in time. St. Lawrence, from the 3rd century is about to tell us a good one."

St. Lawrence clears his throat and says, "I was burned to death on a grill over hot coals, so I called out to my executioners and said this side is done. Turn me over and have a bite."

The room explodes with laughter. Then St. Augustine of Hippo says pluckily, "Lord, give me chastity but not yet."

Again the laughter. Their wings sway about when they laugh. I will never get used to that. I love it. Ambriel is in stitches. She twirls her beads when she laughs. St. Augustine says to me, "St. Philip Neri, the 16th century priest, likes to make fun of himself to keep himself humble. That is why he is called the humorous saint." Saint Philip winks at me.

St, Lawrence tells us, "St Francis of the 17 century, bishop of Geneva, is known to say, When you encounter difficulties and contradictions, do not try to break them, but bend them with gentleness and time."

St. Philip Niri says, "Christian joy is a gift from God."

I say to them, "you are all so entertaining. I have enjoyed all of your jokes."

"Do you have to go so soon?" Says St. Lawrence.

"I'm afraid so", says Ambriel.

We leave the merry band of jokesters, onto a tiny footbridge into a park, where swings made from long ropes, and wooden seats hang from tall trees. Ambriel says, "We will swing for a while, and watch as a few more chapters of your life are about to unfold."

It's like being at the movies, except we're outside, and the sky is our screen I especially like the love scenes.

—⁂—

A thin dusting of snow scatters the tracks when the train pulls into the depot in Minneapolis. Two passengers on board are especially excited to be home.

Inside the depot, Kate and Bill Monson wait anxiously for their son Alex and his buddy, Tom, to step off the train. Dressed in full Marine uniform, the two men enter the train station. When the crowd of people sees them, they go wild cheering and applauding. The victory of the war is a welcome relief. People are thankful and proud of the men who fought so hard against the Japanese and the Germans. They know these young men have put their lives in jeopardy to fight for a cause they believe in, and they are grateful.

A little gray-haired man, who bears scars from World War I, is the first to his feet to salute the boys entering the waiting area. There is a young woman, who has two small children at her side, grinning and clapping their hands. Their mother is clapping, so they do too. Everywhere you look, people are cheering for the two

American soldiers who have made it home.

Tom and Alex are worn from battle, but the warmth from the strangers in the room is touching. As they walk through the crowd to get to Alex's parents, people shake their hands and pat their shoulders. It's a moment Tom said he will not forget.

They are on a two-week furlough for Christmas, and the first couple of days Tom plans to stay in the city with Alex and his family before going on home to Fawn Oakes. He says he wants to be able to spend as much time with me at the sanatorium as he can. I bounced back quickly from my toe surgery. I'm anxious to see him.

The Monson's car stops in front of the sanatorium and the two soldiers get out. Tom is in a hurry, and practically runs up the steps to the entrance of the sanatorium.

"Hold on there, buddy," says Alex, "we'll get there. She isn't going anywhere."

"Just try to keep up, will ya'?" Tom says. "I know it's been a while since you've seen each other, but we're not chasing down the enemy here. No need to rush."

"I can't help it. She's my little sister."

"Time flies when you're having fun."

"What war were you fighting in?"

"Uh, wrong choice of words," says Alex. "God, Alex. I can't believe I'm visiting her in a sanatorium, and she's already been here six months."

Tom gets the room number from the woman in the admissions office, and the two soldiers head for the fifth floor. When they step off the elevator, Alex says, "I'll wait by the nurses' station to give you some time alone."

I've been giddy all day waiting for Tom to come visit. When I see him standing in the doorway in his uniform, my breath catches, and tears well up in my eyes.

He practically sprints toward me, but once he is beside me, he acts awkward.

"For crying out loud, Tom, I won't break! Get over here and give me a hug for heaven's sake!"

He tosses his hat onto my bed, and bends to hug me. I feel him tense up. After all, I have lost a lot of weight. I have to be 15 pounds lighter since the last time he saw me. He notices the bandages on my foot, and I tell him about the surgery. My toenail is gone, but my toe is still oozing, kept in a bandage. I hope he can't smell it.

"Hey, Francie! Who's the handsome soldier?" As if, Poppy doesn't know.

I introduce Tom to each one of the girls in the room. they all have exaggerated stories to tell him about me. Margaret's bed is still empty, so Tom sits on the edge to visit with us. The memory of that night is still fresh for all of us, and still seems strange she isn't lying there. Poppy brakes the silence. "Francie says the two of you are pretty close. It must be nice to have a sister you can call friend." "You nailed it, Poppy. We're only two years apart, and once she learned to walk, she followed me everywhere. We got pretty close growing up."

"She told us how you taught her to ride a bike and play softball."

"Oh yeah, Francie could throw a ball as well as most of the guys around our farm. She was a better swimmer too."

Agnes chimes in. "I have a brother, but it seems like all we ever did was fight as kids. It must be the red-haired Irish in us. But now we get along pretty well."

"I never had a brother," says Izzy, "just two sisters. I can't imagine what it would be like having a brother. What do you say, Francie, mind sharing Tom?"

Before I have a chance to answer, Tom says, "Of course she wouldn't. I've had a lot of practice being a big brother, and I could always use another little sister—that is if you don't mind being part of the Carver Clan."

"Part of the Clan?"

"Sure. We soldiers get lonely being so far away from family, and letters from home really cheer a person up. What do ya say?"

I was so proud of Tom at that moment.

"I'd like that. We can be pen pals."

"Pen pals it is then. I'll make sure Francie gets my new address as soon as I'm stationed. In the meantime, though, maybe you can keep an eye on Francie for me. Did she tell you she's having a birthday soon? She's catching up to me fast."

—⚬⚬⚬—

Meanwhile, Alex is leaning against the nurses' station with his hat in his hand, when Nurse Kirschner comes out of a patient's room. She stops in her tracks when she catches sight of him. She walks up to him and extends her hand. "You must be Tom. It's so nice to meet you. I'm Nurse Kirschner."

Alex jumps to attention when he sees her, and eagerly takes her hand.

"Well hel-lo Nurse Kirschner."

Nurse Kirschner smiles. He doesn't let go of her hand, so she gently pulls it free. "Francie has told me so much about you. She's been counting the minutes for you to get here. How was the train ride?"

Alex scrambles for the right words. "Ah, yes—the train. The train ride was good. A little delay over the mountains because of snow, other than that it was good. There was quite a welcoming committee at the depot. I wasn't expecting that."

"A welcoming committee?"

"Yeah, you know, soldiers coming home from the war and all that."

"Oh, of course. That's wonderful. I know there's been a lot of enthusiasm in welcoming the soldiers back home. You deserve it."

"It does feel pretty good to be back on American soil." He is quiet for a moment with his eyes fixed on her, and then he says, "And even better to be here."

"Well, I just have to tell you, I've really enjoyed getting to know your sister, these past few months. I only I wish it was under different circumstances."

"Do you take care of her?"

"I do. Francie is very special. She has such a positive attitude—you hardly know she's ill. You can be very proud of her. She's had a real impact on everyone around here."

"You don't say. Have you worked here long?"

Nurse Kirschner winces slightly at the question, and says, "I've worked here ever since nursing school. Once I walked through these doors, I couldn't leave."

"You must be very dedicated."

"I love the work I do here." She tries shifting his attention back on to me. "Have you been in to see her yet?"

"No, not yet. I've just been waiting out here."

"Well come with me. You can't keep her waiting one minute longer."

Nurse Kirschner heads for my room. Alex just stands by the desk watching her. "Aren't you coming?" she asks.

"I sure am," he says, grinning.

This time, she scowls.

Tom is still sitting on Margaret's bed. When I see Nurse Kirschner come in, I can hardly control my excitement. "Nurse Kirschner, come here and meet my big brother!"

"Your brother? But…" She looks toward at Alex, who shrugs his shoulders, and grins.

Tom stands to meet her while I introduce them. Alex takes his time, and then swaggers toward us.

Tom talks first. "Hey buddy, it's about time. Francie, Nurse Kirschner, everybody, this is my good friend, Alex."

Nurse Kirschner looks agitated. Alex is very animated and ignores Nurse Kirschner for the moment. "So this is the lovely Francie I've been hearing so much about. I see she has all the good looks in the family, Tom. Good thing she doesn't take after you."

I roll my eyes, and Tom punches Alex's shoulder.

"Francie, I feel like I already know you. Your big brother here talks about you and the rest of the family nonstop."

"Ah, c'mon. I do not," says Tom.

"Well put it this way," says Alex. I can name every kid in your family and I know that you and Tom here were inseparable as kids growing up."

"It sounds like he's got you, Tom," I say.

Just then, another nurse comes to the door and says, "Nurse Kirschner, you have a phone call."

"I'll be right there. Tom, it's nice to meet you. I'm sure I'll be seeing you again." She leaves the room without a word to Alex.

Alex's eyes are alive with mischief, and watching her every move as she leaves the room. "Whooee! Now there's a nurse! Buddy. I think I'm coming down with something. Maybe I need a check up. It might even be an emergency."

"Slow down there, Pal. We're not here to harass the nurses. I'm sure she has better things to do than worry about your sorry shenanigans."

"But Tom, I think my pulse is going through the roof. Who knows, it could be my heart. I think I should have her check me out."

By this time, he has everyone giggling.

"Tom, when you told me Alex was a handful you weren't kidding."

"Yeah, you have to look out for him. He's got a weird sense of humor, that gets him in trouble most of the time."

"How 'bout it, Francie," says Alex, "you must have some pull with her. Maybe you could ask her to listen to my heart."

Alex is acting like a lovesick cow. He certainly is getting the attention of everyone on the ward. We all actually find him entertaining. "How about I give you my expert opinion, Alex?" I say.

"Okay and just what would that be?"

"You're probably suffering from travel syndrome."

"Travel syndrome?" He says it like it's a nasty disease.

"Sure, you know. A long journey that has left you exhausted and not quite in your right mind." I hope he knows I am kidding, and then I say, "A lot of the soldiers are coming down with it, but the good news it's curable. I think if you just sit down in that chair over there and relax, you'll be fine."

"What? That's it? No pulling the alarm and having Nurse Kirschner rush to my side and cure what ails me?"

"Nope. I have x-ray vision and can see right through you. No need for any further intervention," I say with authority.

"Well, okay then. I can see I'm outnumbered here, so I guess I'll sit. But I just want you to know that this battle isn't over yet. I'll sit but I'll be planning my attack."

The girls laugh.

"Francie, you better warn Nurse Kirschner," says Tom. "I've been in battle with this guy, he's ruthless."

"I have a feeling by the way she left here—she doesn't need a warning."

Chapter 27

*"The shortest distance between two
people is a story"*

*Patti Digh, Four-word Self Help:
Simple Wisdom for Complex lives.
Self -Help: Simple wisdom for
Complex lives*

Heaven: We're still swinging, when Ambriel says, "Have you ever heard the saying, It is easier for a camel to go through the eye of a needle than it is for a rich man to get into the kingdom of God?"

"No, I've never heard that. Why do you ask?"

As quickly as I ask the question, I see a huge camel grazing on the grass, then another, and other and another. One of the camels squeezes through a needle. I almost flip my lid! Then the second camel squeezes, then the third and then the fourth, until all four squeeze through the needle.

I say to Ambriel, I have never seen anything like it. And I suppose I will never see anything like it again." Ambriel falls to the ground in laughter. When she comes to her senses, she says, "This next coming attraction is going to give you a preview of Nurse Kishner's private life."

"Sounds juicy."

—ᴥ—

It's been a long day, and Tessa Kirschner seems to have conflicting thoughts while sitting on the bus to her destination.

"He made a fool of me, she whispers to herself. Why can't I get him out of my thoughts? He was so arrogant. Just let him show up again—I won't give him the time of day."

She gets off at the next bus stop and, and walks the incline to the entrance of Hilltop Nursing Home. Its brilliantly decorated for Christmas, but the nursing home has a different atmosphere compared to the sanatorium.

Working at the sanatorium, a person endures disinfectants, blood, emesis, suffering, and even death— not very different from the nursing home.

However, as lovely as it is, it's the final chapter for people who live here.

Once inside, she sees a man named Jacob, who walks with a cane, and mumbles to himself. He is a retired farmer, with four children and thirteen grandchildren. Tessa stops to say hello, but today, he doesn't know her.

Passing by the double doors of the cafeteria, Tessa notices a party going on. A woman sits at the piano playing Jingle Bells. There are patients seated in wheelchairs, some seated in regular chairs, and others meandering around the room visiting with one another. Some of the residents listen to the music, some sing along, and others look off into space.

Tessa inhales deeply, bracing herself for her visit with her mother.

Five years earlier, an argument between her parents ended in a one-car rollover that killed her father, and left her mother bound to a wheelchair. Ruth and Arden Kirschner, regardless of their wealth, had been wallowing in a loveless marriage.

"It's about time, what kept you?" snaps Ruth.

"Well hello to you, too, Mother. In case you haven't noticed, it's snowing out and the roads are getting slick. Why aren't you at the Christmas party?"

"I told that nurse I didn't want to, and made her bring me

back to my room."

"It's the holidays. Don't you think singing and enjoying a glass of punch with the others would be fun?"

"No, I don't."

"There are a lot of people here that you could be friends with. Alice Winters for instance. She's very nice, and has invited you many times to join her and her friends for a game of cards."

"I don't like cards."

"If you would just try, I'm sure you could become good friends."

"I don't need them. I have you."

Another battle lost.

"Are you going to do my shopping on Saturday like promised?

"I am."

"Go early to avoid the crowds, and be sure to wear something nice. All I ever see you in is that nurse's uniform."

"It's a long bus ride to Hilltop from the sanatorium. No time to change."

"I don't see why you have to work at that awful sanatorium anyway. It's full of sick people."

"Yes, mother, it is full of sick people—people that need my help. They are very sick…and they depend on people like me. I'm sure you can understand that."

"What I don't understand is why a pretty young thing like you needs to work in a place like that. You should find yourself a rich husband, who would take care of you."

"I can take care of myself. I don't need a 'rich husband.' Besides, working at the sanatorium makes me feel like I'm doing something right with my life. I enjoy working there. It's very satisfying. You know all that. We've had this conversation before."

"But to put your mind at ease, since It's my day off, I will wear something appropriate, just for you. Then I will come and have lunch with you. How does that sound?"

"Okay."

"I don't want to fight with you any more, Mother."

"I don't want to fight either. I just get lonely when you're not here."

"Well, I'm here now. Why don't we look at some of the decorations before we go to the party? By the way, I saw Martha Robinson sitting at the piano. She plays really well. I'll bet if you asked, they'd let you play for a while."

"I don't remember how anymore."

"Oh, sure you do. You used to play so beautifully. I remember when I was little how I'd sit next to you on the bench just watching you play. It was magical watching your fingers glide up and down the keys. Do you remember that?"

"That was so long ago."

"You can't have forgotten. I know with a little practice, you could do it again. Wouldn't you like that?"

"I don't think so. Martha does a good job. The people like her."

"Well, maybe one day just you and I will sit at the piano, and you can play for me again."

"You're such a good girl, Tessa. I don't know what I'd do without you."

"You'd do just fine if you'd let yourself, but I'm not going anywhere, so let's go join the others for a while."

—⁓—

The next morning, Nurse Kirschner is bringing our meds to us. I'm anxious to talk to her. "So, Nurse Kirschner, what did you think of my brother's friend? Pretty cute, huh?"

"What friend? You mean that soldier with your brother Tom?"

"Yes, Alex."

"Was that his name?"

"I think he likes you."

"Why do you say that?"

Nurse Kirschner moves around the room delivering meds to each of her patients, ignoring me.

"When you left, you were all he talked about."

"Oh?"

"Mm-hmm. He said his heart was pounding, and he wanted you to listen to it."

"He did, did he?"

"He even said it was an emergency."

"I found him quite arrogant."

"Maybe he was just trying to impress you."

"He certainly did not!"

"Tom told me they were best buddies in Okinawa, and watched out for each other. Tom said there isn't a better soldier than Alex."

She sighs. "Well, he may be a good soldier, but his manners need a lot of work."

I ignore her disinterest, because I love playing matchmaker. "I think you should go out with him."

"Go out with him? I don't even know him. Why would I want to go out with him?"

"You could call it your contribution to the war effort."

"The war is over, Miss Carver."

"Oh. Well then, you could support the homecoming of our troops."

"Okay, little lady, that's just about enough out of you. Open wide and swallow."

I choke a little on the water.

"Take a breath and cough, she says. You must have ingested some into your lungs. Slow down, and don't talk so much."
Once I was able to breathe normally again, I start up ignoring her last remark. I'm on a roll. "I think he's coming back with Tom again today. I'll bet he asks you out."

"I think you've been reading too many romance novels, or maybe Lydia has rubbed off on you. Whatever it is, I want you to lie here and behave yourself." Do you hear me?"

Just then, Dr. Wagner comes into the room holding my chart.

Chapter 28

"Never deprive anyone of hope—it may
be all they have."

Unknown

Heaven: We are swinging again. I say, "I think I'm wearing
Nurse Kirschner down."

Ambriel says, "Like I say, your words and actions are making
a ripple."

"Oh Yeah, that stone in the water and the ripple effect.
Gotcha."

The swinging is making me dizzy, so she says, "Hop down,
and let's play on the teeter-totter for the time being. While we
teeter, I am going to play teacher for a moment."

"Sounds like fun. "Teach me."

"The subject of this flash course is Purgatory. She says, "The word
Purgatory is sometimes taken to mean a state between hell and
heaven. It is the condition of souls which at the moment of death
are in the state of grace, but which have not completely expedited
their faults nor attained the degree of purity necessary to enjoy the
vision of God." "Do you understand?"

"I think so, but why are you telling me this?"

"Hop down."

Once again, I follow her into another part of heaven. I look
around to see if I can figure out what the connection of her lesson,
when I see a man sitting on a rock. He seems to be suffering. He
keeps rubbing his head, and then starts to cry. He stands and paces,
still rubbing his head. It goes on forever. Literally.

Ambriel says, "This man has been here for centuries." He is

undergoing punishment for his sins. If people on earth pray for this man, he may be cleansed of his sins and would be able to see the face of God."

What did he do?" I ask.

"His sins were egregious."

"He seems so sad. I feel bad for him."

"Well then, what should do about it?"

"Um, pray for him?"

"Are you asking me or telling me?"

"Oh, of course, I will pray for him."

"The more prayers, the closer his suffering will ease, and he can obtain his just rewards."

She puts the Christmas Lily in her teeth. Its time to go back to the sanatorium."

—⁂—

"Did I hear someone say Miss Carver has been miss behaving?"

Nurse Kirschner says, "Miss Carver has three more days to misbehave, and then she turns eighteen, and must act like an adult."

"That's right. In three days you will see a new me!" I say.

"Well, don't change too much," says Dr. Wagner, "I kind of like the old you.

He sits next to me and I brace myself. Miss Carver, I have great news! I just received a very important call from the Mayo Clinic. "There's a drug!"

"What do you mean?"

"There's an experimental drug. It's still being worked on, but there is a drug." He catches his breath and continues. "Because your TB hasn't been responding to any treatment so far, I've been searching every possible avenue for an answer, and I found out some time ago, there are researchers at Mayo Clinic, in Rochester, who have been working on a drug to cure tuberculosis, and are having very favorable results."

I feel a blood rush. I suck in my breath, forgetting all about my matchmaking. "A cure?"

"Possibly, but I can't stress this enough—it's only experimental! I'm not sure how it will affect you or what side effects it might have, but yes, there is an experimental drug that could possibly be a cure."

"I can't believe this. This is the answer to all my prayers."

"It could be. I've been keeping your parents informed of your condition, in that the treatment you've been receiving so far isn't working. Some time ago, I told them about the experimental drug. They were interested, and said they wanted to do anything they could to help, so they wrote a letter to the Mayo Clinic to try the drug on you. The more involved we all are, the better our chances of obtaining some of the drug. I have also been in contact with Mayo, and have recently spoken with a Dr. Hinshaw. I told him about your condition, and he's in agreement that you would be a good candidate for his drug."

I can't believe my ears. I have to ask again. "You mean there's a drug that could cure my TB? What's it called? Why haven't I heard about it? Why isn't everyone on it?"

"Whoa, whoa, whoa, slow down. Those are all good questions. It's called streptomycin and, like I said, it's just in the experimental stages right now. The trouble is there isn't enough of it to go around, and everyone who's heard about it is trying to get some for their patients. It's very hard to obtain. I've written many letters and have been in constant contact with Dr. Hinshaw, and I am very happy to tell you that he has agreed your case warrants a trial."

"He did? I could be cured?" I still have a plethora questions. "But what about the other girls?"

"The other girls are improving with the treatments we have available here at the sanatorium, and new surgical procedures are being tried every day with very favorable results. But, I'm sorry to say, you're TB has progressed, and nothing we've tried is helping. We need to get more aggressive before it has a chance to spread any further. The good news is, I've convinced Dr. Hinshaw to try some on you."

By this time, I'm shaking.

"I've spoken to your parents and explained the risks involved. I told them it looks like I will be able to access some of the drug, and asked them if they are still willing to let me try it on you. They wanted me to talk to you first, and if you're willing they give their permission."

Before he can say another word, I say, "Yes! Yes! Yes!"

"I thought you might feel that way, so I've already asked Dr. Hinshaw to send it. But because of the shortage, it might take a while before we get it, but they will be sending it."

"Oh, Dr. Wagner, this is wonderful news!"

"Yes it is. Let's call it an early birthday present. I just wish I could tell you exactly when we'll be able to get started, but we're on their list and hope is on the way."

Chapter 29

*"The only blind person at Christmas
time is he who has not Christmas in
his heart."*

Helen Keller

Heaven: Ambriel takes me to a stream and parts the water.
We enter heaven, where I get another glimpse of Jesus. Little
children gather at his feet. Ambriel says "Jesus is about to tell them
the Christmas story. "Would you like to stay and listen?"

Oh, could we?" I sound like the little children. Jesus begins. I
can hardly compose myself. He starts.

"Oh, come all you children, oh come one in all."

Hundreds of children gather in anticipation. When He
finishes, the children cry for more. Ambriel says, "We have to leave
now."

"I will never forget this. I just heard Jesus tell little children
the Christmas story."

"Only in heaven you will hear Jesus tell the story."

"Now back to business.

"You were a great match-maker," she says, talking about Nurse
Kirschner.

"I knew she would go out with him". I say.

"You have just put a lot of wheels in motion. Because of your
influence on Nurse Kirschner, her whole world will change."

"All because of me?"

"If it wasn't for your interfering in her personal life, she may
have taken another path. Let's see how this plays out, shall we?"

I tie the last bow on the gifts I've been wrapping, and proclaim, "There. I'm done. Now I'm just going to sit back and wait for my gifts to pour in." I light up when I see Jonah appear in the doorway. Life is good.

It has been three months since we shared our first kiss at the movies, and Jonah has not missed a day since to be with me. My heart lifts, and I feel tingly at the sight of him. He is my soul mate.

Secretly, I wish the other girls would disappear, so we could have some privacy. But privacy at the sanatorium is a luxury. I know courting me this way is tormenting him. However, Jonah is patient, and says I'm worth it.

There are some visits, we do have the ward to ourselves, and can talk freely. But eventually, the room is full again. Occasionally, he will take me on a gurney. In addition, we find a quiet hall where we can be alone. He will lean in close and kiss me softly. It's always just a few stolen moments here and there.

We also like going to the movies on Wednesday nights, where we will mostly stare into each other's eyes and whisper.

But most of the time our courtship is spent in the ward with the other girls and their visitors. It's like one big happy family. Despite the surroundings—our love is deepening.

"Jonah, hi," I say.

"Hey there, Sunshine. Looks like you've been busy. Anything in that pile for me?"

"Maybe. Maybe not. You're just going to have to wait like everyone else."

"I don't like to wait. I'm still a little kid at heart."

"I know you are—that's what makes it so much fun. Guess what?"

"First you make me wait, and now you're going to make me guess. What I don't go do for you."

"Poor baby. Okay, I won't make you guess. I'm too excited anyway. Actually, I have two things that I'm excited about. You're not going to believe this, but Dr. Wagner was just here and told me there's a drug that can cure tuberculosis."

Jonah's mouth drops. "What? Are you kidding me?"

"No. He just told me. But he warned me over and over that it's experimental, and it's very hard to get. He's been in contact with Mayo Clinic, and well, long story short, they're sending some to try on me!"

"When? How soon? Is it going to be used on everyone?"

"I laugh. We think alike. I had all those same questions. Dr. Wagner says the other girls are all getting better, but my TB isn't responding to treatment. He says it's in short supply, and very hard to get. But they've agreed to put me on a trial. Hopefully it won't be long before it's available for everyone in the world who has TB. Isn't it just swell news?"

"Francie, this is a dream come true. How soon do you start?"

"Well, Dr. Wagner doesn't have it yet. It's called streptomycin. But as soon as some is available, Mayo is going to send it."

Jonah kisses me, long and hard, ignoring everyone who is in the room. I am happy to kiss him back.

"Okay, now that you've got my heart pounding, what's the other good news?"

His kiss puts me on cloud nine, and I almost forget about Tom. "Tom is here, and he's coming back this afternoon to spend the day with us. I can't wait for the two of you to meet.

"I heard Tom was here, he says. Oh and I also heard you're playing matchmaker."

"What? How could you possibly know that?"

"News travels fast around here, you know. Let me see… what's his name? Oh yea, Alex. I hear he might be sweet on Nurse

Kirschner, and you're playing cupid.'"

You tell me right now how you come to know that.'"

"These walls have ears.'"

"Okay, now you're just teasing me. You tell me right this minute.'"

Poppy walks in, just then, from having breakfast in the cafeteria. Her privileges are allowing her more freedom every day. It won't be long, and she will be walking down the aisle with Ken.

"Oh, hey Jonah. You're here already," says Poppy. Your boyfriend and I shared a cup of coffee together. I filled him in on your visitors yesterday."

"Jonah, you sneak!" You had me going there for a minute. I was scared everyone knew, for heaven's sake. Nurse Kirschner would have been livid if she thought I was spreading gossip about her."

Jonah laughs. "You're so easy, I can't help myself."

"That's all right, Jonah. I don't get mad, I just get even."

"Should I be scared?"

"You've been warned. That's all I'm going to say."

His mood changes and he says, "Um, Francie, I have something to tell…"

Just then, Tom and Alex walk in, interrupting.

"Tom!" I light up like a Christmas tree. "Come quick. I want you to meet someone."

The three boys shake hands, saying all the well-mannered greetings. Meeting my large family is challenging, but I know Jonah will get through it—only four more to go plus their families. No problem.

"Dr. Wagner told me you can take me to the visitor's lounge for a while so our time doesn't have to be spent in here. He said he'd make an exception as an early birthday present to me. I also have some exciting news to share with you, but I don't want to tell you until we get to the lounge."

Tom says, "Well let's get going then. I wouldn't want you to bust a gasket."

"Very funny. Also, later this afternoon, we can go to the auditorium. There's a special program for the holidays. Lawrence Welk and his Champaign Music Makers are performing. I guess he's supposed to be a pretty good band leader."

"Oh, I've heard of him," says Alex. He's from North Dakota. I think he's been around for some time now."

"It sounds like we have a great day planned," says Tom.

"Hey kids, thanks anyway, but I won't be able to stay," says Alex. "My parents have plans for me. I just wanted to stop in and say hello before I drop Tom off."

"I'm glad you came," I say.

"Oh, by the way, is Nurse Kirschner working today?"

Jonah has to hold back a smile and says, "I saw her in the hall when I got here about a half hour ago."

"I'll walk with you to the visitor's lounge and then maybe see if I can find her. I probably should apologize for yesterday," he says.

The group of us make our way out the door and down the hall to the lounge, but no sign of Nurse Kirschner on our journey.

I am bursting at the seams to tell Tom about the streptomycin, and when I do, I think my big brother is going to cry. He always was a softie. Jonah reached over and tuned the radio to KNUT. Christmas music is playing. Instantly, the mood changes.

"Oh, I just love Christmas music," I say. "Doesn't it just put you in the Christmas spirit? Tom, remember how good the house smells at Christmas with all the cooking and baking Ma does?"

"Oh, yeah. My favorite part would be coming home from Midnight Mass, and smell her meat pies warming in the oven for our midnight snack."

"Oh, that makes me so homesick. I can almost smell them now," I say.

The three of us talk about how Christmas was when we were kids, and all the Christmas traditions.

—⁓—

Meanwhile, Alex meanders out into the hall, trying to find Nurse Kirschner. He hasn't gone too far when he sees her. She is going over a chart with a doctor.

Alex dips around the corner, where she can't see him.

The doctor writes in the chart, and gives it back to Nurse Kirschner. When they finish, she turns in his direction. Alex starts whistling, rounds the corner, running smack dab into her!

"Oh my gosh! I'm so....she stops. "You!"

Their collision knocks the chart from her hands, and sends it crashing to the floor. Before she can say another word, he crouches down to pick up the papers that came loose from the metal folder. He hands them back to her, and says, "You really should watch where you're going."

"I should watch where I'm going? How dare you? You're on the wrong side of the hall. You should be over there."

Alex looks toward where she points. "Well, I'll be darned. I am in the wrong lane, aren't I? Now, now, don't get your water hot. It was an honest mistake."

Nurse Kirschner immediately regains her composure. Its obvious he's trying to goad her. It seems she isn't going to give him the satisfaction. She smiles politely and veers around him. "If you'll excuse me, I have work to do."

Alex turns on his heels right behind her, like a puppy wagging its tail. "You know, I could let you make it up to me by having dinner with me tonight."

She frowns, and keeps walking.

"Ah, come on. You know you want to. I'm not such a bad guy. Just one dinner. What do ya' say?"

"Mr. Monson. I have neither the time nor the desire to go to dinner with you. Now please, I have to get back to work."

"Okay, okay. I can respect that. You're busy and I shouldn't be bothering you. So why don't you save us both a lot of time and trouble and just say yes. I know a great little place not too far from here. A little music, some wine, a nice dinner. How 'bout it? That's all I ask."

"I have somewhere to go after my shift."

"Tell me where you're going, and I'll pick you up there. What do you say?"

She stares into his powder blue eyes, and says, "All right."

"All right? You'll go out with me?"

"I said I will, didn't I?"

Before she can change her mind, he says, "Okay then. Tell me when and where.

"Hill Top Nursing Home by eight."

"I won't be late. Should I meet you in the lobby or somewhere inside?" All of a sudden, he looks nervous and rambles on like an adolescent.

"Come inside, I won't be long."

"I'll meet you inside Hilltop Nursing Home at eight, he mimics.

She smiles coolly.

Chapter 30

*"When the future hinges on the next
words that are said, don't let logic
interfere, believe your heart instead."*

Philip Robinson

Heaven: "Have you ever wondered how many people around the world that have the same birthday as yours? "Asks Ambriel.

"Come to think of it, I haven't."

"Come with me."

We stop swinging and enter birthday heaven. Millions of people are gathered, all speaking in different languages, but can understand one another. The mood is festive. There is music, and dancing. I see Mrs. Flores. She's playing guitar. She winks at me. Piñata's hang from trees and people try hitting them. When they break, candy spills in abundance. Laughter and music rings through birthday heaven. "I love this, Ambriel," I say. There is ear pulling, smash cakes for babies to mess, bumps and punches, colored ice yogurt on the forehead, butter on noses and socks hang at the house of a bachelor. The Mexican song, "Laminitis, is heard. Clocks and watches are given freely for good luck.

"Do all of these people have the same birthday as me?"

"Every one, and just look at all the different traditions.

"Seen enough?"

"So many traditions, how fun!"

"Let's go back to the sanatorium shall we?"

"You say that a lot."

—⚬—

Tom and Jonah bring me back to my room. In time for the

evening meal. We had a great time, but I'm feeling rather tired, and a lot of pain in my ankle. Tom and Jonah say their goodbyes, and I find I can hardly keep my eyes open.

—∭—

Alex gets to the nursing home early. He wanders the halls whistling a strange little tune and talking to anyone and everyone he meets. He ducks into the cafeteria for a cup of coffee. Instead of coffee, he is distracted by a baby grand piano. The room is empty. He slides onto the bench, and begins to play. He starts out with a couple of fast-paced Christmas tunes. After some time of playing as many Christmas pieces that he can muster, he decides on a piece that comes to memory *"In the Shade of the Old Apple Tree"*. He bends forward putting his ear close to the keys, and moves his fingers in magnificent precision. His body sways back and forth in time with the music like a mother rocking her baby. The notes from the ivories swell to intensity, then slowly releases into a rhythmical lullaby.

Tessa hears the music from the hall, and pushes her mother toward the cafeteria. Ruth demanded to meet the young man who wants to date her daughter. Tessa wheels her mother's chair through the double doors of the cafeteria, but stops in her tracks when she sees who is inside playing the piano. Its Alex. She looks stunned. She moves cautiously toward the piano, as if she is drawn to it. The tune is familiar. He is playing the same piece her mother used to play all those years ago when she was just a little girl.

"For there within my arms I gently pressed you. And blushing red, you slowly turned away, I can't forget the way I once caressed you; I only pray we'll meet another day."

She watches, and remembers. Music is like that—it has a way of bringing back memories, and placing you in another moment in time. Ruth sits quietly in her chair and listens as the young man makes the piano come alive. The music grows louder, and he sways when the notes soften. He is doing more than merely playing the piece, he's feeling it—The music is in him, and he is the tool that makes it happen. Tears flood Ruth's eyes. For Ruth and her daughter, the music takes them back a lifetime between then and now.

—⁓—

Alex presses his hand to the small of her back, and escorts Tessa out of the building, into his father's '42 Packard, and says "For a while there, I wasn't sure you would come", he says.

"I have to admit, the thought did cross my mind, she replies."

"Well then, we'll just have to make this a night to remember so the next time there'll be no doubts."

"Do you really think there will be a next time?"

"I'm sure of it." "

Even though our first date is at a nursing home. "

It will be a good story to tell our grandchildren."

Up until now, Tessa has only seen Alex in his Marine uniform. Tonight he is dressed in a dark blue suit tailored to his long, lean body and sports a blue striped tie that contrasts against a starched white shirt. His black shoes polished to a spit shine, and there is a hint of Old Spice about him. His military haircut accentuates the strong features of his chiseled jaw.

When they are well on their way, he turns the radio on and begins tapping his thumbs on the steering wheel to the beat of the music. He doesn't ask any questions.

"My mother is a patient at Hill Top. I visit her nearly every day."

"What happened to her?"

"She was in a car accident a few years ago that resulted in a spine injury. My father was killed."

"I'm sorry to hear that. That's gotta' be rough. It must be hard on you too."

"I've adjusted. She needs me, and I'll always be here for her."

—⚯—

The waiter comes with their wine.

Alex picks up his glass and says, "To many more surprises" They clink glasses. "You've been awfully quiet. I know we've only just met, but I had the impression you were a little chattier."

"Chattier?" She laughs at his choice of words.

"Yeah. You know, I thought you were a woman who has a lot to say."

"Well, I'm usually not at a loss for words, but I've been sitting here trying to figure you out."

"Oh no, don't do that. If you figure me out, it won't be fun anymore. I need to remain a mystery to keep you interested."

"Well, you've succeeded at keeping me interested, I'll give you that."

"Good. For a minute there I thought you might have figured out that I'm really quite predictable."

"Well so far, I've find you to be entirely unpredictable."

"Does this mean you're not mad at me anymore?"

"I know there are reasons why I should be mad at you, but for the life of me I can't remember what they are right now."

"Good, then I won't remind you that I tricked you into thinking I was Tom, and purposefully bumped into you in the hall. That would be foolish of me to get your blood running hot again. It was fun though, don't you think?"

He smiles a Cheshire grin.

"In an adolescent sort of way—maybe," she teases.

"Heck. We can't be adults all the time can we? Where's the fun in that?" She is looking at his twinkling eyes and expressive mouth.

Then he leans into her, and kisses her gently on the lips. She is still holding her wine.

"I thought we should get that awkward first kiss out of the way," he says "And just so you know, I'll let you make the next move."

Maybe it was the wine or his unpredictable behavior, but she starts to giggle like a teenager.

"See, isn't it more fun to play? That's the first time I've heard you laugh. You're beautiful when you smile. You should do it more often."

"Thank you. It felt good. I can't help it, you surprise me and it makes me laugh."

Their evening is fun. The food is good, the wine robust and the music tantalizing. Every song beckons them to the dance floor where he holds her close—even after the music has stopped. When it does, she is the one to make the next move. She stands on her toes, and puts her lips on his.

When the music starts up again, Alex is still holding her. They move in time with the melody and then he asks, "What are you doing for Christmas?"

"Christmas, hmm, other than the festivities at the sanatorium, I've hardly given the holiday much thought. I was just planning on going to spend it with my mom."

"Come with me to my parent's house. Spend Christmas with me. I only have until after New Year's, and I'll be shipping out again. Please. Spend Christmas with me."

"Gee, I-I don't know."

"Tessa, don't over think it. If you over think things, it takes the fun out of it. Let's be spontaneous. I promise—you won't be sorry."

"Alex, I don't think I can do that. I can't abandon Mother."

"We'll spring your mom and bring her with us. My parents

would love it if the two of you come. Don't say no. Say yes."

Their bodies move as one to the rhythm of the music and she says, "Yes."

—∞—

On Christmas Day, Alex guides Ruth's wheelchair through the front doors of his parent's home. There is no ramp to assist him. Maneuvering is difficult. Once inside, Alex helps her with her coat. The aroma of turkey roasting in the oven, along with the sweet smell of apples and cinnamon wafting from the kitchen meets them as soon as they enter the house. The home is warm and inviting, with a cheery atmosphere. The table is set with china and wine glasses, and a centerpiece of candles and poinsettias on top of an intricate hand-made lace tablecloth. Kate Monson has seen to every detail, and she opens her home to Tessa and her mother, as if they have been lifelong friends.

There is an immediate connection between Tessa, and Kate. Spending Christmas together is fun for everyone. Even Ruth doesn't object.

—∞—

On the ward at the sanatorium, an eighteenth birthday party is already underway. It's for me, of course. Ma, Tom, Pa, Sarah, Lily, Johnny, and Michael are there, along with the girls on the ward and Jonah. Even Dr. Wagner pops in. We are celebrating my birthday first, then Christmas.

But I'm getting a funny vibe from Jonah—I can't quite put my finger on it. It's as if he wants to tell me something, but struggles to get the words out. I decide to wait until later when everyone leaves. I will ask him about it then.

Lydia waltzes into the room carrying a gigantic birthday cake. She puts the cake on a small table, she has placed by my bed, and lights the candles. Everyone sings "Happy Birthday".

"Okay, Francie Girl. Says Pa. Make a wish."

I look at Jonah. Then I close my eyes, and blow the candles. However, I don't have enough strength, and miss four. Michael blows the rest for me.

Chapter 31

"What is time? The shadow on the dial,
the striking of the clock, the running
of sand, day and night, summer and
winter, months, years, centuries—these
are but the arbitrary and outward
signs—the measure of time, not time
itself. Time is the life of the soul."

Henry Wadsworth Longfellow

Heaven: "I did have a good time at my birthday "I say, even though I wasn't feeling the best."

"Time doesn't wait," says Ambriel.

We are back where she has shown me earlier. I see the suffering man again. He's still sitting on the rock, crying in agony. I hear him say, "I'm sorry. Someone comes running toward the man. It's the little boy. The man sees the boy and cries even more hysterically.

"I have something for you," says the little boy to the man."

The man stands and paces back and forth. The little boy says, "Look, look what I have." The man still does not look at the boy.

"See here?" "Look what I have, please look, Mr. Gunderson, the boy says. In my sack, I have enough prayers for you. I have been praying for you. God told me I have enough prayers for you, and you don't have to suffer anymore. "Now you can see the face of God. I forgive you, Mister Gunderson." "You don't have to suffer anymore. See?"

"Oh Frank," says the man, I am so sorry."

We leave, and I say, "That was some powerful stuff."

Ambriel says" Prayer is powerful.

I ask, "How long do you think he has been suffering?"

"Maybe five minutes, or even five centuries. Time can be anything in heaven.

"For now, let's go back to the sanatorium where you will be in fast forward."

She levitates and puts the Christmas in her hair.

—⁂—

Dear Diary,

January 2, 1946: The holidays are over, and I am now officially an adult. My birthday party was a humdinger and Ma brought her famous meat pies to share with everyone for Christmas. It sure was swell. Turning eighteen doesn't really feel any different than being seventeen. I don't know what I was expecting—maybe a larger bosom and longer legs-ha. Just kidding!

Now I know why Jonah was acting so strange during Christmas. On January 1, his tuberculosis is said to be completely cured, and gets to go home. The news is bittersweet—it is for him too, that's why he had a hard time telling me. I am so happy that he's cured and gets to leave this place, but the selfish part of me wishes he is still here. He promises to come and visit every chance he gets. He's going to start college this next semester and work at his dad's newspaper part time. In the meantime, I have to work on getting out of here. Swell day, feel fine.

January 3, 1946: More snow has fallen in the past couple of days, and the ice on the lake has gotten thicker. They put my knee in a cast to immobilize it. The pain never stops. I miss Jonah. Nurse Kirschner walks around here like she's floating on a cloud. She went out with Alex every night while he was here. He and Tom got stationed at Camp Pendleton in California. They left right after the holidays. Nurse Kirschner told me they are writing to each other every day. Tom writes to Izzy. Today I made a scrapbook and went to confession. I sure hope Dr. Wagner gets the streptomycin soon. Swell day, feel fine.

January 4, 1946: We are having a January thaw, nice and warm out. Dr. Wagner came in and took my pulse. I took lamp today. Father gave us communion this morning at six o'clock. I feel very sleepy this morning. I wrote a letter to Ma. Still no word on the streptomycin. Swell day, feel fine.

January 5, 1946: Bea had a kidney operation. My friend, Millie, stopped in on her way to Mankato with her boyfriend, Pat, and brought me some yarn. I started a sweater for Dorothy's boy, Ronny. Yesterday, the ice on the roof melted and fell. Boy was that noisy. Feel swell and warm today.

January 7, 1946: It's Monday, and I started a college course today. I can only take one subject—it's Problems in American Democracy, and I get two credits for it. Jonah is coming to visit tomorrow. Took lamp, feel swell.

January 10, 1946: The wind blew today but otherwise kind of warm out. I went to Mass this morning so didn't take lamp. Jonah came and took me to our favorite deserted spot down a hall by some offices. He told me about his classes but says he misses me. Swell day, feel fine.

January 11, 1946: Lucy went for a ride with her husband. She will be going home soon. Helen doesn't feel so well. I almost finished the back of Ronny's sweater but ripped it out again. Mrs. Carroll came and showed me how to hemstitch. She also gave me some pincushions to work on. Agnes dangled her feet for the first time since the 4th of February, 1944. Dr. Wagner called Mayo again, but they're still isn't enough streptomycin right now—soon I hope. I am very tired tonight. I'm going to listen to Danny Kaye. Swell day, feel fine.

January 13, 1946: Jonah came to see me and took me to the

auditorium for a program. We left early and went to be by ourselves. OOH LA LA! Swell day, feel fine.

January 21, 1946: It snowed a lot today. Dr. Wagner came up to see me at dinnertime and gave me the news. Dr. Hinshaw from the Mayo Clinic handed over the burden of who gets streptomycin to the National Institute of Health. There just isn't enough to go around, and it has been decided that they will not be sending it to me. I feel bad for Dr. Wagner; he looked crushed when he told me. He said he would keep trying. Feel kind of sleepy.

January 22, 1946: It's my sister, Dorothy's, birthday today. Jonah visited, and I told him about the strep. He said he is going to write a letter to the National Institute of Health. He's such a good writer. I hope he can persuade them. Swell day, feel fine.

January 23, 1946: Izzy sits up out of bed for the first time today, kind of weak. Bea walked over to Izzy's bed. I studied this whole week's lesson today. Izzy got some records from the men in 541, kind of nice. Millie surprised me tonight and came to see me. I sure was glad to see her. Tonight is Helen's last night before her operation. They are going to remove two of her ribs. Feel swell, kind of sleepy.

January 24, 1946: They called Helen's operation off until next week. Poor kid. I wrote a letter to Jonah and listened to Red Skelton tonight—pretty good. Today I had thirds on French fries (pig.) Dr. Evans was up and was very nice to me. Nurse Kirschner and I have gotten close. Sometimes I call her Tessa, and she calls me Francie. She is so happy since she met Alex. Swell day, feel fine.

January 25, 1946: Swell day but a little windy. Tonight it is 10 below zero. I listened to Danny Kaye and Molay Mystery tonight. Izzy started sitting up for two meals a day. Izzy got a letter from Tom. I didn't take lamp today, studied for class. Dr. Wagner came in to see how we we're getting along. Swell day, feel fine.

January 29, 1946: I am madder than a wet hen today, 'cause yesterday I put olive oil in my hair, and didn't get it washed out. I took lamp and cried all the way through it. Bea walked over to my bed today. Dr. Evans came in and cut my cast. He sure is nice. Helen went downstairs today. She is going to have her operation tomorrow. The Catholic Ladies came and gave us Holy Cards. Swell day, feel fine.

January 30, 1946: I took lamp and feel a lot better today. Dr. Evans helped me take my leg out of the cast and I had x-rays taken. I had my hair washed, thank goodness! Dr. Wagner was on the elevator when I came up. He sure looked cute. Father Alphonse came to hear our confessions today. We are having real winter weather now. Helen had her operation today. I will pray for her tonight. Good night, Dear Diary.

February 4, 1946: Took lamp and had more x-rays taken today. Dr. Evans came and asked me if my cast was okay, if not he would try to fix it. I had my first English class today with Miss Parker. Kind of hard. Feel kind of tired tonight, but it's a swell day, (19 degrees above).

February 6, 1946: It rained and thundered out this morning. Dr. Wagner called me down for a chest examination and said my blood count is normal. When I first came in, my sedimentation was 66 mi, now it is 44 mi. It is supposed to be 20 mi. My lungs are improving. Dr. Wagner said Dr. Evans would be sure and look at my leg next Wednesday. Lucy's husband came in when I was in my brassiere. Was I ever embarrassed! Good night Dear Diary.

February 8, 1946: Izzy got bathroom privileges. I had English and tried to stay awake. I started a green and white beanie for my niece, Donna, today. Boy, am I tired. The sweater business has me all tired out. Lucy's husband said I'm the busiest girl he has ever seen. I am too! It feels like spring out. Good night.

February 12, 1946: The big three were in today, Dr. Wagner, Dr. Evans, and a new doctor, Dr. Lind. Tessa washed my left leg. We talked about Alex and Tom and Jonah. Swell day, feel fine.

Thursday, February 14, 1946: It's Valentine's Day. Poppy gave me a teal headband and I gave her three sticks of gum. Lydia brought us all treats. I got a bouquet of gladiolas from Ma, Pa and the kids. Millie sent me a bottle of Jealousy. I received eleven red roses and one white rose from a secret admirer today. Guess who? He came to see me, and we went down to the tunnel for old time's sake. That's all I can say about that, Dear Diary. There was a big teddy bear setting on the desk at the nurses' station. Alex sent it to Tessa. Lucy got discharged today. What a great Valentine's Day for her. Lucky kid! A new girl, Michelle Klein, took Lucy's place in the last bed across from Helen. Her family visited and brought us hot dogs and pickles, and then her dad, Floyd, passed around cookies. It was lots of fun and a swell day. Dr. Wagner told Poppy she gets to go home soon. I feel fine.

February 16, 1946: Today, I have been here eight months. I went to Mass this morning and then went down to x-ray for my eight-month check up. Five shots. I finished the green and white beanie. I also sent for a pattern book—hope it gets here soon. I studied my English for a little while tonight but couldn't concentrate because Izzy was playing her phonograph. I put red lipstick on my face in the shape of a heart. I am having a lamp on my leg tonight to dry my new cast. I don't feel so good tonight.

February 22, 1946: I started to make slippers and broke two hooks; one was Poppy's. It is George Washington's birthday today, so didn't have class. Darn it! After all that studying.

February 23, 1946: I had a pretty tough night last night. I couldn't sleep and my left heel ached. We asked about Helen, but the doctors and nurses don't tell us much when someone isn't doing well. I guess they don't want to bring us down. I don't like looking at her empty bed. Lydia told us one of the men in 541 has to have his leg cut off. Agnes gets bathroom privileges and Poppy and gets to go home next month. What will I do without her, Dear Diary?

February 27, 1946: Well, today was a red-letter day. I went down to see Dr. Evans, and he is going to fuse my knee. Dr. Evans is a swell doctor and I like him very much. Swell day, feel fine.

March 6, 1946: Today is the first day of Lent. Ma sent me a Lenten book. Agnes gets to sit up for three meals a day and bathroom privileges. Jonah is coming up and we're going to the movies tonight. There is pea-soup fog outside. Swell day, feel fine.

March 16, 1946: Today is Saturday, and I have been here 9 months. I still think about Margaret from time to time.

March 17, 1946: Today is St. Patrick's Day and we got a little green on our grapefruit and a basket with candy in it. Lydia told us that Helen died last night. Sad day. I don't feel too swell tonight, Dear Diary.

March 24, 1946: I saw my first robin today. I think I have spring fever. This is the sunniest and warmest day we have had this year. I found out today that I will be having surgery soon. I can't wait. Good night, Dear Diary.

March 27, 1946: I took lamp this morning. I am getting ready to go downstairs for my operation soon. I called Ma this afternoon—it was so good to hear her voice. Everyone in 530 has been so nice to me. Dr. Wagner put my cast on today. Swell day, feel fine.

April 1, 1946: We have a new girl on the ward named Grace Magnuson. She moved into Helen's bed. She is very nice. Poppy left today. It feels like an April fool's joke on me. I miss her already.

April 8, 1946: I had a urine specimen today and am getting ready so I can go downstairs for the operation on the 10th. I talked to Ma this afternoon. Wednesday is the big day. Feel fine.

April 9, 1946: Dear Diary…

Chapter 32

"People have one thing in common: they
are all different."

Robert Zend

Heaven: Ambriel leads me to the edge of a river where we sit and watch the water twist and turn. There's a flock of white birds nestled on the other side. I tell her I'm enjoying looking at my life play out and am beginning to understand how my actions play a role in other people's lives. She smiles. I see so many people in heaven. They are all different but the same.

Ambriel says, "All these people either had cancer or, polio, or, hepatitis, or Parkinson's or aneurisms, or tuberculosis, just to name a few. But they are cured in heaven. They are free to dance, and play, and sing, and paint, whatever, or all those things. Their suffering is gone." "The differences in nationalities has even melted away."

"I wonder if the differences on earth could ever melt away."

"With the right people and a lot of prayer."

"Time to go" she says.

—∞—

It's April 9, the day before my surgery. I have been writing in my diary. Lydia comes to get me, and moves me downstairs to three-east. When we get there, I can see Little Agnes waving to me off the porch of five-main. Lydia goes back to the ward to gather my things, and is about to bring them to me, when she notices my diary shoved part way under my pillow.

"Whoops, better not forget this. I'm sure she's going to want it after her operation." She reaches for the diary, but it slips through her fingers and lands on the floor. She bends to pick it up, when she notices her own name scrawled at the top of the page. She quickly looks around the room to see if anyone is watching. The temptation must have been too great. —It's as if her name whispers for her to peak. She doesn't stop herself.

April 9, 1946: Dear Diary,

Lydia is so excited. Kinsley's Department Store got a shipment of nylon stockings today, and she wants to be first in line tomorrow morning to buy a pair. She heard a rumor that hundreds of women are supposed to show up to buy them, so she's going to get there by four in the morning to be first in line. Isn't that crazy? I hope she gets a pair, though, because I know how badly she wants them. She's planning a trip to Hollywood soon, and says she needs them to make a good impression on agents. I think she already makes a good impression. She has beautiful legs, and doesn't need nylons to make them prettier. But more than that, Lydia is smart. She knows more about our illness and our needs more than some of the nurses. The patients like her, and the doctors respect her. She has healing power. She goes wild when I tell her that, because she wants to be an actress not a doctor.

As for me, Dear Diary, tomorrow is my big day! After months of waiting, I'm finally going to have my operation. Dr. Evans is going to perform a procedure called an arthrodesis, which means he is going to fuse my knee. I'm so anxious to have it done, because I can't wait to start getting better. The doctors say the surgery will take six months to heal, and then my work-up with privileges will take eight months before I can even think about going home. I've been here so long already. That seems like such a long time to be in a place like this.

My operation will start at seven o'clock, but I won't have to wait in line like Lydia will for nylons, because I'll be the only one on the table. (That is a joke, Dear Diary). I think the rage over getting a pair of nylons has warped my thinking just a bit. The way people talk about them, you would think they would just die if they don't get a pair. But I guess people don't die that easily. Anyway, that's what Dr. Wagner says.

Lydia freezes. She is still squatting on the floor with the open diary in her hand. She closes the book, and stands up slowly. It's getting late, and she needs to get my things to me down on three-east.

—⚐—

The next morning, Lydia's alarm goes off at three-fifteen. She moans, and slams her hand down on her alarm. "What time is it?" She rolls over, and buries her face in her pillow, muffling her voice. "What am I doing?" After a grueling moment, she flips over and rubs her hands over her face. "Come on, Lydia, old girl. Get out of bed. This is what you've been waiting for, isn't it?" She drags herself into the bathroom without much enthusiasm, as she did a day earlier. "Get a move on it. Those nylons are calling." She grabs her thermos of coffee, her purse, and runs out the door. The bus drops her off in the parking lot of Kinsley's at three fifty-five. To her dismay, there are already women milling around to be first through the doors when the store opens at nine. The sidewalk to get in line is a long one. Hopefully, there won't be any trouble like what happened in Chicago, where a skirmish broke out at a large department store—it had been a regular hand-to-hand fight, and the police had to be called to regain some semblance of order.

She attaches herself to the end of the line, and pours a cup of coffee. It's going to be a long wait. She busies herself by watching everyone and sipping her brew. After three hours, It's evident that drinking coffee has been a huge mistake. There is no way to relieve herself, and get back to her place in line. It's every woman for herself. This will be trickier than anticipated—two more hours until the store opens.

What was she thinking?

The lines are growing longer, and newspaper photographers and radio station reporters are on the scene. Lydia is more than glad to flash a smile for a young photographer, and even consents to an interview. Being in the limelight is what she aspires to. But, for some reason, she doesn't seem as excited as I thought she would. She is not the bubbly Lydia that we all know and love. She checks her watch—It's seven o'clock.

—⁂—

At seven o'clock they wheel me into the operating suite. I'm nervous, but at the same time anxious to be having the surgery, hoping it will stop the pain and swelling in my leg. Dr. Evans told me a small group of TB germs has reached my bones and joints by way of my bloodstream. They are growing due to a breakdown of my body's own resistance. They have spread and inflamed the lining of the joint. Fluid has collected, and destruction of my bones has begun.

Dr. Evans is there to greet me with a comforting smile. I sure like him. I told him that, at this moment Ma is in the chapel praying to God to guide his hands during the surgery. He tells me that he knew Ma's prayers would be answered, because he feels confident. The next few hours will prove that.

—⁂—

The next few hours prove difficult for Lydia, standing in line needing a bathroom. She actually crosses her legs and jumps around. She looks at the mounting line that has grown the length of the entire city block. It's madness. The chill of the early April morning keeps the crowd moving around to keep warm, but everyone seems to be in good humor. People are making jokes and bursts of laughter breaks out up and down the sidewalk. The crowd is giddy with anticipation.

All of a sudden, there is a commotion, and someone screams from at the end of the line. A young man runs in the opposite direction with a woman's pocket book. The woman screams, "My purse! He took my purse! Someone stop him! He's got my purse!" It turned out he wasn't the brightest thief on the block, because there were extra policeman on duty just in case the crowd gets out of control. As soon as the woman started screaming, officers are on the dead run and tackle him to the ground. The last thing Lydia sees of the ignorant thief is a police officer stuffing him into the back of a squad car.

—w—

The last thing I remember is counting backwards from 100. Once I am under the effects of the anesthetic, Dr. Evans does a preliminary survey. "On palpating the knee, there is swelling with prominence of the suprapåtellar pouch, and filling of the fosse on either side of the quadriceps tendon," he says. As he is talking, a technician is taking dictation. "There is tenderness along the medial and lateral joint line. The x-rays show erosion of the articular surface and narrowing of the joint space." Dr. Evans tells the team he will have to remove the articular surfaces of the joints, and then hold the bone ends together. The next couple of hours will be tedious.

—w—

The next couple of hours drag on for Lydia with the mind-numbing reminder of how badly she needs a restroom. Finally, at nine sharp Kinsley's opens its doors and the nylon shoppers cheer like a crowd at a ballgame after a homerun. Finally, the line begins to move.

There is security at the entrances to keep the crowd from becoming a mob. Lydia is finally at the counter making her purchase. The war has literally halted purchasing nylons, except maybe through bootlegging, and now here she is, purchasing a pair of the coveted nylon stockings. But she doesn't seem to be enjoying her purchase like I thought she would.

Walking out of the store, she passes a young woman sitting on the curb pulling on her new stockings, and stroking her leg as if it was gold. Of course, she is putting on an act for the photographers, as camera lights flash at her from all sides. Normally Lydia would have done flip-flops to be that woman, but instead she walks sullenly past the cameras to catch the next bus home. She looks at her watch again.

—⁂—

It's nine-thirty. The surgery has taken two-and-a-half hours. The portable x-ray machine is in place taking pictures, to make sure my bones are in proper alignment. My vitals are stable, and I tolerate the procedure well. They move me to the recovery room.

Chapter 33

*"The tragedy of life is not that it ends
so soon, but that we wait so long to
begin it."*

Anonymous

Heaven: I'm enjoying the river. I like the way the water twists and turns. Kind of like my days in the sanatorium, twisting and turning, never stopping.

"You are becoming a philosopher, says Ambriel.

"I have a good teacher." The path into heaven she takes me is a bumpy one. She glides along smoothly, but my teeth chatter over the bumps. We come to a wide-open space on a countryside where a mass of elderly people are enjoying themselves. Some are sitting painting the landscape. Others are writing their life stories. Ambriel says, "They find peace in looking back. And it also helps with grieving." Another group of adventurous folks are sky diving. I hear a man cry out loudly, "When you least expect it, adventure finds you."

I have to laugh. I look further and see a crowd of men and woman white water rafting, having the time of their life. Another group are running a marathon. A group of hikers is hiking the Grand Canyon.

A woman taking piano lessons tells me, "I like to say hello to a new adventure."

"The world is full of adventure," says a man organizing a rock band. Another says, "Adventure fills the soul."

—⁓—

When I wake up, I am in room three-eighty-four. Ma, Pa, and

Jonah are here. Ma brings me some new pajamas. They have poodle puppy's on them, I am in a lot of pain, and mostly keep my eyes closed. I don't feel much like talking. Jonah sits by my bed holding my hand. Pa is munching on a piece of chocolate someone brought for me. Doctors come and go a dozen times each. They say I'm running a temperature, and my pulse is high. Dr. Wagner assures my family I am doing fine. By two o'clock, Ma and Pa have to leave. They tell me my older brother, James, and my sister, Dorothy, are coming to visit the next day. I'm too sick to say much about it.

As the days and weeks pass, I have no appetite, and trouble sleeping on my right side. My leg again, smells just awful, and even bothers the other girls. It's getting so I can't stand it myself. By June, the doctors are talking about sending me to Mayo Clinic for plastic surgery. I'm still having pain and oozing coming from my knee, and the healing is like watching waiting for water to boil—pretty slow for someone who waits.

June 16th rolls around, making it one whole year since I have been at Glen Lake. Looking out the window from my bed, I try to see Birch Lake through the tangled trees, and think about the events of the past year. Pa bringing me to the sanatorium, the bombings of Hiroshima and Nagasaki, meeting Jonah in the tunnel, Margaret's suicide, Tom coming home from the war, my surgeries— and the talk of a drug that could possibly cure my disease. What did I know about any of these things a year ago, and how much longer do I have to wait?

Out at the nurses' station, Nurse Kirschner's wait is just about over. She is putting reports into the patients' charts, when she hears a familiar voice.

"I need some help over here, good looking."

She spins around so fast she drops her papers. "Alex!"

"Well, are you just going to stand there, or are you going to come over here and give me a hug?"

She goes to him, and he picks her up and twirls her around. Nurse Jones is at the nurses' station looking through her orders, getting briefed for the evening shift. She glances at Nurse Kirschner and Alex, but goes back to what she is doing. It's business as usual with her. What other people do is their business. Nurse Kirschner is beaming with excitement. She holds on to him as if she is never going to let him go. It's obvious how happy she is to see him.

"Alex, oh Alex! What are you doing here? I thought you weren't coming until tomorrow."

He lowered her to the ground and they stand facing each other still holding hands.

"I was able to get an early furlough, and I wanted to surprise you." He pulls her around the corner where they have more privacy. He tells her he only has a week, and then he and Tom will be shipped back to Okinawa for clean-up duty. "So let's make the best of the time we have. I'll pick you up after your shift."

"I'll be ready," she says.

—⁂—

By August, I'm still not improving, and Dr. Wagner is running out of ideas. "We need Streptomycin, and we need it now." He says to my parents by phone. "I'm waiting on a call from The National Institute of Health."

"Dr. Wagner, the call you've been waiting for." Nurse Jones holds the phone for him. He takes the call. "Hello, Carl Wagner here."

"Dr. Wagner. This is Stanley Doss from the National Institute of Health returning your call. What can I do for you?"

"Dr. Doss, how good of you to get back to me. I'm hoping you can help me out. I'm desperate here, so I'll get right to the point. I'm calling in hopes of obtaining Streptomycin from you. I'm sure you're aware of the hullabaloo in the newspapers lately calling it the miracle drug."

"Yes. It's been impossible to keep it out of the headlines."

"I have a patient…a young girl. She's eighteen. She has pulmonary TB that has progressed to her bones. Her entire right side is infected. She failed conservative treatment. We tried aggressive treatment when we did an arthrodesis on her knee. That was four months ago. Since the surgery, she's been going downhill. Is there any way we can test the drug on her?"

Dr. Doss lets out a sigh. The hint of a cure for TB has leaked to the newspapers, and since then, researchers have been overwhelmed with requests from all over the world from families and physicians trying to save their patients. "Dr. Wagner, I have to be honest with you. We have an inadequate supply of the drug. Even though there are eight separate pharmaceutical companies in the United States that are producing it, there's still only enough for one out of four hundred patients with TB."

"I'm aware of the shortage and the need, Dr. Doss. I have been in contact with Dr. Hinshaw from Mayo, who was ready to send me some, when The National Institute of Health took over the responsibility of who gets the drug and who doesn't." Dr. Wagner isn't giving up easily. "I know you're doing clinical tests. Couldn't my patient be considered for testing?"

"You realize of course that we're just in the early stages of testing. There's still a lot of risk to the patient. We're finding that ten percent of the patients who have taken it for a year are now deaf. There's just so much that we still don't know."

"I'm in a race against time here, Doctor. My patient has run out of options, and without your drug she's going to die."

"It sounds like she's in advanced stages. Streptomycin alone might not even be effective."

Both men are quiet, and then Dr. Doss says.

"I'll tell you what—I don't want to get your hopes up, but I can make some calls."

It's so frustrating, so many in need with so few resources, and they all keep telling him the same thing.

"I'll see what I can do."

"I appreciate your effort, Dr. Doss."

The wound on my leg is growing uglier every day. It smells like something that has crawled into a corner and died. The other girls in the room notice but try to pretend otherwise. They hide their faces when the offensive odor drifts across the room to their beds. They make small talk, and busy themselves with other things to put on a good show, but I know how bad it is. I can't stand it myself. My whole leg from my thigh down to my heel aches constantly.

Tessa's touch is gentle. She rinses the cloth in the antiseptic, and then washes my leg in small even strokes, being careful not to tear the raw oozing tissue.

"Am I hurting you?"

"No, Tessa, that feels good. It's just that it smells so awful, but it actually feels good when you wash it."

"This antiseptic should help fight the infection. Hopefully, it'll start healing."

"It's been four months since my surgery. It seems like it's getting worse instead of better."

"When I'm done here, Dr. Wagner wants me to take you downstairs so he can put it in a cast again. That should stabilize it, and maybe help conceal the odor."

"I hope you're right. I feel sorry for the other girls. They pretend they don't notice it, but I know how bad it is. I know they can smell it."

"Don't worry about the other girls, Francie. They just want you to start feeling better. A little foul odor isn't hurting anyone."

"For once I'm glad Jonah got discharged. I'd hate to be around him with my leg like this."

Tessa keeps rinsing the cloth and washing my leg. "What do you hear from him since he's been gone?"

"He's working part time in his father's newspaper and taking full classes at the university. It's just as well that he's busy. I need time to heal before he comes back to see me again. My smelly, oozing leg kills the romance."

"What's he studying?"

"Journalism—of course. He's such a good writer. He hopes to follow in his father's footsteps and take over the paper one day."

"How about you, how many classes are you taking now?"

"Two. English and Problems in American Democracy. Miss Parker gave me an A on my last Democracy paper, but I don't think the next paper will be that good. I haven't been studying the way I should. I've been so tired lately."

"I think the knee surgery has taken a lot out of you. Maybe after Dr. Wagner gets it into a cast, you'll start feeling better."

"I hope so," I perk up, "I want to be able to dance at your wedding."

Tessa's expression lifts. "Don't you think you're getting a little ahead of yourself? We haven't even set a date yet."

"Well what are you waiting for?"

"We want to wait until he's officially discharged. Since he and Tom deployed back to Okinawa after their last furlough, things have been a little up in the air. It'll be easier to make plans once he's home and out of the service. I'll let you in on a little secret though. I have my heart set on a summer wedding. That should give you plenty of time to get this leg healed."

"Oh, Tessa, that's so exciting—first Lydia and now you."

"What do you mean? Is Lydia engaged?"

"Oh—no. Haven't you heard? She left on a trip to Hollywood. She and a friend went together on the train, and they're going to stay with her cousin. She's hoping to meet some agents and try to get her career started."

"Well, I'll be darned. I knew she always talked about wanting to become an actress, but I figured it was just talk. I never thought she would actually do anything about it. I just hope she's careful."

"Why, what do you mean?"

"Well, trusting the wrong people for one thing. Hollywood is full of characters that prey on young naïve girls like Lydia. It could be dangerous if she were to meet someone who wasn't on the up and up."

"I think Lydia is too smart to fall for a con job. She's has too much spunk. Besides, she's with her friend, Mark, and he'll be looking out for her. I guess her cousin knows some people who might be able to help. Hopefully they're legitimate."

"I hope so. But, just the same, she should be careful."

Chapter 34

"In the book of life every book has two
sides: we human beings fill the upper
side with our plans, hopes, and wishes,
but providence writes on the other side,
and what it ordains is seldom our goal."

Nisami

Heaven: Ambriel says, "Let's go to the movies." I follow her into heaven, and the aroma of popcorn makes my mouth water. We take our seats in the front row. I giggle, "I am actually watching a movie with my guardian angel on a gigantic outdoor screen.

"It's the big screen of heaven, "Ambriel says. I laugh, "Hubba, hubba!" The movie starts with girls my age walking with angels. There are Eskimo girls, Chinese girls, all nationalities, who are just like me.

When the movie is over, I say, "How fun was that, I've never thought about the similarities before. God did make us all the same with hopes and dreams."

"Let's see what's happening with Lydia."

I hurry and finish my popcorn. Ambriel smells the lily.

—⁓—

"You can take the window seat, Mark. I know you like to look at the scenery. On the other hand, I am a people person. I love to watch people." Lydia bursts with excitement. "I can't believe we're actually on our way to Hollywood, Mark. I've dreamt about it for so long, and now it's finally happening. I hope I haven't forgotten anything."

"Hey, you need to take a breath and chill. We've got a lot

of hours ahead of us on this train. You have plenty of time to get excited once we get there."

"You're no fun." She elbows him in the side. "Being excited makes the journey more memorable. And that's what this whole trip is about—making memories."

"Well, I don't know about you, but I'm going to put my seat back and take a snooze. An early bird I am not. Wake me when it's time for breakfast."

"What? I can't believe you. How can you sleep at a time like this?"

"A time like this is exactly when I sleep. It's five-thirty in the morning for crying out loud. My day starts much later. So, if you don't mind, it's lights out for me. Good night." He leans back, and sleeps.

"Suit yourself."

Lydia told me this will be her first ride on a train. She sits in her seat, drinking in all the sights and sounds and smell. She seems to be enjoying everything it has to offer. The seats are spacious and comfortable. She listens to the clacking of the tracks. Before too long, the conductor comes through to take tickets, announcing the next stop. People constantly move about from car to car. The dining car is one car in front of them, and the observation car is a few cars back. She plans to check them out, as soon as it is daylight. It's supposed to have swivel seats facing each other and large windows from top to bottom so the passengers can visit and look at the scenery.

A plump woman with a shiny black face wearing a white shirt and blue uniform comes by with a clipboard signing people up for breakfast. Lydia and Mark are on the list for the second shift. The woman says she will announce when it's time.

A middle-aged woman in a bright-red saucer hat with

matching gloves occupies the seat next to Lydia. She wears one of the trendy new looks by Christian Dior. Her dress has padded shoulders, narrow waist, and a full skirt, accentuating all her curves. Her clothes look very expensive, and everything from her shoes to her purse matches. I know how much Lydia loves fashion. That would be the kind of outfit she would wear in Hollywood.

"This is my first time on a train. I'm going to Hollywood, California," Lydia says to the woman.

The woman smiles, and says in a flaccid voice, "That's nice." She is reading a magazine.

"I'm traveling with my friend, Mark." She points in his direction. He's snoring quietly, from underneath his hat. "It's too early in the morning for him," Lydia laughs. "How about you, where are you headed?"

The woman seems a little annoyed at Lydia's interruptions. Her crimson lips articulate the words, "I'm going to Billings, Montana, to visit my sister."

Lydia doesn't seem to notice the woman's tone or just doesn't care, because she remains her same perky self. "Oh, Billings. How nice. I can't wait until we get there so I can see the mountains. I've never seen mountains before." When the woman doesn't reply, Lydia jumps back in. "I'm hoping to become an actress when I get to Hollywood. I've been dreaming about it all my life."

The woman's grin is a little larger this time. She must want to humor Lydia. "I suppose becoming a movie star would be more glamorous than being a housewife or a secretary or a nurse now, wouldn't it?"

Lydia cringes a little at the woman's remark. "I guess so," she says. This time Lydia is the one feigning interest in a magazine, flipping through the pages—so much for small talk.

The temperature is in the eighties when she and Mark arrive

in Hollywood. Lydia's cousin, Ruby, meets them at the depot, and heads straight for an afternoon of sightseeing. Lydia looks awe struck by the landscape of the city. She walks with her head tilted back looking at the tall, slender palm trees, the busy streets, and the richness of the foliage. She even pinches herself to make sure she isn't dreaming.

They drive along Sunset Boulevard, have a view of the ocean, and drive through Beverly Hills to look at the homes of the stars. They enjoy an early dinner at a posh Hollywood restaurant, relax over coffee, and then it's time to head back to Ruby's where they will sleep before her next day's career-hunting venture. Ruby has a friend of a friend who made a call to an agency to put in a good word for Lydia.

Ruby says, "It's all about who you know out here."

Lydia walks into the agent's office the next morning looking like she stepped off the cover of Woman's Day Magazine. Her appearance is cool and chic, as she saunters through the door, in a green street dress. It has a black collar with black contrasting pockets over each breast. Black heels and nylon stockings accentuates the curves of her tanned calves. Her curly brown hair pulled back at the nape, and held in place with a black velvet ribbon. Her perfectly manicured nails matches her cherry-red lips that are full and pouty. She is ready to knock them dead.

After an hour of sitting in the agent's waiting room, she finally gets in to see him. The agent seems in a hurry when he talks to her. He asks for her resume, headshots and a portfolio of any work she has done. Lydia hands him a skeleton copy of her life's work, which is almost laughable, and a few photos Mark had taken with his Brownie. The man breezes through the portfolio, thanks her, and says he will call her. The interview lasted five minutes. So much time and energy in getting here, and it only lasted five minutes.

Mark tells her to brush it off, and says, "It's not the only talent agency in town. Let's hit them all. So, off they go until Lydia's feet ache from pounding the sidewalks. She is getting tired and, Mark tells her this will be the last agency for the day.

The name on the door reads, "Vincent Tucker." Some of the paint has chipped away from his name. The office is dimly lit, and the magazines in the waiting area are more than a year old. The girl at the desk is filing her nails and says, Mr. Tucker can see you now. She escorts Lydia inside the office.

"Good afternoon, Mr. Tucker. It's so nice of you to see me. My name is Lydia Browning." She extends her hand.

He shakes her hand, while studying her face. "Good afternoon, Miss Browning. How nice to meet you. Have a seat."

She sits in the chair facing his desk and crosses her legs at the ankles. She lays her handbag across her lap and folds her hands. She is on her best behavior, and musters up all the good manners she has ever learned in Miss Petrie's School of Etiquette. The man's eyes drink in her appearance from head to toe. "So, tell me, why do you want to be an actress?"

She is quick to answer. "Because I possess powers to entertain and make people laugh."

"I see. And have you ever done any acting?"

"In my hometown. I'm a member of a local theatre group where I have performed in many shows and even starred in a few."

He rises from his chair, and comes around to the front of his desk. He leans back on the desk and sits down, folding his arms across his chest grinning at her. "A theatre group," he mimics, "I'm impressed. What kind of education do you have?"

"After I graduated high school, I got a job at a sanatorium and have been taking acting classes at the University in the evening."

"Well, well—very ambitious. It sounds like you're focused on your career."

His eyes drinks her in. "Would you stand up for me?"

"What?"

"I'd like you stand up so I can get a better look at you. You know, to see how your posture is, how you handle yourself—get a better look at your whole persona. I'd like to see if I can visualize you up on the big screen."

There is an awkward moment. He is too close to her. She looks him straight in the eyes and stands.

He walks around her like a vulture circling road kill. "Very nice, yes, very nice indeed." His voice drips with praise that sounds rehearsed. "I think you have something…something special. I can definitely see you on the big screen, Lydia. Do you mind if I call you Lydia?" He places his hand on her shoulder.

"Not at all, that's my name," she quips.

"A sense of humor, I like that. Yes, I like that. "I'll tell you what, Lydia. I'll need to get some still shots of you. You know, for professional reasons. How about you come back later tonight, I'll have my photographer get some shots, we'll have dinner, and then we can talk about things. How does that sound to you?" He still has his hand on her shoulder.

Lydia steps to the side to be free of his touch, and clears her throat. She follows her gut. "Mr. Tucker…do you mind if I call you Mr. Tucker?" Before he can answer, she continues talking as she walks toward the exit. "I don't think your agency is at all what I'm looking for. In fact, I'm not even sure what it is that I'm looking for, but I know it's not this. Just to be clear, I won't be back to be photographed. Good day, sir." She holds her head high, and walks out the door, leaving him with his mouth hanging open.

Lydia and Mark spend the rest of the week traveling around Hollywood and seeing all the sights. As fate would have it, Mark decides he won't be traveling back home with Lydia. He wants to stay in California and pursue a career in interior design. He says he can start with Ruby's two-bedroom flat. It is calling him. When the week is up, they say their goodbyes at the depot. Lydia boards the train, taking a window seat. This time she looks at the scenery.

Chapter 35

*"Three o'clock is always too early, or too
late for anything you want to do."*

Jean-Paul Satre

Heaven: I say to Ambriel "That was fun watching Lydia. I
knew she could take care of herself. She has spunk."

"Her instincts for right and wrong kept her safe", says
Ambriel.

"Speaking of right and wrong, you have shown me so much of
heaven that has got me thinking."

"That's my job getting you thinking. "She says, "You are
curious about hell."

"Yes. In School, Sister Jane Frances touched on the fires of
hell, the weeping, and the gnashing of teeth. I've seen pictures of
the devil with a serpent tail, looking toward fire. But is he real?
Where is he, I don't see him. Where is hell?"

"You really have been thinking." "Let me put it this way". "It
is a state as it is a place which is true for many things." It has many
levels or degrees according to the needs of the occupants, both in
this world and the world to come. Again, only God decides who
goes to heaven and who goes to hell. It will all be clear when you
see the face of God." For now, let's get back to Lydia."

"Ok. She seems a little conflicted of late."

"Your influence is at work."

Really?"

"Let's find out, shall we?"

"We shall."

—ᴡ—

Lydia marches straight to the guidance counselor's office at the University, the moment she gets home. After that, it's back to work as usual. It's great seeing her again, but something is different. She seems a little quieter, serene, if you will. She doesn't say much about her trip the way I thought she would. She did tell us about all the places they went, the beautiful scenery, and the ocean. But there is an edge to her voice. Oh, she still jokes and clowns around with us, but at the same time, appears to have a lot on her mind. I think the trip to California has changed her somewhat.

Lydia isn't the only one experiencing change. At the sanatorium, things are about to worsen quickly. It's late afternoon, you know, that weird time of day where you don't always know what to do with yourself—too early for supper and too late to start a fresh project? For someone with idle hands, it's a time of day that means catastrophe.

Nurse Jones takes the thermometer out of my mouth. "Ninety-nine point three. Your temp is elevated somewhat," she says, recording my vitals in the chart. "Dr. Wagner wants another chest x-ray."

"It seems that's all I do lately is have sputum cultures and x-rays. You would think the sanatorium would have enough pictures of my chest and leg to last a lifetime."

"Dr. Wagner is a curious fellow. He wants to see how you're improving."

"Or not improving," I say, as I struggle to sit up.

It's hard for Nurse Jones to lift me. My entire right side is painful. Any movement makes me wince.

"I know it hurts, Miss Carver. I'll try to be careful. You help me lift so I don't touch where it hurts." Nurse Jones slides her arms under my knees, and places me onto the gurney, trying to avoid any pain." You're light as a pillow."

"I must be losing weight."

Nurse Jones maneuvers the gurney out into the hall, heading towards the elevator and destination X-ray, with me in tow.

—◇◇◇—

The radiologist sticks the films onto the viewing box, switching on the light. Dr. Wagner is looking on, and the two discuss the findings.

"The infiltrate in her lungs has increased, and spread to her entire right side, says the radiologist. The wound on the leg has broken down, and there is more drainage. The fusion in the knee is still showing cavitations. See right there? Pointing to the film.

"We'll have to skin graft her knee," says Dr. Wagner. This is getting more serious by the hour. Her temperature is elevated and she's still losing weight. There's obvious spread of the disease that is not responding to therapy."

"The radiologist asks, have you heard back from The National Institute of Health?"

"Not yet. I spoke with a Dr. Doss, who is part of the clinical testing and research team. If it turns out he can't help, I've already written a letter to the Merck Company asking for their help. Some how, some way we have to get Miss Carver started on a trial of Streptomycin. It's her only chance. The clock is ticking and we're getting nowhere fast. In the meantime, I'm going to set her up for the skin graft on her knee."

—◇◇◇—

Nurse Jones gathers her things, getting ready to leave for the night, when the phone at the nurses' station rings.

"Five-main, Nurse Jones speaking."

"Hello, Mavis. This is Pete McDonald, your neighbor."

"Yes, Pete. What is it?"

—⚒—

"Mavis…I don't know how else to tell you this.

"Tell me what?"

Your house caught fire this evening."

Nurse Jones gasps. "What? How? Is Roy okay?"

"Roy is okay. He's okay. I happened to step outside when I saw the flames. I ran over as fast as I could. The fire wasn't too bad at that point, so I went inside, and that's when I found Roy sleeping in his chair. He had a cigarette in his hand that must have rolled onto the floor, and caught the curtains on fire. I was able to drag him to safety.

He's okay," says the caller, "Flora is taking good care of him at our house."

"Roy's okay? He's not hurt?" She asks again.

He's not hurt. But, Mavis…" his voice trails off.

"What Pete? What is it?" She keeps her composure.

We called the Fire Department right away, but the fire spread so fast, they couldn't save the house. I'm sorry, Mavis, It's pretty much gone."

"I'll be right there. I'm on my way!"

—⁓—

By the time she gets to her house, smoke fills the air from the charred remains. Firefighters scurry about the yard, running back and forth to their fire trucks. A barking dog scampers past, chasing something flipping through the air. The firemen douse the smoldering embers. Mavis stands bewildered, staring at the ugly mess. Her whole life has literally gone up in smoke billowing toward the evening sky. Charred walls stare back at her. Black film smears broken windows, and electrical wires dangle aimlessly. There is a hole in the roof where flames still have hold, finally— destroying the remains. Curious neighbors are milling around in the darkness watching the drama. They stand side by side with heads close, discerning the cause and pointing in the direction of the tragedy. Then she sees Roy. He's sitting on Pete's porch step with his head buried in his hands. She is unsure what to do next, when Pete's wife, Flora, comes to her side. The two women embrace. Mavis says, "I don't want to see Roy just now I'll stay in the nurses' quarters."

Flora says, "He can stay with us."

Mavis looks at the ashes, asking why. However, ashes don't talk, they whisper.

Chapter 36

*"Everyone journeys through character
as well as through time. The person one
becomes depends on the person one has
been."*

Dick Francis

Heaven: We're still at the river. I love it here. The river is
constantly changing.

Ambriel says, "We are on the streamside, called the Riparian
zone."

"Good to know", I say, rolling my eyes. She ignores my
sarcasm.

"On earth, it seems most young people think they are
invincible only to find out they didn't achieve their goals, and envy
for what they don't have. Eventually some change and just know
they can do it. But like the river, they lose some and they gain some.
It depends on who they are and what they want."

"Interesting, But what happens to Nurse Jones?"

"Patience little one. From here, we will meander around the
bend. Get it? The bends in the river is called meanders."

"So much information," I say.

Ambriel inhales the aroma of the Christmas Lily. All right,
let's look in on Nurse Jones

—⋙—

Nurse Jones keeps to herself since the fire. The buzz around
the sanatorium is, she left Roy, and moved into the nurses' quarters
at the sanatorium. She is able to live on campus, and gets paid forty
dollars a month, plus laundry services.

At the nurses' station, Dr. Wagner is talking to Nurse Jones. "The extra hours you've been putting in are a tremendous help for the rest of the staff. You're dedication is admirable."

"Thank you, Dr. Wagner, but, I'm not so sure it's really dedication. I just have a lot more time on my hands these days." You know, Nurse Jones, you're among friends here. Maybe a few of us could get together over coffee some time. Think of it as a life saver—it won't stop the waves but it might keep your head above water."

Nurse Jones actually smiles at his profound attempt of an invitation.

"That's very kind of you. Maybe when Nurse Kirschner gets back."

"Is she sick?"

"Yes. She called in yesterday, and again today."

"I hope it's nothing serious", he says.

"I don't think it is. I talked to her this morning, and she said she might be feeling well enough to come in this afternoon."

That afternoon, Nurse Kirschner manages to come back to work. She brings me outside for after noon sun therapy. I sense something different about her. She has a glow. I watch her out of the corner of my eye as she pushes me out onto the veranda. She's humming, You Are My Sunshine.

"You're sure in a good mood. You must be feeling better."

"I am. It's s such a beautiful day, I just feel like humming."

It's nearing the end of August, where the weather is warm and humid. The temperature is already up to eighty-nine. Nurse Kirschner pushes me to a spot on the veranda where there are large pots of petunias, snapdragons and geraniums placed on a ledge, and hanging baskets of pink, white and red impatience dangle from hooks in the shade of the pillars.

I love to watch the humming birds suck the nectar from the flowers, flapping their wings at lightning speed. I hear the buzz of their tiny wings when they fly past.

"Well then, I say, how about staying a while", I ask her. "I'd love to have the company."

Nurse Kirschner pulls a veranda chair close to my bed.

"I can spare a few minutes. It's been kind of nice since Nurse Jones has been helping out. It lightens the load for the rest of us, although I feel horrible over what she must be going through."

"Losing her home in that fire must be so devastating", I say. "In addition, everything she ever owned—gone just like that. I wonder what she'll do."

"I'm not sure. You know Nurse Jones …she doesn't open up much about her personal life."

"She's been married such a long time, hasn't she?" "It would be sad to see it end."

"She has some hard decisions to face. But you know what? I believe that things have a way of working out."

"You sound pretty optimistic. You must have gotten up on the right side of the bed this morning. I'm glad to see you're feeling better."

Nurse Kirschner is quiet for a moment, biting her bottom lip as if contemplating what she is going to say next. "Francie, if I tell you something, will you keep it a secret?"

"I love secrets! Cross my heart and hope to die."

"Since it was you who got Alex and me together, I feel we are kindred spirits."

She lowers her voice and whispers, "I'm pregnant."

"Pregnant?"

"Shh. Not so loud." She looks to see if anyone hears.

"Oh, a baby! I knew something was different about you! Is that why you missed work? "

"Yes. I've had morning sickness, so when I suspected, I went to see a an obstetrician. I'm due in March."

"Does Alex know?"

"I haven't had a chance to tell him yet. You're actually the first to know."

"What are you going to do?"

"Well, we're already planning on getting married. I guess it'll just have to be sooner rather than later. But with Alex still in Okinawa, I just don't know when that will be. It's going to be hard though. You know…once I start showing. People are going to talk."

"They always do. But, Tessa, a little baby. You must be so happy!"

"You have no idea. It's all I can think about."

She looks at her watch. "The others are going to be wondering where I am. I better get back." She puts her finger to her lips and says, "Remember, our little secret."

I pretend to lock my lips together and throw away the key.

Once Nurse Kirschner is gone, I bathe in the sunlight, hopefully healing my tuberculosis. I close my eyes, and think about Tessa, Alex and their little baby. It makes me happy. I hope someday Jonah and I will marry and have kids. Then I drift to sleep.

—◊◊◊—

Later that same day, Lydia is at home getting her mail. She hears her telephone and runs back into the house to answer.

"Hello, I'm here. Don't hang up!" She's out of breath.

"Hey, Lydia. This is Ruby. You sound out of breath."

"Hi! I am. I was outside when I heard the phone. Whew! Hey, how are you? I've missed you."

"I'm great. I have some news that will blow your socks off."

"Okay then, don't keep me hanging."

"You're not going to believe it."

"What? Ruby, tell me before I grow old, for crying out loud."

"An agent just called here looking for you. You know...the one my friend told you about, anyway, he left a message saying that he might have a job for you doing a hair commercial, and you're supposed to call him right away. Isn't that wild?"

Lydia looks too shocked to speak.

"I told you it would blow you away. Do you have a pencil? Here's his number." Lydia writes the information. It's what she has been dreaming about her whole life, and now it's finally happening. It's just a commercial, and she will have to audition, but if she gets it, it could lead to more jobs. It could be the start of her career.

Lydia plops down on a kitchen chair, looking through her scattered mail. She threw it down in her excitement to get to the phone. One of the envelopes is thick, and has the return address of the University. She opens it and reads

Dear Ms. Browning:

We are happy to inform you about your acceptances into the Medical Program. Without reading any further, she lets the letter drop into her lap. "Someone, pinch me," she says aloud.

Chapter 37

*"Everything that happens in the world
is part of a great play of God running
through all time."*

Henry Ward Beecher

Heaven: We're sitting at the river again. It scares me a bit, so I say to Ambriel, "I'm having some dark feelings."

"Care to share them with me?"

"Well for one thing, why do bad things happen to good people?" Why did I have to die so young? Why do my parents have to have all these worries? I just don't understand."

"These questions are part of earth, the answers are in heaven. " Let's go for a walk, there are some people who might be able to clear this up for you."

I follow and find we are in the Garden of Eden again. Eve is still by the tree of knowledge, and the serpent is still slivering in the tree branches. Adam appears and says,

"Ambriel tells me you are conflicted about the tragedies of human suffering."

Eve steps out and says, "Hello again, Francie. "To answer part of your question, a transformation on earth occurred when Adam and I disobeyed God in the Garden of Eden."

Adam says to me, "The world on earth is now stained by a physical evil that often puts pain and disaster in the lives of its inhabitants."

I ponder that for a moment, then I ask, "But why does God let these things happen?"

Adam says, "Physical evil comes into your lives for a bunch

of reasons. One of them is freedom of choice. People on earth sometime make bad choices, ending up in a heap of trouble. It doesn't mean they are wicked. Just bad choices."

"But what about little children with no fault of their own who get cancer and suffer horrendously?"

Eve says, "When you see the face of God, that question will be answered."

Ambriel thanks Adam and Eve, and tells me we have to go. As we are walking, Ambriel asks me "Did they answer your questions?"

"Somewhat. The part about the freedom of choice makes sense, but some things are still a mystery to me."

"It looks like Lydia has a choice to make." Says say Ambriel.

"She needs to follow her heart", I say.

"Again, your influence."

"I'm getting pretty good at this, aren't I?"

"You're almost there."

—✕—

Lydia calls the agent in California and politely thanks him for his offer. She tells him she has decided on another career choice. She follows her heart, and enrolls into med school. I can't be happier for her. I'm sure she would have made a wonderful actress, but I know for sure, she will make a better doctor. Besides, I don't know any lady doctors—she will be my first. She will still work at the sanatorium on a part-time basis, so we will get to hear her lame jokes, and the antics of college. I think we all live vicariously through Lydia—her future is bright.

As Lydia is leaving the sanatorium for the day, a storm is brewing outside. Thunder rumbles in the distance, and the leaves left on the branches dangle listlessly. The air is still and eerie. I'm having trouble breathing, but mesmerized by the color of the plants and rocks when the clouds move. Everything seems so brilliant and tranquil. I realize there really is calm before the storm. I try to get comfortable but can't sleep on my right side—it hurts too much. The thunder is getting closer, The angry skies finally burst into a constant pounding of raindrops splattering the windowpanes. The leaves on the trees frantically sway against every drop. The rain falling on the lake looks like a million tiny feet dancing on the water, orchestrated by the vertical lightning flashing in the sky. It's exciting to watch.

Between the thunder, the lightening, and the pain, I'm on the verge of tears. I'm exhausted, and feel trapped. I hear voices in the hall.

Two nurses walk by the nurses' station talking about Nurse Kirschner and the condition she is in. The months have passed quickly, and just as quickly, Nurse Kirschner's belly begins to swell. Her pregnancy is obvious, and so do the whispers and disapproving stares. They are judging her. — Except for Nurse Jones, that is.

"Pay them no mind," Nurse Jones says. "Let them say what they want. What do they know? Having a baby is a blessing."

"You surprise me, Nurse Jones. I know from the stares and whispers how people feel about a girl getting pregnant out of wedlock."

"Out of wedlock or in wedlock, your baby will be born out of love. That's all that matters. People can look, stare, and judge all they want. In the end, you're going to have a beautiful little baby to love, and he or she will love you back. What can be more wonderful that that?"

Nurse Jones seems to have softened since her separation from Roy.

"You don't know how good it feels to have someone say that to me. It's hard showing up for work every day thinking everyone is against me."

"If they're so perfect and never made a mistake, then they should stare. I say the heck with them. You just be happy." Then she turns the subject onto herself. "Maybe things would've been different between Roy and me if we had had children. We tried, you know."

"You did?"

"Since that didn't happen, I've kind of adopted our girls on the ward. I know they don't know this, but I love each and every one of them as if they were my own. I know I'm strict, but it's only because I love them so much. I just want them to get well. I'll do whatever it takes to help them follow the rules so they can walk out of here strong and cured. It's what I would do for my own child."

"You have a good heart, Mavis", says Nurse Kirschner.

Nurse Jones smiles at the intimacy of names. "I think I'll sit with Miss Carver for a bit. She's been in a lot of pain lately, and this storm might be a little unsettling for her. It doesn't sound like it's going to let up any time soon."

"That's a good idea. Lydia used to be good at cheering the girls in a storm. But since she's taken on full classes at the university, we don't get to see as much of her anymore."

"That girl used to drive me crazy with her shenanigans, says Nurse Jones, and now here she is going to become a doctor. I swear—this sanatorium has influences on all of us in one way or another."

"I think you're right," Nurse Kirschner laughs. "But you have to admit, she is good with our girls."

Nurse Jones then goes to the ward.

—⋘—

Nurse Kirschner is alone at the nurses' station. An angry sky throws lighting bolts, followed by thunder, opening up to the pouring rain. The elevator doors open, and two people step off. Nurse Kirschner is charting, and doesn't hear them—the sound of the storm drowns their footsteps. There is an icy chill. She is about to reach for her sweater, when she sees them standing at the nurses' station.

"Mr. and Mrs. Monson...? What are you doing here?"

Kate Monson looks drained, and doesn't speak. Bill Monson says "Tessa, can we go somewhere and talk?"

Nurse Kirschner pushes her arm through the sleeve of her sweater. She is shivering. "Why, what's going on? Is something wrong?"

They would never have come to her workplace, especially in a storm.

"Is there a quiet room where we can go?" Bill looks around.

"I'm here alone right now. I guess I can call Nurse Jones. We can go to the nurses' lounge."

"Why don't you do that, dear," he says.

"Bill, you're scaring me. Please tell me what it is." She looks at Kate and sees eyes filled with tears. "Is it Alex? What is it? Is he okay?" She runs from behind the desk to meet the Monson's face to face. "You have to tell me right now. Please!"

"We had two Marine officers come to our door this afternoon with a letter from the War Department—an apology."

"For what?"

Bill steps closer, and holds Nurse Kirschner by the arms. She grows impatient, and pushes him away. "Bill, an apology for what? Alex? Is it Alex?"

"They say he's missing in action."

Nurse Kirschner stiffens.

"They couldn't give us the details of what actually happened, but there was a skirmish, and Tom and Alex didn't return."

Nurse Jones and I can hear the commotion.

"I'll be right back," she says to me.

Nurse Kirschner looks as if she is going to faint. Bill grabs her and holds on to her.

Kate Monson explains to Nurse Jones what has happened. "We want to take her home with us tonight, she says."

Nurse Jones says to Nurse Kirschner, "You go with them. I'll handle things here."

The storm subsides somewhat to a drizzle, tapping against the windows.

Chapter 38

"Let your heart guide you. It whispers,
so listen closely."

Unknown

Heaven: We're still at the river. I say to Ambriel, "It's been months since Tom and Alex went missing. "I dream about Tom every night. I worry about him, and miss him so much. It's agonizing." To make matters worse, Nurse Kirschner's baby is due soon. She and I must both be going through our own tortured problems."

Ambriel says, "Things are only going to get worse."

"I'm not sure I want to see what comes next."

—∞—

Months have rolled by, and predictably, and the icy winds of winter are upon us once again. A man passes her on the sidewalk, pulling his collar up around his neck to block the chill. The wind picks up, and Nurse Kirschner crosses her arms tight against her body to keep warm. Her baby is due in a few short months. Shortly after the news of their disappearance of Tom and Alex, the head honchos at the sanatorium fired Nurse Kirschner when they found out she was pregnant—they have rules. Life is so unfair. God has given her so much, and now has taken so much away. She has cried a pool of tears, and yet there they are ready to spill over at the mere thought of Alex. She holds back and continues walking, lost and alone.

"Oh," she says aloud, and puts her hands on her belly and caresses her unborn child. A part of Alex still lives—And soon she will be holding his baby in her arms—but alone without its father.

As hard as she tries to block it, reality creeps in. Alex is missing. But she holds on to hope.

There has been no word on Alex or Tom. There is no turning the clock to bring them back. Having to go on without Alex, into a society that frowns on bearing a bastard child. It's the reality of her situation.

When she gets back to her apartment, the phone rings. She throws down her keys and answers, always hoping for the news that Alex is still alive.

"Hello?"

"Hello Nurse Kirschner, this is Dr. Wagner.

There is sadness in his voice.

"It's Miss Carver. She's slipping away."

"Oh dear, I've expected this call."

"She's been going downhill for some time."

She asks, "What's her condition?"

"Serious but stable—I'm praying for a miracle, but maybe you could come? I know how close the two of you have gotten. Her family is on the way, but I think a visit from you would help."

"I'll be right there."

Dr. Wagner hangs up the phone, and puts his face in his hands. A doctor isn't supposed to take the death of a patient personally, or get too involved or feel too deeply. A doctor is supposed to remain objective to make the critical decisions that are in the best interest of his patient. But I know his heart is breaking. He has wanted so badly to save me. He has written mountains of letters, and numerous phone calls to find a cure for me. But he is losing the battle. I am now too sick to eat, and growing weaker day by day. My condition is serious.

I can't sleep because of the pain in my side, and I am having a lot of trouble breathing. They have me in a private room, as is the case when a patient is critical.

I turn my head and stare out the window. I think about the first day I looked out the window at the sanatorium and watched a squirrel wind its way through the branches—that is almost two years ago. Now the trees are bare and, ice covers Birch Lake. Everything looks cold and barren. My eyes move to the skyline where the colors are changing in layers, from pale yellow to a soft gold. I always loved the magic of the sky, as if God is splashing paint on canvas. How many times I wondered at the beauty of a simple sunset, or the sun dancing on the water or the call of a loon, and now these things seem so clear, almost surreal. It's all so fragile, and precious, and a heartbreaking, feeling of loss and loneliness. I grieve for my brother, Tom, and for my parents. How heavy their hearts must be. I feel so much compassion for everyone and everything around me, and, strangely, I feel at peace.

Then, there is a tap at my door.

I roll my head toward the door and see Nurse Kirschner, and the fullness of her belly. "Oh, Nurse Kirschner, look at you." My voice is weak.

"Hey, you. Don't look at me, look at you in your cute little poodle pajamas," she whispers, as she sits down beside me. She reaches for my hand, and holds it gently in hers. "I have to admit, they are my favorite pajamas, but I can't take my eyes off your tummy, you look like you're going to pop." I'm having a hard talking, so I close my eyes.

"I feel like I'm ready to pop. She places my hand on her tummy. "Feel that?" The baby moves, as if it welcomes my touch.

I smile, and whisper, "It feels like its rolling. Something tells me it's a girl."

"You know what? I think you're right."

Nurse Kirschner says, "I feel her kicking."

At the same time, Nurse Kirschner shivers from the touch of my hand bittersweet—like birth and death holding hands.

"If it's a girl, I'm going to name her Alexandra Francine."

"That's a beautiful name." I pause a moment for impact, and to let my strength rebuild and say, "Things are going to work out for you and your baby. I can feel it." I close my eyes again.

"Miss Carver is right", says Dr. Wagner entering the room. "Things have a way of working out when you least expect it."

"Nurse Kirschner is going to make a wonderful mother, isn't she, Dr. Wagner?" I say in slow, panting breaths.

"She is."

"Your baby is going to be so lucky", I say, as I drift off to sleep.

She and Dr. Wagner continue their conversation, still standing in my room.

"I'm holding onto the hope that he's coming back, "she says.

Dr. Wagner says, "Life has backed you into a corner, but I'm confident things will change for you."

As if someone turns on a light, the colors in the room shift with the clouds. The warmth of the sun streaming through the window beams on Nurse Kirschner.

I can see the heaviness in her heart is starting to lift. I then sleep as peacefully as her unborn child.

Chapter 39

*"Death leaves a heartache no one can
heal, love leaves a memory no one can
steal."*

From a headstone in Ireland

Heaven: The River is raging all around us, giving me a weird feeling. Ambriel senses my unrest, and says, "Do you want to talk about it?"

Without hesitation, I unload my wrath on her. "Almost year and a half of my life in the sanatorium and still no cure!" I tried as hard as I could to follow the rules and where did it get me?"

"Who are you mad at?"

"Myself, why did I even go through all of it?" It seems so unfair. Ma and Pa don't deserve this. Two of their children gone in a blink of an eye! Tell me, where is the justice in that?" After a quiet moment from my rant, I say, "Will it really be better in heaven?"

—⁂—

When Dr. Wagner and Nurse Kirschner left my room, Nurse Jones sits with me, trying to make me as comfortable. I love her for that. I always could see right through her. She has reconciled with Roy, but is still staying in the nurses' quarters while he is getting help for his problems. They are taking it slow.

When I wake up later, Nurse Jones is gone, and Lydia is beside me.

"Well hello there, you're finally waking up. I see you're wearing your favorite little poodles."

"These pups have seen their better days, but I can't seem to part with them."

"How are you doing?" She asks.

"Better now that you're here. I've been hoping you'd come. I want to give you something."

"You want to give me something?"

"Yes, I've been thinking about the first day we met. You were so sweet to bring me a welcome gift."

The nap has rejuvenated me somewhat, and I am able to reach under my pillow and, pull out the diary she gave me nearly two years earlier. "It has been such a wonderful gift, and now I want to give it back to you. "You saved my life many times since I've been here, and giving me this to write about my feelings is just one of them. I thought maybe you'd like to have it back, as sort of a remembrance of this chapter in our lives."

"Oh, Francie, I don't know what to say." She gently takes the diary from my hand.

"You don't have to say anything. I just want you to have it in case, well you know."

"Don't you talk like that," she says sternly. "You are one of the strongest people I know. I'm thinking only good thoughts, and one is that you're going to get better."

"I'll hold you to that."

"Since I have this in my hands", Lydia says, "I do have a little confession to make", feeling the leather of the diary. "I hope you don't get mad—I read part of this once. I knew it was wrong, but, Francie, I just have to tell you, reading it was a turning point in my life."

"It's okay, I'm not mad." I smile and look up toward the Heavens.

"You've had such a huge impact on me, Kiddo. I used to get so darned irritated when you'd say I'd make a good doctor. I always thought I wanted something else, but you made me realize I was chasing the wrong dream. Thank you for the diary. Whenever I have doubts, and I know I will, I'll pick it up and read it and be inspired by you all over again."

"Lydia, I know you're going to spend a lifetime saving lives just like you did mine." I close my eyes again. She kisses the top of my head before leaving. "You're the lifesaver, Francie."

The doctors say I am critical, and throughout the day, everyone I know has been popping in and out to see me. Poppy comes with Ken, but he stays outside the door.

"Poppy," I whisper.

"Shh. You don't need to talk." She holds my hand.

"I know, Poppy, neither do you."

We have an unspoken bond. It's the same camaraderie Alex and Tom have on the battlefield. We have fought our own war, and have been each other's strength. Just as she is now, sitting silently at my bedside.

I sleep for a while, I don't know how long, but when I wake, I smell aftershave. It makes me think of the tunnel. It's funny how scents jog our memory. When I open my eyes, I think I've died and gone to heaven, but It's only Jonah lying next to me. His body is warm, and he has been holding me as I seep.

"If this is what heaven is like I can't wait."

He strokes my hair and kisses me. "It's so like you to make jokes."

"I'm not joking. Loving you feels like heaven."

"I want this moment to last forever", he says.

I did seem to regain some of my strength. Jonah always does that to me. "I love you so much, Jonah. I think God would have taken me a long time ago, but then he gave you to me, and I got stronger. Thank you for loving me."

We don't talk. I drift in and out of sleep with Jonah holding me. When I open my eyes again, his voice is dry and husky. "I remember the day I rescued you from the tunnel—I wish I could rescue you now." He trembles as he strokes my cheek.

"Don't be sad, Jonah. You have rescued me. This might sound strange, but in spite of it all, I've been so happy this past year and a half, and it's all because of you."

Jonah and I haven't experienced the true depths of our passion—but it doesn't matter. We have given ourselves to each other in every other way that matters, and the root of our love is buried deep in both of us. We have faced each day together with hopeful hearts. We played and laughed and had fun just being together, and we helped each other forget the rawness of our surroundings.

"You're in my heart," he whispers. You're going to get better."

—◊◊◊—

Its Christmas Eve, the day before my 18th birthday and Ma sits close to my bed with her rosary spilling through her fingers, only moving her lips. She says she feels God's presence, and knows He is watching over us. Bing Crosby's White Christmas softly plays in the background while I doze in and out of consciousness.

Since I am so critical, Father Alphonse comes and administers the Last Rites. Extreme Unction. He bends over me, and anoints my forehead with oil and prays. "Through this holy anointing, may the Lord in his love and mercy help you with the grace of the Holy Spirit." He touches my eyes, ears, nostrils, lips and hands and says, "May the Lord who frees you from sin save you and raise you up." I am too tired to open my eyes.

The room they have me in, is small. With all the family gathered together, it's crowded. The kids move about the room, and take their turns touching me and kissing me and telling me to fight, as did Millie and Poppy—my old friend and my new friend.

After Father leaves, leaves, Pa lingers in the doorway. I am lying quietly still among my blankets and pillow. He comes to me and takes my hands—they are ice cold. He kneels beside me so I can see him without straining.

My eyes flutter, and my voice is barely a whisper. "Hi, Pa."

He strokes my cheek. "You're so soft and sweet." He puts his head on mine, and cries. "Please God, make this all go away."

Because I am so cold to the touch, he pulls the covers over my shoulders. But I'm actually too warm, and push them away. My breathing has become labored. It makes me perspire. I have regular episodes where I stop breathing. The doctors call it Cheyne-Stokes respirations.

I pat his hand. It's my way of telling him it's okay.

He pulls himself together, and hugs me. I think he can feel the grip the other world has on me.

The clouds move about, and pale moonlight seeps through the windows. Pa is still holding my hands, I stop breathing altogether.

Chapter 40

"Here is the test to find out whether your mission on earth is finished: If you're alive, it isn't.

Richard Bach, Illusions

Heaven: We are on the edge of the riverbank where Ambriel and I are sitting. The air has cooled and a low-lying fog has set in. Ambriel keeps silent while we sit watching the white air take shapes, like wild horses kicking up clouds of dust. The flock of white birds that has been nesting on the other side suddenly lifts their wings and fly—something has scared them. That's when Ambriel takes my hand and leads me to a shallow part of the river. Silently we wade to the other side where the fog is thicker. Ambriel drops my hand and we stand at the edge of a forest hidden by the dense fog. Dry twigs snap and branches bend behind the billowing white haze, and then out of the murkiness a man appears.

"Tom!" I gasp.

He looks dazed but smiles when he sees me.

"Tom, it's you! Where have you been?"

He rushes toward me and takes my hands, and holds them tightly in his and says, "I can't believe my eyes! It's so good to see you," and then he hugs me as tight as he can.

"What are you doing here?" I ask. My breath catches when I realize the answer.

Ambriel stands silently in the distance.

"Where's Alex?" I ask.

He squeezes me tighter, and puts his hands on my shoulders. "Alex is safe."

"Does Nurse Kirschner know?" I don't know what questions to ask first.

"No, not yet."

"What happened?"

"We were on clean-up duty when Alex and I got separated from our squad in a skirmish. Some of the Japanese didn't know the war was over and took us as prisoners. They held us for weeks and weeks in an abandoned cottage with hardly enough food and water to stay alive. We always had hopes that our guys were still looking for us. But then one night the guards took Alex to another shack to separate us, and for one brief instant in a moment of confusion, I was able to escape. I hid out for a while until I came up with a plan. So I went back."

"What did you do?"

"There weren't too many of them, only a handful, but without a weapon I didn't stand a chance against them. So I started a fire to throw them off guard. Things got crazy, and, just as I hoped, they went nuts trying to put the fire out. I went in from the other side and took the one guard by surprise, and that's when Alex and I managed to get away. Alex made it back safely, but then something happened that I didn't count on—I didn't see the land mine."

"Oh, Tom!"

"It's all right, Francie. I know I made the right decision when I went back for Alex. We had each other's backs, and he's needed back on Earth."

"But, Tom."

"No buts, Francie. It all goes back to our childhood. It's how we were brought up. Everything Ma and Pa taught us as children molded us into who we are today. They taught us about courage, and loyalty. And to do the right thing. Alex was in trouble, and he needed my help. My instincts just kicked in. I did what I had to do."

"Tom, no! What about you? What about our family?"

He lets go of my hands and backs away from me. "Our family will be fine. Ma and Pa will understand. Their faith will get them through. They will come to realize I did the right thing, and they will find peace in that. But, they're going to need you now more than ever, Francie."

I look curiously at Ambriel.

"It's time for you to go back, Francie," is all she says.

Tom begins to fade from sight. I'm losing him. "Tom, come back, don't go."

"I'll be fine, you know that. This is my destiny. But you've got to hurry Francie. Go, now! You're needed." Then he is gone.

Ambriel says, "Tom is where he's supposed to be, Francie. It's God's Plan."

The feeling is bittersweet. "Time is running out," says Ambriel. We will meet again years from now." But know I will always be with you. She puts something into my pajama pocket. It's time, Francie.

I look down and see Dr. Wagner and a nurse doing CPR on me. Another nurse tells the kids to step out of the room. Another escorts them. They're crying. Ma sits motionless with her rosary in her hands, tears spilling onto her cheeks. Jonah is leaning against the wall, staring into space. In the corner, Pa stands holding my gray patent leather pumps tight against his chest. They are the shoes I so proudly showed off on the bus that first day.

Out at the nurses' station, a package has been delivered to Dr. Wagner, something he has been anticipating for months.

Suddenly, I feel a magnetic pull that over powers me and sends me whirling into a white space, spinning me around. Then gravity catches hold, and a huge vacuum pulls at me with a force like being squeezed through a keyhole, until all of a sudden I land with a thump back into my body so abruptly, it feels as if I'm being slammed against a brick wall.

"I've got a pulse!" Dr. Wagner exclaims. Everyone is frantic. I can feel the electricity in the air as my family let's out collective sighs.

My eyes flutter, and I begin to cough uncontrollably, gasping for air. I suck in hard until I pull in enough air to inflate my lungs, which sends my blood rushing hot through my veins. Voices become clearer and shapes come into focus, as I fight my way back. Instinctively, Jonah rushes to my side before Dr. Wagner and the nurses are done with me. He puts his hand on my face—it feels like heaven. You're awake! He says triumphantly. Ma and Pa are touching me and Ma is still crying. When I see the faces of my mother and father, I see the hope in their eyes. "Oh Pa, I say. That's when I notice the Christmas Lily on my bed stand.

THE END

CPSIA information can be obtained
at www.ICGtesting.com
Printed in the USA
LVHW011420221219
641388LV00001B/162